THUNDER GOD

(Joe Hawke #2)

Rob Jones

ISBN-13 978-1523702756
ISBN-10 1523702753

Other Books by Rob Jones

The Joe Hawke Series

This novel is an action-adventure thriller and includes archaeological, military and mystery themes. I welcome constructive comments and I'm always happy to get your feedback.

Website: www.robjonesnovels.com

Facebook: https://www.facebook.com/RobJonesNovels/

Email: robjonesnovels@gmail.com

Twitter: @AuthorRobJones

DEDICATION

For Snow-White, Again

THUNDER GOD

CHAPTER ONE

London

Joe Hawke woke with a start. In the darkness of his London flat the telephone was ringing, and he scrambled to pick up the call before it rang off.

"Hawke," was all he said. He squinted at the small clock beside his bed: 01:17.

"This is Eden." His voice was level and inscrutable.

Hawke felt a surge of uncertainty course through his veins. He had no idea why Sir Richard Eden would be calling him in the middle of the night, but he knew he wasn't inviting him to a birthday party.

"What's wrong?"

"It's Lea," Eden said firmly. "She's gone missing."

Hawke paused a beat to let the words sink in. He was still half asleep, and part of him wondered if all this was nothing more than a terrible dream. Eden was talking about Lea Donovan, his personal security chief, and the woman Hawke had started to fall in love with. He swung his legs out of the bed and switched on the light. The past few weeks had changed his life completely – he'd hunted down a Swiss megalomaniac, ending his insane dreams of world domination, and met Lea, the first woman he'd felt strongly about since the cold-blooded murder of his wife. Now, Eden was telling him she was gone.

"What does *missing* mean, Richard?"

"We don't know. She was on assignment for me in the Far East and she's dropped off the grid. A few days ago I sent her to Hong Kong to look into something that could be a potential problem for me – for us all. She always sticks to protocol, which is to make contact with me every six hours, but contact was broken around ten hours ago."

"I'm listening."

Eden continued, calm and measured, but clearly concerned and trying to hide the fact from the former SBS man. "I have a feeling something pretty big is about to kick off, Hawke, and I'm trusting you to sort it for me. I know there are some things you don't trust about me, and I know you're aware that I'm not telling you everything, but I'm asking for your help, and in return you'll get the knowledge you've been searching for."

Hawke listened carefully to what Eden was saying. Since the very beginning he'd known something big was being kept from him, and that Sir Richard Eden was where the mystery began and ended. He also knew the deceit had something to do with not only Scarlet Sloane and Sophie Durand but also Lea Donovan herself – the woman who had broken contact with her boss and was now missing in Hong Kong.

Now Eden was confirming that his intuition had been right all along and that there was more to all of this than he knew. The old English politician was also telling him that he was closer than ever to finding out the truth about it all, but Hawke didn't need any of that as an incentive – the fact that Lea was missing while on assignment was enough to motivate him.

"Can I take your plane?" Hawke asked.

"No. I sent the plane to Dubai to pick up Scarlet Sloane. I know how well you worked together and I asked her to help you. You'll have to fly on a commercial airline, and that means waiting until the morning."

"I'm on it."

A second after Eden had hung up, Hawke was on his feet.

He got up and paced into the bathroom where he picked up his pre-packed kit bag and brushed his teeth. Light off and back in the bedroom, he tossed the bag on the bed and pulled some clothes off the back of an old chair at the side of his bed.

The agony he'd felt after Liz's murder had ruined him for years, and left him a broken man. He'd long ago lost count of how many booze-soaked nights it had taken to get over Liz – nights full of tears and insomnia so carefully hidden from the rest of the world, and yet he knew you never really got over something like that, not completely.

Worst of all was the knowledge that her killer was now dead himself, taken out by a Special Forces raid in Thailand. Instead of celebrating his death, Hawke found it had robbed him of the most primal of desires – revenge, and that meant a never-ending cycle of hatred and regret without any closure.

All this had left him scarred and with a greater fear of losing those he loved than he had ever had before Hanoi. Now, faced with the thought of something similar happening to Lea, his fists tightened and he clenched his jaw, totally rejecting even the thought of such a terrible nightmare.

Whatever he felt about Eden and his game of secrets, he knew he was an extremely professional man with serious contacts in the intelligence communities, as well as a highly respected archaeologist and discoverer of ancient treasures. None of this made him inclined to take his word with anything but the gravest seriousness.

Whatever had happened to Lea, he would undo it.

Whoever was responsible, he would punish.

He slammed his door on his way to the cab and told the driver to get to London Heathrow Airport as fast as possible.

It was all kicking off again.

CHAPTER TWO

Paris

Art historian Felix Hoffmann sprinted through the foot tunnel of the Kléber Metro station. The cold air burned the back of his throat as he desperately searched for a way to escape his pursuer. He had known they would come for him one day, but not like this. Not with such ferocity. Not in the middle of the night.

A moment ago he was enjoying a simple apéritif with friends in the Club Kléber, but then his world had changed forever when the stranger whispered in his ear: *the God of Thunder has returned.* He knew what that meant. He knew what they wanted.

Now, he stumbled down the tiled steps and ran deeper into the deserted station, straining every fiber of strength he could find in his desperate bid to outpace the much younger and stronger assailant chasing him through the Paris night.

Below in the darkness, he heard the sound of a train on the line. For the briefest of moments he thought he was going to live, to see his family again. But when he reached the platform he saw it was not an arrival, but an outbound train leaving the station.

Desperate and scared, he looked up and down the platform for someone to help him, but there was no one there – just the roving eye of a security camera fixed to the wall, cold, remote and powerless to stop his terrible fate from unfolding. Behind him he heard the footsteps again, the breathing. The assailant was getting closer.

There was only one course of action now, and he took it.

He climbed down into the tunnel and moved through the darkness. He was fearful now not only of the lethal threat behind him, but of the potentially fatal consequences of touching the third rail. He weaved as fast as he could along the guiding rails of the tracks, his feet occasionally brushing against the rubber-tired lines.

Hoffmann was a specialist in Chinese art in everything ranging from Shang Dynasty bronze work to Zhou Dynasty artwork and he was proud of his ignorance of the technical world. But he had read the signs all over the Paris Métro warning against urinating on the third rail often enough, and he needed no further explanation as to why doing such a thing would be a bad idea.

But now he was actually down on the tracks, running for his life and breathless with panic at the thought of what would happen to him if he was caught. Maybe even electrocution in this dark, cold tunnel would be preferable to that.

Now, he heard the familiar rumble of an approaching train. He strained his eyes in the low-light of the tunnel and saw something that filled him with dread. Ahead of him, one side of the tunnel was being illuminated by the ghostly yellow light of an approaching Métro train. His only chance of escaping being crushed to death by it was to turn and run back into the arms of his pursuer. As he thought about options, he watched the rats scatter in fear of the imminent danger.

Then he heard the voice. "You can't escape, Felix!" It was cold, and emotionless, and bounced icily from the tiled walls of the grimy tunnel.

"Why can't you people leave me alone?" he screamed, his voice hoarse with the effort of sprinting and the sheer terror he now felt coursing through his veins. "Haven't you taken enough from me?"

"You have given us very much, yes," said the voice. "But it is what you are keeping from us that we are more interested in. Where are the papers?"

Hoffmann's mind raced with indecision. In one direction was certain death, brought by the crushingly heavy twin steel bogies of the Métro train now rumbling toward him with terrifying speed. In the other direction was also certain death, brought by the people he feared more than anything.

The train driver sounded the horn. It was shrill and deafening in the enclosed tunnel.

"Give us this one last thing, Felix," the voice said, calm even in the face of the on-coming train. "Join us!"

"Never! I will never involve myself with such sacrilege!"

"You don't know what you're talking about, Felix. This is what you've always wanted. Now is your chance! Help us, and you will taste eternal life."

Hoffmann stared at his pursuer's silhouette. He looked at the train – thousands of tons of metal racing towards him. He knew what acquiescing to them would mean. It exhilarated him, but it terrified him more.

"Last chance, Felix! Give us what we need and join us. Join the Gods!"

One more look at the train and Felix Hoffmann obeyed his deepest instinct and ran away from it, sprinting closer to his pursuer with every step. He might stand a chance on the platform, but if he stayed here on the tracks his life was certain to end in seconds.

"You made the right decision, Felix."

"Somehow I doubt that..." he said. He would live today, he thought, so he could run tomorrow.

But he didn't have long to think about tomorrow,

because then his future took a drastic change for the worse.

As he crawled up on to the edge of the platform to get out of the tunnel, he felt his assailant move quickly behind him, and then suddenly it happened.

The cord flicked around his neck and tightened, cutting an agonizing groove into the soft flesh of his throat and cutting off his air supply. In vain, he tugged at the cord, but it was too tight around his neck for him even to get his fingertips beneath it.

Behind him, the train raced past in a howling gust of grit and grime.

"Where are the Reichardt Papers, Felix?" the voice said. Cool, authoritative. In complete control.

"Please!" he croaked hoarsely.

"Where are they?"

Hoffmann flailed about in a vain attempt to free himself, but he grew weaker with every missed breath. His eyes were bulging so much he thought they might burst from his head, but he somehow managed to get the words out. *"You said I could join you..."*

"I lied. Give me their location or your family will die just like this."

"They're... they're... *here!* I have them on me now. Please don't harm my family!"

As Hoffmann felt his pursuer reach into his jacket and pull the papers from his pocket, he knew he had betrayed not only himself but the entire world. "I've told you now, please... please just let me breathe and let my family live!"

But the assailant didn't let him breathe. Hoffmann struggled but there was no escape. The last thing he saw was the glowing strip lights of the Métro station through his painful, bulging eyes, and then he felt himself slip away. They had won at last, and the world would pay a terrible price for his failure.

CHAPTER THREE

Hong Kong

Hawke knew when he was being followed, and now was one of those times. He and Scarlet Sloane had been in Hong Kong less than one hour and already there was someone tailing them. For all he knew, they could have been watching him on the plane from London – the first flight to leave London for Hong Kong after Sir Richard Eden had woken him to tell him about Lea's disappearance.

They cut through an alley and entered the Temple Street Night Market in a bid to lose their pursuer. Years ago, Hawke was stationed in the city as a commando in the British Forces Overseas Hong Kong. The Royal Marines had been stationed in the city since the very first days of British colonization, and it was a great posting loved by most of the military who went there.

But as Hawke looked for a way to lose the tail, he saw things had changed. For one thing, the night market was different. Once it offered excellent food, a great atmosphere, singers on the sidewalks – but now not so much. It looked tacky and tired, the singers had disappeared into the cool, subtropical night and the food was cheap and salty.

And the man was still behind them.

The tourists in the market grew in number as the night grew older and the familiar smell of fried meat and plum sauce filled the air. All around them people laughed and took selfies of their night in the exotic city.

9

They passed some prostitutes outside a noodle bar and moved deeper into the crowd to consider their situation. Only one person knew they were in Hong Kong – Sir Richard Eden. Hawke knew he would never betray him.

They crossed Saigon Street. Red bunting flapped in the wind and a man was arguing with a fortune teller, raising his voice to be heard over the noise of a nearby karaoke bar.

News of Hugo Zaugg's death less than two weeks ago had been presented to the world as a tragic suicide, but how many knew the truth outside of Eden's official circle and certain elements of the American Government was unknown.

When he'd landed in Hong Kong things had gotten even worse. Eden had contacted him to brief him about another murder. A private researcher in Paris who was somehow linked to Lea's disappearance was killed shortly after Eden's first phone call to Hawke, and of grave concern to Eden was the simple fact that Lea had been tasked with putting this particular man under surveillance while he was recently in Hong Kong.

Hawke wondered if the death of Felix Hoffmann and now his new friend a few hundred yards behind him were connected to the Zaugg affair, but instantly put it out of his mind. He was in Hong Kong to find Lea and now work out the Hoffmann connection, and he knew where he had to start.

"Check out the guy in the black shirt." Hawke jabbed his thumb over his shoulder.

"We're being tailed?"

"Pretty sure we are, yeah. He's been keeping around a hundred yards behind us since we turned into the market."

Scarlet turned slowly and pretended to look at a passing 747 as it climbed into the orange clouds above the city. It looked like it could rain at any minute, and as she followed the path of the aircraft she covertly surveyed the street.

"Black jeans and shades on his head?" she asked.

"That's the chap."

"If it's a tail he's not very good," she said dismissively. "Could be anyone."

"Or he could be someone," Hawke said.

"So, make him sing for his supper, darling."

They stopped walking and pretended to check the menu in the window of a Nepalese restaurant.

"Definitely a tail," Hawke said, watching the man's reflection in the window. "He's pulled up outside that jewelry store on the other side of the street. If he's half as smart as he should be, he's looking at us in the reflection of that window the same way we're using this one."

A moped puttered down the street, weaving in and out of shoppers and tourists as it spewed a cloud of filthy blue smoke into the air behind it. People were going about their business in the early evening like any other night in the city.

Scarlet sighed. "So what now?"

"Let's have a word with him," Hawke said coolly.

"He's probably armed."

He turned to her with a sarcastic smirk on his lips. "Yeah, but I've got *you*."

They turned from the restaurant and aimed for the man, but before they could even step into the street their pursuer knew he'd been rumbled and immediately pulled a gun from his pocket. He fired it twice at them in what looked to Hawke like a dangerous piece of improvisation.

They both ducked and jumped behind a food stall for cover as the bullets smashed the restaurant window and exploded a shower of glass splinters all over the people inside.

People across the market screamed and ran for whatever cover they could find. A man in a down-market barbershop picked up his phone and made a call, presumably to the police. Then a young security guard in a nearby jewelry store ran into the street. He pulled a Glock 19 from his hip holster and aimed it at Hawke and Scarlet.

"Arms up and don't move," he shouted in stilted English.

Scarlet raised an eyebrow. "Well, which one do you want me to do, darling?"

Hawke watched powerless as the man in the black shirt turned and fled into the market crowd.

"We haven't got time for this…" he said.

"You do arms up, now!" shouted the security guard. "You try and rob store!"

Before the security guard knew what day it was, Scarlet knocked the Glock from his hand with a ferocious Krav Maga slap kick and sent it flying into the road with a metallic smack. Hawke retrieved it and the guard immediately raised his eyebrows and then, a second later, his hands. "Please, don't shoot!"

"Look at it this way – you're still breathing," Hawke said to the guard. "That means she likes you."

Then without wasting another second, they gave chase to the fleeing man.

They sprinted into the crowd, darting through the busy night market as fast as they could, but seconds later Hawke stumbled over a crate of cheap bracelets beside a stall and sent them flying all over the place. The stall owner shouted and waved his finger, but Hawke and Scarlet left him in their wake and continued in pursuit of the man.

Suddenly, Hawke's plan had changed from tracking down Lea and now Hoffmann's killer for Eden, to chasing an unknown assailant through the Hong Kong night. For all he knew, the three were connected, and now he had to find out how.

"Come on, Joe!" Scarlet shouted. "We'll never get him with you falling all over the place like a drunken twat. If only Lea could see you now..."

Lea. In the two weeks since Zaugg had met his maker, Hawke and Lea hadn't seen much of each other, but now she was missing he wished they had. After they returned to London from Geneva, they had spent a few days together before Lea went alone to Ireland to see family.

She surfaced only once to text Hawke and ask him when they should meet again. She told him she was at home, and he guessed the west coast because she had spoken to him that night in Zermatt about a cottage she owned there. But now Eden's call in the middle of the night to tell him she had gone missing had come like a sledgehammer.

But Hawke had been busy too. The affair at the British Museum had not exactly helped his reputation in the world of private security, and while his resolution of that problem would have won him endless contracts, he had no choice but to keep the whole business to himself. So he had divided his time between looking for work and improving his parkour across the London skyline.

Until, that is, this latest nightmare had arrived on his doorstep. First Lea's disappearance and then when he landed, the news of Hoffmann's murder. The briefest of briefings had sketched a rough picture of a private German researcher who had dedicated his life to the discovery of something described by Eden only as the Reichardt Papers. He was a loose associate of Eden until they found him garroted to death on the Paris underground.

Now, their man had left the market and was sprinting

for his life down a smaller side street. Hawke was certain the man probably knew the city like the back of his hand and if he let him out of his sight he would vanish into the night forever. But his parkour training meant there was little chance of the man getting away in an urban environment.

Away from the main drag, Scarlet fired a shot at the man with her Beretta Storm, a nifty little subcompact pocket pistol she packed when she was going away to enjoy herself. The sound of the gunshot melted away fast in the busy night. The hunted man ducked down instinctively to avoid being struck so she fired five more, deliberately high. These shots were louder, and followed by the sound of people screaming behind them in the market.

"That's just fantastic," Hawke said, sighing. "Every cop in the city will be here in five minutes."

"So let's get on with it then."

Hawke was beginning to regret asking Cairo Sloane to lend him a hand, but once again, her assistance was heavily recommended by Sir Richard himself. Clearly they had a complex relationship – neither had decided it was time to tell him what was going on but with Lea missing he would take whatever help he could get his hands on.

The man now scarpered to the end of the side street and ran around the corner but Hawke and Scarlet were closing on him. In the next street a few seconds later, Hawke squinted in the brightness of the neon shop signs – no one was running any more.

Scarlet caught up with him a second later. "Anything?"

"He's slowed to a walk to blend into the crowd."

Then, the sound of police sirens. Hawke looked over his shoulder and saw a Mercedes Sprinter van in police markings cut along the end of the street behind them. They too were on the hunt tonight.

"Looks like the plods are out to spoil our fun," Scarlet said.

"And we need to get to our little friend before they do," Hawke said, surveying the crowd. "There! He's stepping through the crowd again – I see him trying to get away down an alley."

They chased after him once again, pushing their way violently through the crowd of shoppers and tourists as the police sirens closed in around them.

"He's getting away, Joe!"

"Not if I can help it."

"He's disappeared again!"

"Damn it!" Hawke muttered, and climbed halfway up a traffic sign for a better view. Seconds later he saw the man weaving slowly in and out of a group of people watching a street performer playing a guitar and singing through a cheap sound system.

"There he is!"

The man glanced back and saw Hawke up the stop sign. He immediately darted into the next alleyway and was gone from sight once again.

"It's now or never," Hawke said. "I think this guy's going to disappear into the night if we're not careful."

"And for all we know he's our only lead to Lea or maybe Hoffmann's killer."

Hawke and Scarlet raced into the alley and allowed a second for their eyes to adjust to the darker atmosphere away from the neon brightness of the main drag. Then they saw their man, but now he was no longer alone, and he was no longer running away from them, but toward them.

"Bastard must have called for back-up," Scarlet said. "They're mob-handed now – must be at least eight of them."

"I don't fancy our chances," Hawke said. "Not with so many members of the public all over the place."

The men approached, and Hawke saw the flash of a blade in one of their hands.

Scarlet looked at the Beretta. "Only three left in here, Joe."

"But they don't know that."

She sighed. "As much as I want to kick their balls in, I think eight versus two, and their having the home advantage too, means maybe it's time for a tactical retreat, no?"

Hawke agreed.

Reluctantly.

CHAPTER FOUR

The gang chased after them, emboldened by their new strength in numbers. They moved with their concealed blades deftly through the oblivious crowd of shoppers and tourists like sharks cutting through a shoal of guppies.

Ahead of them, Hawke and Scarlet Sloane had gone from hunters to hunted in a few short seconds and were now racing back along the city streets in a bid to find a place to hide from the armed men. It was at times like this Hawke regretted getting involved with the enigmatic Richard Eden, but in his view, being chased through foreign cities was better than watching paint dry, and he would go to the end of the earth if it meant saving Lea.

He glanced back over his shoulder when they reached the end of the road and saw the gang was gaining on them. They clearly wanted a silent and fast end to Joe Hawke and Scarlet Sloane, preferably in a quiet alley in the darker corners of the city.

"What now?" Scarlet asked.

Hawke's mind raced. Ahead were just more shops and tatty market stalls, tourists milling about and casually looking at the cheap jewelry.

"We need some speed," Hawke said.

"I never knew you were into that sort of thing."

Hawke rolled his eyes. "You know what I mean, Cairo."

Then the heavens opened.

"Bloody fantastic!"

The storm clouds unleashed a heavy subtropical

monsoon onto them, and seconds later the sky was full of lightning and rainfall. A deep peal of thunder boomed above the city as Hawke spotted their chance. A young man was sliding off the saddle of an old Vespa and going inside a snack bar for shelter.

Hawke pointed at the dilapidated moped. "That's our ride!"

"That thing?" Scarlet said with contempt. "I'd rather be dead than seen on that."

"Which is very convenient because right now that's exactly the choice you have."

Behind them, the gang was closing in. Scarlet pursed her lips as she pretended to deliberate over the situation.

"Stop pissing about and get on the bike, Cairo!"

Scarlet gripped Hawke around his waist as he revved the Vespa and released the brake. The moped lurched forward and skidded out into the street, Hawke desperately trying to maintain control as the narrow wheels slipped about on the greasy road.

He watched the men in the small, cracked rearview mirror and saw two of them dragging a taxi driver from his cab and stab him. He fell to the floor in a heap while they jumped into his car and gave chase. Seconds later the cab's headlights were just yards behind them, lighting the heavy rain in their yellow beams as the engine growled and revved in the background, the grille like a snarling jaw.

"Bloody hell, Joe – can't you go any faster? They're almost up my arse."

"*Well...*"

"Don't even think about finishing that sentence or I swear I will throw you under the wheels of that cab."

"Got it."

Hawke made a sharp right turn, holding his leg out to stop the thing from tipping over. The new street was narrower than the last, but this didn't stop the cab. They closed the gap and began firing at them. A second later a bullet ricocheted off the tin license plate on the rear of the Vespa. It made a comical pinging sound before flying off into the rain.

Scarlet pulled the Beretta from her pocket and with one arm looped tightly around Hawke's waist, she coolly fired a shot into the windshield of the pursuing taxi. Through the torrential rain she made out the tell-tale sign of a bullet hole in the glass.

The car skidded and swerved in the narrow street, its right fender striking a low brick wall and sending a shower of golden sparks into the damp air, but they were soon on their tail again.

With a renewed sense of purpose, the taxi now pulled up close enough to hit the rear tire of the Vespa and seconds later Hawke was fighting to control the light-weight moped as it spun all over the slippery road, narrowly missing a line of garbage cans at the rear of a restaurant.

"Another shot please, Cairo!" he shouted. "And make this one count."

Scarlet turned on the moped again and fired a second shot, but just as she squeezed the trigger the moped hit a pothole and the bullet fired off high, sailing above the cab and disappearing into the Kowloon night. "Damn it, Hawke! Can't you drive?"

"Eh?"

"You ask me to take a shot that counts and then you drive right over the top of a fucking pothole."

"You might have noticed that we're in the middle of a damned monsoon, Cairo, and my vision is limited to about half an inch. Take another shot."

"Only got one bullet left, Joe. No more potholes, all right darling?"

Hawke slowed down, allowing the cab to gain on them once again. Scarlet held on to Hawke again as she turned and aimed the Storm subcompact for a final time at the pursuing cab.

And fired.

This time the bullet went through the windshield again, but lower, and hit the intended target. The driver slumped forward and the engine revved wildly as the dead man's foot pushed down on the throttle.

Hawke pushed the Vespa to the max in a bid to outrun the more powerful car, but just as it was about to ram into their rear tire once again, the narrow road came to an end and Hawke spun out to the left. Behind them the cab raced onward in a straight line and smashed head first into a giant billboard advertising a luxury gift store.

"That's them all wrapped up then," Hawke said.

Scarlet sighed. "For fuck's sake."

"What?"

"Just enough with the nasty one-liners, all right?"

"Sure, if you say so, but..."

"What is it? Why are you slowing down?"

Hawke came to a stop and switched off the engine. "We've got company."

He pointed to a long, black car parked in front of them. Leaning against the hood was a man holding a shiny black pistol as casually as if it were a banana.

"Inside the car please," said the man, and pointed the gun at them.

*

The car was a stretched Mercedes limousine and a second later the rear door opened.

"In here!" Hawke didn't recognize the voice, but then the driver held a tiny paper dragonfly out of the window for him to see. "It's this or die, Mr Hawke."

"How does he know your name? Who are these people, Joe?"

Hawke sighed. Of all the people to be rescued by, it had to be *her*.

"Come on," he said. "This car will take us where we need to go."

They climbed inside and shut the heavy door on the rain. The man with the gun sat opposite them, gun raised at their chests. Without another word being spoken, the driver pulled away. They drove through the city for an hour and finally pulled up outside a seedy-looking strip club. Inside they were shown up a flight of stairs and they entered a semi-lit room.

The woman's voice was cool and slightly husky.

"It's been a long time, Joe."

Hawke peered into the shadows where the figure of a lithe, young woman emerged into the room. He recognized her perfume – orchids and vanilla.

"Dragonfly," Hawke said, putting his gun away.

"Always and forever," said the woman. She blew him a kiss.

Zhang Xiaolu moved forward and offered the Englishman an ambiguous smile. She was wearing mostly black and her lips seemed impossibly red in the half-light. She held a Type 84 loosely in her hand, but slid it artfully into a shoulder holster as she stepped into the warm glow of the lamp.

"You look good, Joe," she said.

Known in the West as Lexi Zhang, the woman was a card-carrying member of staff in the Ministry of State Security, the intelligence agency of the People's Republic of China. Hawke never took his eyes off her, and not just because he didn't trust her. The good news was that the phrase *smoking hot* was invented for Lexi

Zhang, the bad news was that she knew it. "Too bad I didn't break into your bed as well as your hotel room back in Geneva. You looked so peaceful when you were sleeping. I had the urge to... *ruffle your hair.*"

Hawke smiled. "But we all know what to do with urges, don't we, Lexi?"

"Yeah," Scarlet said, stepping forward. "And I am actually in the room with you two right now, you realize that?"

Her words startled Hawke, who had apparently forgotten she was actually in the room with him and the beautiful Chinese agent.

"Sorry," he mumbled unapologetically. "Lexi, this is Cairo Sloane, Cairo – meet Lexi Zhang, otherwise known as Dragonfly. She recently broke into my hotel room in search of information relating to Poseidon..."

"Pleased to meet you," Lexi said.

"Likewise, and it's *Scarlet*," she said, frowning at Hawke. "No one calls me Cairo anymore. Now we've got that out the way, perhaps we can get to business?"

"Business?" Lexi said, turning to Hawke. "And here I was thinking you had flown to Hong Kong for pleasure." She ran a gentle finger up the length of his arm all the way to his shoulder.

Hawke frowned. "Sorry Lexi, but this time it really is business."

"*This* time?" Scarlet said, raising an eyebrow.

Lexi smiled. "Joe and I go way back. We met in Zambia where... well, let's just say our interests collided."

"Oh, *God*," Scarlet said. "Is there a drink around here?"

Lexi glared at Scarlet for a second and then turned to a drinks cabinet. She poured three glasses of iced vodka with mint and handed them to the others. They sat down and Hawke tried hard not to notice the flash of her tights in the lamplight as she crossed her legs.

"Why did you kill Felix Hoffmann, Lexi?" Hawke was blunt and to the point.

Scarlet shot a glance at Hawke. "What are you talking about, Joe?"

"Let her answer."

Lexi was unfazed. She sipped her drink and took a moment to watch the gentle whirring of the ceiling fan which cooled them silently from above.

"What makes you think I killed him?" she asked.

"Come off it, Lexi. A friend of mine sent me the Paris Métro CCTV – it has him being chased off a platform and into a tunnel by what is pretty obviously a woman of your height and build. Not only that, a policeman found a tiny origami dragonfly blowing along the tracks."

"It looks bad, I know," Lexi said. "But you know me, Joe. If I had killed him and wanted the fact to remain unknown then I would not have done those things."

"Maybe, or maybe you just can't help yourself. The thrill of the hunt and all that."

Lexi smiled. "You are such a cynic, Joe! But I'm being serious – I did not touch Hoffmann, I swear it. I would admit it easily enough if I had. You know me, Joe."

"You mean you're not exactly backward in coming forward?"

Lexi shrugged her shoulders and finished her drink. "I swear to you, Joe. I did not kill Hoffmann."

Hawke evaluated her for a moment, using his NLP training to check for any small sign she was lying.

Lexi spoke next. "This friend of yours is Sir Richard Eden, right?"

Hawke nodded. "You know it is."

"And he sent you after me, right?"

"No. He sent me here to find a missing friend. After I arrived he told me Hoffmann was murdered just after we spoke and I thought of you. He was chased out of a nightclub in Paris in the middle of the night and tried to flee into the Métro."

"And I was here in Hong Kong the whole time. How could I have killed him?"

"Easy enough with a private plane at your disposal."

Lexi said nothing, and sipped her drink.

"Well?"

"Obviously, someone framed me – presumably the same people who were tailing you in the city tonight. When Lao briefed me about Hoffmann's death he told me he wants to know who's behind all this as much as you and your boss. Tell me, how is the enigmatic Sir Richard these days?"

"I wouldn't know," Hawke said. "He's not my boss."

Scarlet leaned forward and joined the conversation. "You could say Hawke's on probation, darling."

Now it was Hawke who shot Scarlet the glance.

Scarlet ignored it. "Now, do tell us what you know about this poor Hoffmann chap, and why I was dragged from my bed in Dubai to fly to Hong Kong in the middle of the night."

"Oh, I don't think I like *you* at all," Lexi said, and turned to Hawke. "We've been watching Hoffmann for some time."

Scarlet raised her eyebrow and sank back into the chair.

"And by 'we' you mean the Chinese Ministry of State Security?" Hawke asked.

"Many agencies were watching Hoffmann due to the nature of his research. He left a trail of flagged keywords behind him like a line of bread crumbs – he was probably oblivious to the attention he was drawing to himself."

"And what were these keywords, my dear?" Scarlet purred.

Lexi continued talking only to Hawke, never taking her eyes off him for a moment and not once acknowledging Scarlet. "Mr Hoffmann was a private researcher of limited funds, and it was obvious someone else with considerable means was funding his research, Joe. He used those funds to fuel a lifelong obsession with ancient Chinese mythology."

"And what's wrong with that?" Hawke asked flatly.

"Nothing... and *everything*."

"Explain."

"You see, Felix Hoffmann started digging too deep into something that has concerned certain – how shall I put it – powerful agencies here in China for a very long time."

"Like who?" Hawke finally felt as if he were getting somewhere for the first time since landing in the city.

"My boss will explain more in the morning."

"And what about Lea Donovan?" he asked firmly. "Have you heard anything about her?"

"Sorry, no. I didn't even know she was in Hong Kong."

Hawke frowned and absent-mindedly scratched the back of his neck. He found this hard to believe, but either way it was another dead end for now.

"Like I said, you need to talk to my boss." Lexi handed them a business card. "Be there on time."

Outside, Scarlet lit a cigarette and exhaled a cloud into the warm air. "Interesting woman. If I could ask her, what would your little Nightingale friend tell me about the Dragonfly?"

"She would tell you that Lexi Zhang is a ruthless assassin working mostly for the Chinese Ministry of

State Security but not above private contracts. Oxford-educated at Christ Church College, fluent in several Chinese dialects, Japanese and English. Family history unknown, at least to Western intelligence agencies. Probably responsible for the death of at least three presidents in the last five years."

Scarlet nodded her head appreciatively. "And you think she's the one who killed this Hoffmann guy?"

"Maybe. I know she protested her innocence, but Lexi Zhang could lie her way out of quicksand."

"I have no trouble believing that. Listen, Joe..."

Hawke watched a wave of doubt cross Scarlet's face – not an emotion that spent a lot of time bothering Cairo Sloane. "What's the matter?"

"There's something you need to know."

"Don't tell me... something about Sir Richard Eden?"

Scarlet looked at him sharply for a moment. "Why would you say that?"

"Just a crazy hunch..."

"Well yes, there is something you don't know about Eden. In fact there's something you don't know about any of this, but I'm not authorized to tell you. It's just that with Lea missing I think it's important you know the truth."

"Well?"

She stopped herself. He sensed something powerful was preventing her from going any further. "I really can't. I shouldn't have brought it up. That was very unlike me. Talk to Eden about it if it's really stressing your nuts off."

Hawke sighed. So near and yet so far. "What I love about you most is your finesse."

CHAPTER FIVE

The following morning, the cab raced through the tunnel under Kowloon Bay and emerged on Hong Kong Island just as the sun was breaking through a thick bank of clouds to the east. Hawke's mind once again turned to Lea Donovan, and he wondered what was happening to her at this moment – if she was still in Hong Kong... If she had read his text telling her how he felt about her – and who had taken her, and why.

He was knocked from his speculation by Scarlet Sloane nudging him in the ribs.

"Pay the man, Joe."

Hawke paid the fare and moments later they were taking the elevator to the tenth floor of the skyscraper Lexi had described the previous evening.

Jason Lao's office was stark and professional. One framed picture of a woman Hawke guessed was his young wife, and a couple of simple pot plants, both plastic. The main attraction was the breathtaking view of the bay and the humming chaos of Kowloon rising up behind it.

For a few moments after Lexi had made the introductions, the atmosphere in the office was awkward, and things got even worse when Lao buzzed through on the intercom and had his personal assistant bring another person into the room.

The man was roughly the same dimensions as a grizzly bear and by the look on his face shared many of the same personality traits. He had a straight-forward crew-cut, silver at the sides, and wore a blue blazer with cream-colored chinos.

"Please meet General Frank McShain, he's with the US Army and is here representing certain interested parties inside the American Government."

"Just what the hell is going on?" Hawke asked.

"Take it easy, Joe," Lexi said.

Lao and McShain shared a concerned look.

"We only wish we knew," Lao began. "All we know is we've picked up chatter pointing to something big that's about to reach boiling point in the underworld here and on the mainland."

"Something big?" Scarlet said. "Gee, thanks. Now we know *that* we can get to work."

Hawke shifted awkwardly in his chair. "How does this tie into the disappearance of Lea Donovan and the murder of Felix Hoffmann?"

"Very recently," Lao continued, "not long after the death of Hoffmann, a piece of famous artwork was stolen from a gallery here in Hong Kong. The picture was a portrait of one of the Four Beauties."

"The Four Beauties?" Hawke asked.

Lexi rolled her eyes and sighed.

"The Four Great Beauties are part of Chinese legend, Mr Hawke," Lao said. "They were four women from various ancient dynasties reputed to be the most beautiful women in the world."

"Never heard of them," said Scarlet.

"Your ignorance of our culture wouldn't surprise any educated Chinese person," Lexi said sharply.

Hawke coughed. "So who were they?"

McShain shifted uneasily in his seat and scratched his stubble as Lao continued.

"The first was Xi Shi from the famous Spring and Autumn Period. She lived during the time you would call the seventh century before Christ. The second was several hundred years later, during the Western Han Dynasty, and her name was Wang Zhaojun. The third was Diaochan, who lived around eighteen-hundred years ago and the fourth and final beauty was Yang Guifei who lived during the Tang Dynasty, a mere twelve-hundred years ago."

"And whose portrait was stolen?" Hawke asked.

McShain cleared his throat and leaned forward in his chair. His voice was deep and coarse, and his Brooklyn accent heavy. "It was a picture of Xi Shi, but the significance of that we just do not know."

Scarlet smoothed the leather on her pants with a slow-sliding hand, cream white, black fingernail polish. "And who took it?"

Lao once again took over the briefing. "The identity of the thief is not known, but we do have a lead. His name is Victor Li, a small-time scumbag pushing heroin around the bottom of the city. His day job is working as a fence for smuggled diamonds and rumor has it he knows something about the missing portrait. He's also worked as a pimp."

"A missing picture is hardly a threat to world peace," Scarlet said.

"Maybe you should listen more and talk less?" Lexi said.

"You *what*?" Scarlet turned in her chair to face Lexi.

Hawke sighed. "Leave it!"

"The point remains," Scarlet said, winking at Lexi and returning to face Lao, "that a stolen portrait is not exactly the plot of Goldfinger."

Another glance between Lao and the American general.

"No, but it doesn't end there," McShain said. "Our intel is pointing to a major and devastating attack on an unspecified city."

Scarlet wished she had listened more and said less.

"What kind of attack?" Hawke asked, straight to the point.

McShain fixed his eyes on Hawke. "We don't know that either, but we're pretty sure it's got something to do with an earthquake."

"I'm sorry," Hawke said, confused. "An earthquake is a natural phenomenon. How can that be used to attack somewhere?"

McShain started to turn a strange greenish-white color and looked distinctly uncomfortable. "What I'm about to tell you is the highest level of Top Secret imaginable and I wouldn't even consider breathing a word of it to you had Sir Richard Eden not instructed my superiors that you should be told."

"Good old Dickie," Scarlet said, and crossed her long legs.

A flick of the eyes from McShain. "The US Government has for some time been able to trigger earthquakes artificially and..."

"Wait a minute," Hawke said, suddenly alert. "You're not telling me those nutcases on the internet were right all along and it's been you guys causing all these quakes everywhere?"

"No, I am *not* telling you that," McShain said firmly. "The technology has only been used in strictly controlled test conditions on an American island in the Western Pacific, far, far away from the prying eyes of the rest of the world.'

Scarlet laughed. "From the human race, you mean?"

McShain ignored her. "The technology in question was evolved by our scientists from an earlier design by Nikola Tesla."

"This just gets better and better," Hawke mumbled.

"I'll say," Lexi said.

"Very recently, and around the same time as Hoffmann's death and the disappearance of your agent and the portrait, the US Navy was transporting the device from the test island to Japan where it was going to be transferred to a ship in the fleet at Yokosuka."

"And don't tell me," Hawke said, "you guys accidentally lost your new toy?"

McShain sighed and looked to Lao, who responded coolly.

"The device in question was taken in a daring assault as the transport vessel crossed the Philippine Sea. The only clue we have was sprayed on the side of the American ship during the raid."

"And that was what?" Scarlet said.

Lao held up a photo of the graffiti. It was two Chinese characters totally unintelligible to Hawke and Scarlet.

"What does it say?" Hawke asked, his interest officially captured.

"These are the characters for Lei Gong."

"I'm still lost, Jason," Hawke said. "What does it mean?"

"Lei Gong is a name, Mr Hawke," McShain said. "It means Lord of Thunder."

"General McShain's right," said Lao. "In Chinese mythology Lei Gong, or Lei Shen to use his other name, was the God of Thunder."

"Sounds like a reasonable chap," Scarlet said.

Jason Lao took a deep breath. "Of all the ancient Chinese gods, the Thunder God was not one to mess with. He appeared to the world as half-man and half-bird, and punished those mortals who transgressed the boundaries of Taoism. His wife was Lei Zi, the Goddess of Lightning."

Scarlet clicked her tongue. "They sound like they'd be real fun at a swingers' party."

31

Hawke rolled his eyes and turned to Lao. "But why was his name sprayed on the side of the American ship?"

Lao shrugged his shoulders. "Maybe whoever took the device has a serious ego problem and thinks he's some kind of god."

"Or maybe," McShain said, "they were giving us some kind of warning about what we're in for."

Lexi nodded. "I think so, yes. Why else waste time doing this during what had to be a lightning raid?"

"Very funny, darling..." Scarlet said.

Lexi looked at her confused. "Sorry?"

"Thunder God, lightning raid..."

"Oh, I didn't mean to..."

Lao interrupted the moment. "This was also sprayed on the ship." He held up another photo of more Chinese characters. "It says the whole world will fear me."

"Not *another* one," Hawke said, recalling Zaugg.

"I'm sorry?" Lao asked.

"Nothing. Carry on."

"Either way," Lao continued, "it's come down to us to get to the bottom of it, and when I say us, I mean you." He looked steadily at Hawke and Scarlet. "Our intel is limited, but we think that the first earthquake attack is merely a prelude to a much bigger strike somewhere else in the world, so it's imperative we find out who's taken the device and take them out before they kill millions of people."

"And then the US Government is going to want the device back in safe hands," McShain said sternly. "And the whole thing remains Top Secret, got it?"

His tone suggested that taking the information to a newspaper might be the sort of thing you'd live to regret. Hawke and Scarlet both nodded in agreement.

"One thing I still don't understand," Hawke said. "What connects the murder of Felix Hoffmann and the portrait of Xi Shi with the stolen Tesla device?"

"Nothing at all," Lao said, "apart from the fact this was found on Hoffmann's body." Lao passed another photo to Hawke and his eyes widened to the max when he saw it. He was looking at an image of Hoffmann's dead body in a morgue, and cut into his corpse were the only two Chinese characters that he now recognized.

"Lei Shen, the God of Thunder?"

Lao nodded. McShain looked nervous.

"This detail was of course omitted from the official public record," Lao said. "According to the official story Felix Hoffmann was killed in an attempted robbery." He smiled briefly. "But these characters were carved into his stomach, and as Eden told you, Agent Zhang's calling card – the origami dragonfly – was left at the scene of the murder as well. Clearly, she was framed for the murder of Felix Hoffmann."

"Clearly," Scarlet said, glancing suspiciously at Lexi out the corner of her eye.

"I did not kill Felix Hoffmann, I swear," Lexi said.

"I believe you," Lao said. "And so will everyone else in here if we are to work together and stop this nightmare from getting any bigger, agreed?"

Hawke nodded. Scarlet made a muffled note of reluctant agreement.

Lao offered an appreciative glance at them all. "So the writing on Hoffmann's body clearly suggests his death is connected to the theft of the Tesla device, and his expertise on ancient Chinese artwork tie everything together with the missing portrait of Xi Shi. As far as your agent is concerned, we know she had Hoffmann under surveillance while he was here in the city recently, so her disappearance is linked to this also, but we don't know the full reason why these things are connected yet. We do know, however, that somehow they are and we have to work out what it is before whoever is behind this murders millions of innocent people."

Scarlet shrugged. "Another day, another dollar."

"You think you can handle this?" McShain asked.

"Pretty sure," Hawke said. "But we're going to need more help so I'm going to make a call."

"And what about you?" McShain said, facing Scarlet.

She sighed. "Don't ask me. I'm still dazed by Joe Hawke using the word *phenomenon*."

CHAPTER SIX

The Blue Orchid was a luxury nightclub buried in the heart of Hong Kong's entertainment district on the east end of Pottinger Street. It was on the same island as Lao's office, so it was just a short ride in a cab through a few blocks of the financial district and they were there, but halfway into their journey Hawke received a text message.

It was from Ryan Bale. He said that he and Sophie Durand had been briefed by Sir Richard Eden and instructed to join him immediately. They were already in Hong Kong and wanted to meet in a bar before they spoke with Victor Li at the Blue Orchid.

Hawke and Scarlet emerged from the cab into a warm subtropical afternoon, the air buzzing with the sounds of a busy city and traffic pollution rising into clouds that hung gray and heavy above the dense skyline.

The bar was busy but there was no sign of Ryan or Sophie yet. Hawke ordered two whiskies and he and Scarlet took a table by the window overlooking the street outside.

"Just like old times," Scarlet said.

"How do you mean?"

She shrugged her shoulders and took some of the Scotch. "Don't you remember Karachi?"

Hawke nodded. Yes, he remembered Karachi. Hart and the rest of the top brass had flown the ultra elite subsection of his unit into Pakistan where they were to meet with local liaison before entering Afghanistan and neutralizing a terrorists' compound in the Tora Bora region.

"Back when you were in the SAS?" Hawke asked.

Scarlet smiled and downed her drink. "The good old days."

"And now you're part of the SIS. A very different life I'd imagine."

She nodded but said nothing. Hawke had known she was lying about being in the Secret Intelligence Service ever since Agent Nightingale had told him so. His former CIA contact had once saved his life and he trusted her a lot more than he would trust Cairo Sloane, and that was for sure.

But all Nightingale had told him was that Scarlet had never been part of MI5, and this cute little bombshell was the full extent of his knowledge about her. He knew she was lying, and he knew she was working for a powerful agency, but who exactly was still a mystery.

The same went for Sophie Durand, the French spy currently shacked up with Ryan Bale in the world's most unlikely relationship. She too had told him she was attached to the DGSE, the French Secret Service. They had first met when they were searching an apartment in Geneva. Her backstory also turned out to be a web of lies, busted once again by the enigmatic Nightingale. Hawke wondered if she had told Ryan the truth about her background since they had been seeing each other. He doubted it.

"So why did you leave the SAS, Cairo?"

She ran her finger around the edge of the glass. Black nail varnish, smooth white hands, beautiful but lethal.

"Some things are better left unsaid, Joe. You know that."

"But..."

Before he could finish his question, he heard a familiar voice call his name. It was Ryan Bale, now walking across the lobby and stepping into the busy bar. He was wearing a Batman t-shirt under a denim jacket and black jeans. He still hadn't combed his lanky hair. Sophie was wearing blue jeans and a simple black shirt. Her hair was up.

"These are your friends?" Lexi asked, eyeing them suspiciously.

Hawke nodded. "Ryan saved my life once. I never forget something like that."

They approached the table and smiled.

Scarlet smiled at Ryan. "Another two whiskies please, waiter."

"Very funny," said Ryan.

"No, I'm serious," she said. "Go and get more drinks, *boy*. We have a serious job to do and I won't work on an empty stomach."

Ryan sighed and went to the bar with Sophie. They returned moments later with a bottle of whisky and five glasses.

Scarlet looked at the bottle and raised an eyebrow. "But what's everyone else going to drink?"

They took a few minutes to catch up. It turned out that Ryan and Sophie had spent the last two weeks together at her place in the south of France in the hills just outside of Marseille. Apparently Lea Donovan wasn't the only woman capable of falling in love with the world's most annoying nerd, Hawke thought.

They talked about Lea's disappearance, and how it was linking up to everything else, but the thought she might have been harmed, or worse, depressed them and they were silent for a long time, each staring into their glasses. If they were thinking the same thing as Hawke then they were wondering if she was still alive.

Ryan nodded his head and sipped his drink. "Then let's get her back," was all he said.

Hawke, Scarlet and Lexi then gave Ryan and Sophie a longer briefing about the last few hours in Hong Kong, and what they had learned about the murder of Felix Hoffmann and his links to the theft of the Xi Shi portrait and the disappearance of the secret Tesla machine.

Ryan's eyes widened like saucers. "This is unreal!"

"Sounds like something from a disaster movie," Sophie said, stunned as Hawke finished describing the potential of the device.

"Hardly," Ryan said. "The US Government has been working on controlling the environment for decades, whether it's tsunamis, floods, rain levels or even earthquakes, like in this example."

"Here we go again..." Scarlet rolled her eyes and started searching her pockets for a cigarette.

Ryan ignored her and pushed his glasses up the bridge of his nose. "Cloud seeding as a form of weather modification has been around a long time. They fire silver iodide into the cloud and this induces precipitation." He turned to Scarlet and spoke very slowly. "That means it *makes it rain*."

"I know what it means, boy. If you're going to bore us to death then at least make it fast."

Ryan was undeterred and sipped hurriedly at the Scotch before continuing. "The American Government's HAARP facility in Alaska is one of the classic conspiracy theories."

"HAARP?" Lexi asked.

"High-Frequency Active Auroral Research," Ryan said.

"Oh, sure," she said. "I know that one."

Ryan continued. "It's built of a massive number of antennas that are there ostensibly to research the ionosphere but theorists have blamed it for just about every disaster from earthquakes to exploding space

38

shuttles."

"Interesting," Scarlet said. "And when you say theorists you mean those sad little wingnuts who sit in the dark with hats made from tin foil?"

Ryan gave her a sideways glance and continued. "All I'm saying is that the US Government, and others around the world, do have active research programs into altering the natural environment. The Tesla Oscillator is just a very early example of this."

"Do enlighten us," Scarlet said, sipping her whisky.

"Tesla invented his oscillator in the eighteen-nineties as a simple way to generate electricity, which at the time was a fairly new idea."

"And what does this have to do with what we're doing now?" Lexi said.

"He'll get there in the end," Hawke said, noting Lexi's confusion.

"Like I said, it was used for generating electricity, but in his later life Tesla claimed he had used the machine to create an earthquake in New York. His comments were reported but largely ignored, and when the powers-that-be decided to discredit him and ruin his reputation, the earthquake claim, along with all his other ideas, simply faded away."

"This is earth-shattering news, boy" Scarlet said.

"Yes, well... ah – very funny," Ryan said. "But seriously..."

"A great album," Hawke said, but urged Ryan to continue when confronted with so many blank expressions all at once.

"The thing is, the original Tesla machine that he claimed had caused the 1898 earthquake was actually very small, only seven inches long and weighing just a pound or two. If this picture is anything to go by," he said, pointing at the size of the crate being loaded into the helicopter on the ambushed vessel, "this new device is tens of times bigger and would cause an earthquake big enough to destroy an entire city no problem at all."

"And that," Hawke said, downing his drink, "is probably the best news we're going to get all day. Let's go."

*

Less than half an hour later they emerged from the bar and walked down Pottinger Street towards the nightclub. Halfway down on the right Hawke was the first to see the sign – a neon blue orchid, bright in the late dusk.

Groups of well-dressed people were already congregating outside the club on the sidewalk, pulling money from their wallets and purses and checking their hairdos.

Hawke surveyed the crowd. "This is the place."

"More up-market than I was expecting," Sophie said.

"My boss has good intel sources," said Lexi. "If he says this is where we'll find Li, then this is where we'll find him."

Inside was a plush entrance hall with stairs leading down to a luxury cocktail lounge and dance floor, behind which was a small door leading through to a smaller part of the club.

Hawke studied the busy club suspiciously. All they had to go on was the grainy picture of Victor Li that Jason Lao and McShain had given them back at the office, but already he was certain his man wasn't in the main area.

"I think our man must be hiding through there," Hawke said.

Scarlet nodded. "So let's go in and find out."

In the corner on a sumptuous semi-circular bench seat

of white leather was a small crowd of people gathered around a central figure. He was dressed in black and regaling everyone with a lengthy tale, a Champagne flute in his hand.

Hawke recognized the man at once from the photo Jason Lao had given him and he felt the old buzz that used to come so often when he was on the verge of accomplishing a mission. Like a hawk swooping for the kill, he wasted no time in weaving through the busy nightclub on his way to Victor Li's table.

The music was intense and the smell of expensive perfume and flavored vodka filled the room as Hawke neared his target. Lights flashed, and a glitterball sent sparkling flashes of silver all over the men and women dancing in the club. A place like this only made sense if you were pretty drunk, he thought, remembering his own turbulent youth back in London.

As they reached the dais with the private tables, two men roughly the size of walk-in wardrobes closed the pathway and raised their hands.

"That's far enough," one of them said.

"This is a private area, so go back," said the other.

Scarlet fronted up to the first man. "I'll kick you in *your* private area if you don't let us past."

Both men laughed. "I must weigh three times what you do, woman. How are you going to get past me?"

Hawke whistled and shook his head.

In a flash, Scarlet delivered her promise, and threw in a free Krav Maga inside chop on his collar bone for good measure. He collapsed in a heap on the floor with his hands all over his balls and screaming like a baby.

Scarlet sniffed. "That's how."

The other guy raised his hands and smiled. "Be my guest..."

Lexi and Sophie covered the second bouncer while

Hawke, Scarlet and Ryan stepped up to Li.

"Victor Li?"

The man looked from his crippled bodyguard over to the strangers in front of him with nervous eyes. "Yeah, who's asking?"

Hawke said no more, but smashed the Champagne glass out of his hand and grabbed him by the throat. Li panicked and went red, and the women around the table screamed and scattered.

"Who stole the Xi Shi portrait?" Hawke asked, his hand tightening around Li's throat.

"Please, I can give you money. My employer has more money than you could ever dream of spending. Please, let go of my throat and I'll give you all you want."

"Do I look like the kind of man who would fly from London to Hong Kong to rob a little scrote like you for money?"

No response.

Hawke shook him violently. "Well?"

"I guess not..." the man whispered.

"One more time and then I'll squeeze your throat until you pass out. When you wake up you'll wish you were dead. Who stole the Xi Shi portrait?"

"Okay, okay...please, just let me breathe." As he spoke, and his concentration was focused on Hawke, Scarlet reached inside his jacket and surreptitiously got his iPhone and passed it to Ryan who uploaded something onto it. Thirty seconds later it was back in Li's pocket.

"A name, now."

A look of surrender appeared in Victor Li's red, bulging eyes. His remaining bodyguard looked on in silent horror as Sophie pushed a concealed pistol into his stomach and Lexi traced her fingers up his neck at the same time.

Li spoke quickly. "His name is Johnny Chan."

"Johnny Chan?"

Li nodded. "I swear it. He's the best thief in Hong Kong."

"Is he really?" Scarlet said.

"But he doesn't like it if you call him that. He calls himself a cat burglar."

"How the hell would you burgle a cat?" Ryan said. "Sounds like it might be illegal."

Scarlet turned and faced Ryan. "I told you never try to be funny."

"Sorry."

"Thanks for that image, Ryan," Hawke said. He returned his attention to Li.

"And where can I find this Johnny Chan, famed burglar of cats?"

"You can make jokes now," Li said, his voice hoarse with the effort of speaking through Hawke's iron-grip, "but you mess with a man like Johnny Chan and you end up in Kowloon Bay."

Hawke tightened his grip and pushed his knee down on Li's stomach, compressing his diaphragm. "Listen, I don't give a damn about Johnny Chan and Kowloon Bay. All I care about is finding the portrait he stole and fast because it's going to help me find someone I care about a great deal. Sadly, I do *not* care about you and I will hurt you if you do not help me. Where can I find Chan?"

"If you have a death wish that's your business," Li said. "But you won't find him in Hong Kong. He took the portrait out of the city as soon as he stole it."

"Where did he go?"

"Shanghai."

Scarlet sighed. "Great. One of the biggest cities in the world."

43

Hawke tightened his grip. "That's no problem, is it Victor?"

"Why not?"

"Because you're going to tell me how to find him in Shanghai." Hawke pushed down with his knee until Victor's eyes were about to pop out like Champagne corks.

"I'll give you what you need," Li said.

Hawke grinned. "I thought you might."

CHAPTER SEVEN

Dragon Island, East China Sea

The man known only as Mr Luk watched the distant sea crash against the rocks of Dragon Island. Somewhere above him, high in the subtropical canopies, was his master's house. From there the view stretched three hundred and sixty degrees, from Hangzhou Bay in the west and the East China Sea in the east.

But down here, on the docking platform, things were less salubrious.

Luk fixed the motorboat to the mooring post and told two guards to take the prisoner into the boatshed. Normally he would take his work into the master's basement where the slaves waited in terrified silence, but on this occasion time was short and the boss had told him to make it fast.

Luk knew why the man had to die. He was a criminal investigator in the Special Branch of the Shanghai Municipal Police. Such a man would be feared by most, but in this case Luk knew this dynamic would be very much reversed. The inspector knew only too well who had kidnapped him from his apartment in Nanhui. He had already begged for his life very convincingly.

All of this meant nothing to Luk. He couldn't feel emotions. Some had called him a robot, but never to his face. He thought of himself simply as pure and neutral. Whatever he was, his master appreciated it and he was paid very well for his unique talents.

They dragged the inspector into the boatshed. His screams were muffled by the oily rag they had stuffed into his mouth when they piled him into the hull of the boat. The men tied him to an old engine block while Luk half-closed the door, but not completely. He liked to watch the Nankeen night herons flying in and out of the Xixi wetland park. They offered him solace in a brutal world.

Then Luk lit the portable paraffin blow lamp.

Yes, the fools had failed in the West, but that was in the past. Now the quest had been passed to him things would be different. He would not make the same mistakes as the others had. His master's desire would bring the sort of savage reforms to the global system that it so badly needed.

Problems like the inspector simply had to go away.

He ordered one of the men to remove the rag, and the inspector gasped for breath. His desperate, babbled pleas for mercy were silenced by a casual wave from Luk's index finger.

"Tell me all about Jason Lao," Luk said quietly, as if he were asking an old friend about a mutual acquaintance.

"I don't know what you're talking about," the inspector said. "Please, my wife is pregnant! Please don't kill me."

"*Shhh*, inspector. You will disturb the herons."

"All I can tell you is Jason Lao contacted the SMP from his base in Hong Kong and I was ordered to put a tail on you. That is all. They didn't tell me why I was to follow you."

Luk smiled gently and stroked the inspector's sweat-soaked face. "That was very rude of them, and very unfortunate for you."

"If I knew anything, I swear I would tell you."

"Inspector, believe me when I tell you that in the next hour you will tell me everything you know and a lot more you don't..."

The men laughed. One of them lit a cigarette and leaned against the boatshed door. The bay was especially hazy today, Luk considered.

"Who were the Westerners that Lao met in his Hong Kong office recently?"

"How should I know? I was told nothing by my superiors except I must follow you."

"The problem I have with that is that a man of your rank is always involved in the strategic planning of such operations. So now you will tell me with whom and why Lao had that meeting. We know the American was a US Army general by the name of McShain, and we know why he's here in China, and of course we know about Zhang Xiaolu, naturally. I want to know who the others were, and who they are working for."

"I've already told you, I don't know!"

Luk contemplated the man's desperate pleas. They meant nothing to him.

He did the kind of jobs other men preferred not to do, but this kind of work had never kept him up at night. When he was nine, the care home where he was growing up in Kowloon had referred him to a psychologist for evaluation after he had stoned a wounded kingfisher to death.

After weeks of discussions, the diagnosis was that he was a sociopath, who could easily turn into a psychopath without extensive counselling. This meant he was among the four percent of people born entirely without a conscience. The standard advice for dealing with psychopaths is to avoid them at all costs. They might not be inclined to hurt you, but if they are, they have no conscience to stop them.

Luk had never found any of this to be at all problematic. In fact, he had found his total lack of conscience to be nothing but conducive to getting ahead in the world. It had proven particularly useful when he was navigating the series of juvenile detention centers and prisons he grew up in after the care home years.

But there was a downside: like most psychopaths, Luk got bored very easily. He often filled the void with drugs and alcohol, only this made him even angrier. He knew no joy, no love, no grief, no guilt. He knew only about gain and loss. Life to Luk was a simple zero sum game which he generally won.

Today, staring at the pathetic and forlorn spectacle of the inspector as he begged for his life, he was reminded of that kingfisher, the one he had killed in the hills of eastern Kowloon.

"Mr Inspector," Luk said quietly, his hand gripping the blow lamp. Its fierce flame was blindingly bright in the half-light of the humid boatshed. "It is unfortunate for you that I do not believe a word of what you say."

Luk stepped forward, his short, bulky frame now looming over the restrained police inspector. He smiled like a kindly teacher and raised the blow lamp. Moments later, the inspector's screams frightened the distant herons and terrified them up into the sky.

CHAPTER EIGHT

Shanghai

Hawke glanced through the window of the Airbus A321 at the countless ships in Hangzhou Bay as the plane descended through wispy clouds on its way into Shanghai Pudong International. With a population over three times bigger than London's, the city loomed up to the west of the aircraft like a terrible, sleeping monster. He hoped Victor Li hadn't sent them all on a wild goose chase.

He checked his watch. The two and a half hour flight meant it was still before lunch and they had the whole afternoon to track down Johnny Chan and the missing portrait, which hopefully would lead them to Lea. But it turned out he'd been optimistic about local traffic and it took over an hour to get from the airport to their hotel. Eden had booked them into the Ritz-Carlton, which Hawke was certain wasn't within the usual parameters of Her Majesty's Government's travel allowance, but that was a question for much later and he filed it with all the other questions he wanted answers to.

The ride had been tedious and stressful so when they finally arrived they took a few minutes to freshen up before starting their search for Johnny Chan. Standing in the heart of the Lujiazui financial zone the hotel offered a breathtaking view over the Huangpu River far below and the endless sprawl of the city beyond its far bank. Somewhere in all of that, Hawke thought, was Johnny Chan and the stolen Xi Shi portrait.

The others joined him on the balcony. Scarlet yawned and stretched her arms, surveying the massive metropolis for the first time. "Where the hell do we start?"

"Your man Lao didn't give us much to go on," said Ryan. "So far all we have is a stolen portrait of one of the famous Four Beauties and a dead German researcher with the Chinese characters for an ancient god of thunder carved into his stomach."

"Who was murdered by someone trying to frame me," Lexi said.

Scarlet raised an eyebrow. "And what was that other thing? Oh yeah, I remember – a missing Tesla device capable of levelling an entire city."

"Oh yeah," Ryan said. "That's the best bit!"

Scarlet perused the drinks menu. "We're going to need some refreshment."

Moments later, Lexi ordered room service – a bottle of chilled vodka and some cigarettes to smoke on the balcony.

The door buzzed.

"That'll be the room service," Lexi said, looking through the spy hole in the door.

She opened the door and Hawke heard her thank the room service attendant. A moment later Scarlet was pouring out glasses of chilled vodka.

Hawke took a long drink and settled his mind. "Any progress on Lea?"

Ryan cleared his throat. "Not really. As we now know, Eden sent her over here to gather information on Felix Hoffmann. He was in Hong Kong researching something but then he flew out suddenly and without any warning. We know Lea never left the city because of passport records, and we also know what happened to Hoffmann in Paris, so the concern is that whoever killed Hoffmann has something to do with Lea's disappearance."

"But we don't know she's actually been taken though?" Scarlet asked.

"No," replied Sophie. "She may have had to drop off the grid. We don't know if she's in danger or not, but it's unlike her to break protocol in this way. That is why Eden has such grave concerns."

"You all seem very well briefed," Hawke said.

"Eden contacted me less than an hour ago," Sophie said in a matter-of-fact tone.

Hawke got serious and slammed his glass down with a smack. "All right, then we know what we have to do. Our priority is the safe return of Lea and to get to the bottom of this Hoffmann murder. Eden says they must be linked and so we're working on them simultaneously."

He turned to Ryan. "You and Sophie stay here at the hotel. We need some kind of temporary HQ and this may as well be it, plus I've asked an old friend of mine to join us – Commodore Hart. I called her when we left Lao's office. If she turns up while I'm away, make her feel at home."

"No problemo," Ryan said, collapsing on the bed and powering up his laptop.

Hawke pulled on his jacket. "Stay in contact with us while you're researching this Tesla machine and anything else in this mess that can throw some light on things. In the meantime, we're going to have a word with Johnny Chan."

"And where is Chan?" Sophie asked.

"According to Victor Li, he lives in a villa on the Hengshan Road in the Minhang district. How long will that take us, Lexi?"

"Maybe a half hour by cab."

*

An hour later, Lexi paid the cab driver and he pulled away into the traffic. They were in a broad, tree-lined avenue in the heart of one of Shanghai's up-market areas. It didn't take long to knock out Chan's CCTV and climb over the wall and then they walked casually up to the front door of his luxury villa.

Hawke paused along the way to peer through a side gate into the rear garden where he saw an expansive swimming pool surrounded by persimmon trees. "Very nice," he said, nodding his head with genuine appreciation.

"Amazing what the proceeds of crime can bring a man," Scarlet said. "I'm obviously in the wrong line of work."

"You think?"

"Uh-huh. Actually, I've been giving that a little thought. After our little sojourn into the vault of Poseidon I was thinking about what would happen if we located a large amount of treasure, only this time we should decide *not* to let the Americans walk away with it."

"Do you ever think of anything besides money, Cairo?" Hawke said.

"Of course. Sometimes I think about sex."

Hawke sighed. "We can talk about your early retirement later, but now I think it's time for a chat with little Johnny."

Hawke moved silently over the fake grass, but despite the lack of noise a man on an upper balcony began shouting and seconds later he was pouring fire down on them from the muzzle of a submachine gun.

Hawke leaped behind an enormous tea tree to avoid the hail of bullets now flitting past his head at the speed of sound and landing with an anticlimactic thud in the ground around him.

Straight ahead he watched another man join the first on the balcony. He wondered which was Johnny Chan and which the hired help. To his right, Scarlet was taking cover behind a low wall and returning fire at the men with her Beretta while Lexi sprinted behind Chan's glistening SUV in the driveway.

He used the cover of the border plants to inch forward out of the view of the men in the house. Scarlet moved forward and went to the right where she hooked up with Lexi before both moved out around the side of the house. They were giving the men two fronts to fight, and he guessed this wasn't going to be the hardest battle he'd ever fought.

He watched a particularly savage exchange of fire between one of the men and Scarlet which ended with the man taking three bullets in his chest and collapsing in agony over the balcony railing. He landed with a terrible thud on the pavement below.

"Damn it, Cairo!" Hawke said under his breath. "What if that was Chan?"

The other man didn't react to the death of his colleague, and wasted no time in emptying his magazine in the direction of Scarlet Sloane.

Hawke took advantage of the moment to run forward and secure a position under the front porch. He snatched up the fallen man's pistol and tried the door – locked. Next move was to pick up one of the plant pots and smash the window to the right of the doorway. Then he was inside.

With the sound of Scarlet and Lexi engaging the man on the balcony in a desperate firefight, Hawke moved up the stairs three steps at a time. On the upper landing he turned left and headed toward the front of the property where Balcony Man was firing at his team and occasionally dodging behind a plaster archway for cover. His footsteps masked by the sound of the gunfire, Hawke stuffed his gun in his belt and moved quickly behind the man, grabbing him by the throat with his left hand while disarming him with the other. A second later he drew the gun and held it at the man's temple.

"Game's Over, Chan."

The man struggled in Hawke's choke-hold. "Who the hell are you people?"

"Think of us as art restorers."

"What?"

"You have some art and we're going to restore it – to the rightful owners." Hawke leaned over the balcony and shouted to the others to join him.

Chan began sweating. "I don't know what you mean!"

Hawke sighed. "It's better you talk now, because in about thirty seconds your worst nightmare is going to walk through that door."

"I don't understand..."

About thirty seconds later Chan's worst nightmare walked through the door.

The art thief looked at the svelte figures of Scarlet and Lexi as they walked casually into his office. "This is my worst nightmare? Looks more like a dream."

"It's no dream, kitten," Scarlet said and kicked him swiftly in the balls.

Chan doubled over in agony and collapsed to the floor in a heap.

"I see you still favor the direct approach," Hawke said.

Lexi glared at Scarlet. "Hey, not fair! I wanted to do that."

"So go ahead," Scarlet purred. "It's not like I kicked them back up inside or anything... *yet.*"

Chan's eyes widened and he gulped in fear. He

glanced up at Hawke, tears in his eyes. "Don't let her anywhere near me, please! You're a man, you understand, right?"

Hawke crouched down and adopted a fake-buddy air, just two old pals in the pub. "What did we say about nightmares, Johnny?"

"Okay, *okay*... What do you want?"

"Like I said, you stole a piece of art recently from Hong Kong and its owners would very much like it back."

"I don't know what..." Chan stopped talking and put his hands between his legs as Scarlet took a step towards him. "All right! It's in there."

"Where?"

Chan flicked his head to a door on the far side of the office. "It's there in the safe room. The first shelf on the right."

Hawke glanced from Chan to the safe and moved forward. Scanning for booby-traps as he went, he stepped into the safe room and took a thin metal box from the shelf.

Back in the study he opened the box and they all peered inside.

They had found the Xi Shi Portrait.

CHAPTER NINE

Scarlet spoke first, and with undisguised contempt. "Is that *it*?"

"What do you mean?" Lexi said. "It's beautiful."

Hawke held the tiny portrait in his hands. It was much smaller than he had expected, and less colorful as well, but there was a certain beauty in its depiction of Xi Shi. She was sitting on a riverbank beside a peach tree in a pale blue dress, now faded by the centuries, and staring at herself in the water.

"So what have we got, Joe?" Scarlet said, and peered over Hawke's shoulder to take a closer look at the portrait while Lexi strapped Johnny Chan into his leather chair and taped his mouth shut.

"We don't want him telling his boss that we've got the portrait," she said matter-of-factly, and shrugged her shoulders.

"But what's so damned special about this particular picture?" Scarlet said. "I just don't get it." She took the portrait from Hawke and turned it over in her hands. "Makes you wish we had a vase to smash."

"I don't understand," Lexi said, confused.

"A long story," said Hawke. "Perhaps another time..."

Hawke took the picture back and studied it in close detail. He already knew it was a job for Ryan, and decided the quicker they got it back to the hotel the better.

"I want Ryan to take a look at this thing," he said at last. "But first we have some loose ends to tie up here."

Hawke stepped over Chan and tore the duct tape off

his mouth.

"Who commissioned you to steal this portrait?"

"I don't know what you mean," Chan said.

"How much did you get paid?"

Chan was silent.

Without warning, Hawke punched him hard in the face, breaking his nose. Scarlet rolled her eyes. Lexi winced.

Chan screamed and spat blood onto his polished floorboards. "You're crazy, man! Why would you do that?"

"He's not very good with words," Lexi said.

"Lets his fists do the talking," said Scarlet.

"Once again, and then I'll reintroduce you to Cairo Sloane's persuasive talents. "Who commissioned you to steal this picture, and where is Lea Donovan?"

"Seriously, I am very professional," Chan said. "I never reveal the names of my clients. If I did, I would be out of business in a day and I have never even heard the name Lea Donovan in my life!"

"And you'll be out of this world in less than a minute if you don't overlook your touching little client-confidentiality agreement right now... *Cairo*?"

Scarlet purred with delight. "I thought you'd never ask."

She stepped forward and pointed Chan's Colt in his groin. The thief's eyebrows went to the moon and his eyes widened like saucers.

"Okay, maybe just this once I could bend the rules a little, just for you, you understand?" He tried to grin through the fear, his eyes crawling from the muzzle of the Colt and up Scarlet's arm to her calm, smirking face.

"I want a name, Johnny," Hawke said. " A name, and the location of Lea Donovan, right fucking now." His meaty fist hovered menacingly at a solid punching-distance above Chan's bloodied face, his arm coiled like a spring.

"Please, I beg of you just one thing," Chan said, his voice breaking with renewed fear. "When – or more likely *if* – you get close to this man, please don't tell him where you got his name. He will kill me in a heartbeat, and when I say kill, I don't mean shoot me like you want to shoot me, I mean he will torture me to death in the most terrible way you can imagine."

"Name, Johnny. Now."

"I was commissioned to steal the portrait by Sheng Fang."

"Means nothing to me, darling," Scarlet said.

"Me neither," said Hawke.

But Lexi spun around and stared at Chan for a few seconds in horror. She spoke to him rapidly in Mandarin, and he returned a few short sentences.

"What are you saying, Lexi?" Hawke asked.

"I just asked him if he's telling us the truth."

"But we have no way of knowing that, do we now, darling?" Scarlet said, looking at Lexi with thinly veiled suspicion.

"It's the truth," she said. "I asked him if he was being truthful and he said he was. He stole the painting for Sheng Fang. He says he was supposed to deliver the portrait to him half an hour ago but couldn't because we've got him taped to a chair. He says Sheng will just send some guys to get the painting and we're all dead, basically, and I believe him. This is Sheng Fang we're talking about, Joe."

"And the significance of that is... what?" Hawke asked.

"Sheng Fang is one of China's richest men," Lexi said. "Ostensibly he made his money in the telecom sector but there are many rumors about him and his activities in the criminal underworld."

Hawke sighed. "Why do I have a bad feeling about this?"

Lexi casually brushed Chan's paperwork on the floor and sat on the desk. "Many people say he made his first fortune in the human slave trade as a trafficker and used that money to invest in real estate before the economic explosion here in the last few years. Among those who know the real man and not merely the public persona he has a reputation for extreme violence and close ties to the Triads."

"And now you understand my reluctance to give you his name," Johnny Chan said, a look of vindication on his face. "I don't know what Sheng wants with the portrait but there's word on the streets – rumors in the wind. Something very big and very dangerous is going to happen, and soon too. A man like Sheng doesn't play games. He wants everything, and he's already halfway there."

"Yeah, you can shut up now," Scarlet said, taping his mouth back up once again.

"This isn't good news, guys," Lexi said. "If Sheng really is behind the disappearance of the portrait and the murder of Hoffmann, then it must be him behind the theft of the Tesla device from the American transport vessel, and worse than that, Lea's disappearance."

Hawke sighed. "This sounds like bad news on a great many levels…"

"I'll say. Does this mean I don't get to shoot his balls?" Scarlet said, jabbing the Colt into Chan's crotch a second time. Chan moaned beneath the duct tape. Hawke wasn't sure if she was feigning the disappointment he heard in her voice or not.

"Afraid so. Cairo – you need to get in touch with Richard and give him an update. I'm going to speak with

Nightingale and see if the Americans know anything about this."

Scarlet contacted Sir Richard Eden. Hawke left Lexi in charge of Chan while he called Manhattan.

A second later Nightingale answered the phone.

"N, hi. Joe."

"Well if it isn't Joe Hawke," she said. "Not heard from you for a while." She sounded happy.

"What can I say? I'm a busy man."

"And here I was thinking that you liked me. You know you asked me on a dinner date when you were flying into Athens. What happened to that?"

"Must have been the altitude," he said. "And as I recall, you still haven't even told me your real name."

She laughed, but now there was a sadness to it. "I think you and I must have the world's most dysfunctional relationship."

"We're in a relationship?"

"You know what I mean, Joe." He heard her sigh. "So I guess you're not calling to ask me on a dinner date this time?"

"Sorry, N, but no. I'm just wondering what you can get me on a guy called Sheng Fang. He has something to do with a case we're on, only this time Lea is missing. He's supposed to be a real..."

"A real bad guy, I know. And you're talking about Lea Donovan, right?"

"Yes. Listen, you've heard of Sheng?"

"Sure. We're not all as ignorant as you, Joe."

"Touché, but I would prefer the word Anglo centric next time."

"Hmm, if you say so. Sorry about Lea by the way. "

'Thanks, but we need information more than sympathy, N."

"I know..."

He heard her firing up her computer and after a few seconds of key-tapping she came back to the phone. "Sheng's a big player in the telecom sector in China – we're talking twenty-five billion dollars here, and that's just the legit end of things. Various covert agencies are pretty sure he still has a few fingers in the human-trafficking pie as well, and how much he makes from that we just don't know. His wealth makes your man Zaugg look like some kind of welfare bum. He has his own private island, and rumor has it that's where he kills his enemies and holds his slaves."

"He sounds like he has reach. Am I right?"

"You most certainly are. Sheng has so many politicians on strings he treats the National People's Congress like a puppet show. Upsetting him is like upsetting China itself. You need to tread carefully here, Joe."

"I will."

"I mean, try not to be *yourself* at any point and you might just get away with it."

"Thanks for the vote of confidence."

"You're welcome. What's your interest in this guy, anyway?"

"We think he's behind the murder of a theological scholar in France and the theft of a portrait in Hong Kong. Oh, and the Tesla machine that you guys were playing with on an atoll in the Pacific."

"The *what*?"

"Maybe you should start to do some research into that, N. I have it on very good authority – a General McShain of the US Army, for one – that someone recently stole a highly classified earthquake machine from the US Navy and now a little bird, call it a nightingale if you like – is making me think the culprit is Sheng Fang."

"I never heard of a project like that, Joe – honest. But

then I've been out of the loop for a long time I guess."
He heard another sigh and then a few moments of silence.

"Are you all right, N?"

"Me? Sure – why wouldn't I be?"

"Just that you sometimes tune out for second, if you know what I mean. What happened to you, N? Why did you leave the CIA?"

"Maybe another time, Joe. I'll tell you over that dinner date we're never going to have."

And then she disconnected.

Hawke didn't have time to think about her last sentence. A second after he hung up, Scarlet ended her call to Eden and began to brief everyone on what he had told her.

"He says if it's Sheng Fang we need to make sure we look after ourselves. He says Sheng is known by various British intel agencies for his trafficking empire, but no one has ever been able to link it back to him."

Hawke frowned. "Why do I get the feeling this is going to spin out of control?"

"He's utterly ruthless, Joe," Scarlet said. "Richard just told me that the last man who crossed Sheng was a Japanese Yakuza rival by the name of Fujimoto. Sheng had him kidnapped right out of the heart of Tokyo and – you're not going to believe this – apparently they found his bloated corpse on a beach in Kyushu. His body was covered in a thousand cuts."

"Death by a thousand cuts?" Hawke said, shocked. "That really happens?"

"Lingchi," Lexi said coolly, as she spun Chan around in the chair with her foot for amusement. "Slow dicing. An ancient Chinese form of torturing someone to death. They sliced off tiny parts of your flesh in non-lethal cuts. They made sure not to let you bleed too much so you would live through it all. Often the victim would even live through amputations of whole limbs. It could last for days."

"Sounds almost as bad as the X Factor," Scarlet said.

"And worse than that," Lexi said, "the Chinese believed that those killed by Lingchi would suffer through all eternity because they would not have their whole body after death. It's how Sheng likes to kill people."

"He sounds like he might benefit from some professional therapy," Hawke said.

"He sounds like he might benefit from a hot bullet," said Scarlet.

"That's nothing," Lexi said. "He's renowned for the pleasure he derives from torturing those who cross him. His torturer is a man named Luk, a former Triad heavyweight from Hong Kong. Not a man to get on the wrong side of. He's a confirmed psychopath and sociopath – born with no conscience. That's why Sheng hired him. He will do things to people no one else would ever dream of doing – that no one else would even be *able* to do even if they wanted to. If he gets hold of any of us then this is what we should expect."

"That's me not sleeping tonight..." Scarlet said. "Anyway, Richard said that if Sheng is behind the disappearance of the Tesla device then the lives of millions could be at stake..."

"There's a but coming, right?" Hawke said.

"But..." continued Scarlet, "he seemed more concerned about the missing portrait. We're all scrambling to find out what's going on but clearly the reference to Lei Gong the Thunder God and the missing earthquake machine are linked. What's bothering Richard is what killing Felix Hoffmann to get the portrait has to do with any of this."

"Doesn't he have any idea what's going on?" Hawke

asked.

Scarlet shook her head. "Not really. He thinks maybe Sheng is after more than just an earthquake machine though, but the rest is up to us to work out."

Hawke cleared his throat. "Lexi – now we know this Sheng guy is involved you can bet your bottom dollar we're not going to be alone in this mystery for long, especially since we seem to have held up his little art purchase. Go to the back of the house and keep an eye out in case we get the kind of company our man Chan here says we can expect."

Lexi went to the back of the villa but returned less than two minutes later.

"I hate to tell you guys this," Lexi said, "but I think we already have a problem."

"What's up?" Hawke asked.

"I don't know who they are but a couple of SUVs just pulled up in the lane at the back and unloaded a dozen guys armed to the teeth. They look like they could take out a small army base."

"I knew this day would come!" Scarlet said, pulling Chan's Type 93 assault rifle from his desk and loading it up. "Seek and ye shall find, Joe."

"Sure, but first take photos of the portrait and email them to Ryan right away!"

"Got it."

Hawke flicked his eyes over Chan's mini arsenal and selected a shotgun. Lexi opted for the Browning Hi-Power. "Looks like the war is about to begin...if only we knew who we were fighting."

"Who cares?" said Scarlet. "Let's just blast their bollocks off so we can get back and have a drink, that way we can...*uh-oh*."

Hawke saw the look on Scarlet's face. "What's up, Cairo?"

"You're not going believe this, Joe, but now I know why Chan was so reluctant to talk about how much he was getting paid to knock off the portrait in Hong Kong."

"How?"

"Because another SUV has just pulled up out the front and the men who are getting out of it are holding Lea."

"What?" Hawke could hardly believe what he was hearing. He raced forward to the window and saw she was speaking the truth. There, in the street outside Chan's luxury villa was Lea, sandwiched in between two of Sheng's goons.

"Looks like he was giving Lea to Chan as payment for stealing the portrait."

"I don't believe it," Hawke said.

"I told you," Lexi said almost in a whisper. "Human trafficking – it's what Sheng does. This is how he pays people, with slaves."

Not on my fucking watch, Hawke thought and pulled a gun from the desk.

CHAPTER TEN

Seconds later, Henshang Road became a war zone. The men assaulting Chan's villa from the front took up what Hawke assessed as fairly professional positions in the street and front garden so he quickly had everyone take up the best defensive positions he could arrange with so little time.

Without waiting for an invitation, the men unleashed a terrific full-frontal attack on the property. Bullets piled into the stucco and blasted chunks of plaster from the walls onto Chan's Astroturf. As they fired, groups of two or three men advanced on the house while their colleagues covered them.

"Cover the back, Cairo!" Hawke shouted.

Scarlet took off down to the back of the villa while Hawke and Lexi fired back at the men in the street, pinning a few of them down in an isolated location behind a magnolia tree. The men with Lea dragged her away to the side of the property. Now they heard Scarlet firing at the back of the house.

"Great," Lexi said. "Looks like we've got the bastards on both sides."

Outside, one of the men primed a grenade and hurled it at the villa's large double doors.

"This just keeps getting better, Joe! They'll be inside in seconds."

The grenade detonated and blasted hand-size fragments of Chan's oak-paneled door into the hall with savage velocity.

Then Scarlet returned from the back of the house. "As

much as it pains me to say it, Joe," she said, "I think we have to admit defeat on this one. There's half the PLA out the back. They're over the back fence and advancing either side of the pool. No way can I hold them off with this thing." She held the Type 93 in the air. "I know I'm pretty bloody amazing but no one's *that* good."

"What I love about you is your humility, Scarlet," Lexi said.

Scarlet smirked. "I'll take that as a compliment."

"You should," said Lexi. "You have so much to be humble about, after all."

Hawke rolled his eyes. "Can we just stop the cat-fighting, please? It feels like Charlie's Angels in here and meanwhile Lea's down there in the middle of a bloody war zone."

Now the men were in the house. They could hear them systematically destroying every room, spraying bullets and lobbing grenades as they cleared the building room by room.

"Something tells me these guys are pretty serious about this portrait,' Lexi said.

"This girl is a *genius*," said Scarlet.

"Can it, Ice Queen," Lexi said.

Scarlet glared at her. "What did you say?"

"Oh, that has to hurt, right?' said Lexi, reloading her Browning. She turned to Scarlet. "I mean with you loving yourself so much and everything."

"Look, in a minute it's going to be *me* shooting you, never mind that lot downstairs!" Hawke said. "We have to focus."

"I'm always focused, darling," Scarlet said. "Didn't the Val Doonicans train you to be focused in stressful situations? Shame..."

Hawke ignored the traditional SAS slur against the SBS and tried to clear his head for a second. "Clearly whoever is behind the murder of Hoffmann and the theft of the Tesla device is also behind this," he held up the portrait of Xi Shi, the First Beauty. "My money's on this Sheng character, and it's pretty obvious he's found out we're onto him and he's not happy about it."

"If it really is Sheng then we've got a real war ahead of us!" Lexi said, her words laced with a lethal mix of fear and anger.

"If it's war he wants then war he gets," Scarlet said. "Eden was very clear about stopping Sheng with whatever it takes. We have carte blanche."

"Why don't we just start with getting out of here?" Lexi said.

Scarlet raised her voice over the sound of the gunfire. "For once I agree with you!"

The sound of men screaming and whooping with joy as they trashed the villa below resounded up the sweeping marble staircase. More shots were fired and more wanton destruction meted out by Sheng's army of thugs.

Hawke ordered Lexi to retreat with the portrait while he and Scarlet covered her from their position at the top of the stairs. There was a French window in Chan's bedroom which opened onto a broad balcony, flanked either side by two mature magnolias. It was at the rear of the house, which was now clear as the men who had stormed the villa from that direction were now inside attacking the new position defended by Hawke and Scarlet.

Hawke took a deep breath and focused his mind. It seemed his life was on a permanent full-speed setting and there was no escaping the fact. Now, only *they* had the portrait and only *they* knew about Hoffmann and the missing Tesla device developed by the US Navy. This meant only they could stop Sheng and whatever deranged plans he had for the world. Now was no time to get killed.

He and Scarlet poured a savage rain of fire onto the men at the bottom of the stairs as Lexi sprinted for safety, but they were gaining ground. There were just too many of them to fight in such an enclosed space.

"Update?!" he shouted over his shoulder.

Scarlet craned her neck and watched Lexi slip through the window, the portrait safely in her grasp. "She's out, Joe."

"Then it's time for you to go too," he shouted. Bullets traced past his head and ripped through a massive abstract oil painting Chan had had hoisted onto the wall at the top of the stairs.

"And leave you here alone?" Scarlet picked off two of the men with startling casualness and watched them tumble down the stairs and collapse in a heap on the polished hall floor.

"Yes, and *now*, Cairo! I can look after myself."

Downstairs one of the men Scarlet had just shot was screaming in pain.

"Damn!" she said. "Thought I'd finished them both off."

One of the man's compatriots fired a short burst of automatic rifle fire into his chest and ended the moaning.

"Can't say their hearts aren't in it," Scarlet said. "And it's time for us both to go, Joe – now!"

Hawke flicked his head to the open window in Chan's bedroom and made a quick calculation. "All right – let's get out of here," he said. "You take the tree on the left and I'll take the one on the right. In three, two, one..."

They deserted their position and sprinted to the large bay window in the master bedroom. As they climbed into the canopies of the magnolias they heard the sound of Sheng's men racing up the stairs and blasting everything in sight.

"Race you to the bottom!" cried Scarlet.

"You're actually enjoying this, Cairo. You're certifiable."

Hawke hit the fake lawn with a gentle thud a second before Scarlet Sloane, which caused her more irritation than the sight of Sheng's men appearing on the balcony and raking them with more machine gun fire. The bullets tore through the magnolia canopies and peppered the Astroturf all around them.

"Over there!" Hawke shouted. "It's Lea!"

He directed Scarlet's attention to the far side of the lawn where Lea was taking cover behind a long hedge. She was holding a gun taken from one of the men who had been holding her before the shooting started, but who was now lying dead on the floor.

"And look there - looks like Lexi's arranged some transportation for us."

They gave Lea the signal to retreat back to the SUV, and they sprinted across the lawn using Chan's mature gardens as cover for most of the way before running through the main gates and climbing into one of the SUVs Sheng's men had arrived in – it was a brand new Jaguar F-Pace. The driver was lying unconscious on the road beside the vehicle, and Scarlet used him as a step to help herself into the car.

"Thanks!" she said. "It would be a shame to bring any mud into such a beautiful car..."

"Are you okay, Lea?" Hawke asked.

She nodded – she looked shaken but not stirred.

"Then hit it!" screamed Hawke, and Lexi floored the accelerator.

The SUV's wheels spun and the car lurched forward in a cloud of stinking black rubber smoke. Behind them, Hawke saw Sheng's men jump into the second SUV.

"Yeah, they're not going anywhere," Lea said with that distinctive smile of hers.

"Alternator?" Hawke said.

"No time for all that," the Irishwoman said. "Blew their bastard tires out. All four of them."

Hawke smiled and nodded in appreciation of her work, but as Lexi steered the SUV roughly around the corner he saw Sheng's men climbing back out of the disabled Nissan X-Trail and kick the tires. One of them crossed the street and fired a shot through the window of a silver Nissan GTR.

"Don't celebrate too soon," said Hawke, "but I think Sheng's goons are more resourceful than we gave them credit for."

"Oh, what *now*?" sighed Lea.

"They've decided to take a nice, shiny roadster for a joyride, and I think we're the target."

CHAPTER ELEVEN

Sophie ordered some coffee while Ryan set up his laptop and started to research the missing portrait. If anyone had ever told her that she would end up falling for a man like Ryan Bale she would have tiger-punched them in the throat, but there was just something about him that she was attracted to.

It started when they were in the engine room of the Thalassa, but when he saved Joe Hawke's life that really sealed the deal. She saw then that he was a just a regular guy trapped in a nerd's body. And then there was his intellect. Her father had been a university lecturer and her childhood was filled with learning and knowledge. Perhaps Ryan was just another extension of that. She didn't know, but she knew she had to protect him in an environment like this. This was her kind of world, not his.

Ryan spoke, his voice full of childish excitement. "Hey, look at this!"

"What have you found?" she said, setting down her coffee cup beside the laptop.

"I decided to start at the beginning – it's only logical, after all."

"Oui, c'est vrai..."

"Hawke's just all over the place sometimes and he needs a man like me to organize him and make sense of things."

Behind his back, Sophie smiled warmly at his words and gently shook her head.

"So where did you start?" she asked.

"It turns out this Felix Hoffmann guy was seriously into ancient China and its folklore and mythology. His main interest was the Thunder God, Lei Gong, although technically that really translates as Lord of Thunder if you're using the Wade-Giles transcription system but in other systems it's Léi Shén, the God of Thunder, which is fascinating because..."

"Ryan?"

"Yeah, Soph?"

"You're doing it again."

"Sorry, Soph. Anyway, I've just taken a look through Hoffmann's research – hacked a couple of his email accounts and so on – you know what they say – walk a mile in a man's shoes if you want to understand him, but read all his emails if you really want to actually *know* him."

"Ah, that old classic."

"Exactly, so he spent a lot of time on some pretty dusty internet forums, and..."

"Wait."

"What?"

"Shouldn't that be *fora*?"

"Well, yes, technically but... and you're just messing with me, aren't you?"

"It's so easy, that's all." Sophie kissed him on the temple and asked him to continue.

"Hoffmann was certain that Lei Gong was real."

"Where have I heard that before..."

"Right – but, Lei Gong was actually born a normal mortal human being thousands of years ago. At some point in his life he discovered a divine peach tree, and unfortunately he decided the best course of action was to eat one of the peaches and *whammo* – the next thing he knew he'd been turned into a god with all the bells and whistles – omnipotence, omniscience, the works. They even gave him a hammer that created thunder."

"A peach tree? Whatever will they think of next?"

"Actually, in Chinese mythology the peach was strongly associated with – and you're not going to like this – immortality."

"I don't like where all of this is going, Ryan. I thought we'd left this madness behind us in Switzerland."

"My feelings exactly, but it looks like we're not getting off the hook that easily. In this Chinese system of mythology the gods ate peaches because they conferred immortality upon them and this is an image which occurs again and again in ancient Chinese art and poetry. The Peach of Immortality was a sacred fruit."

"And this is what happened to Lei Gong – he was a man who ate one of these peaches and became a god?"

"Yup – the God of Thunder, as I say. Lots of ancient cultures developed the concept of thunder gods and they were always very important in polytheistic systems. The thunder god usually was the top man, so to speak, so Zeus was a thunder god, and Thor in Norse mythology. Whoever is leaving Lei Gong's name sprayed on the side of ships clearly thinks a lot of himself."

"He sounds like a total maniac to me," Sophie said.

"A total maniac with a god-complex and a top secret earthquake machine. Not exactly a match made in heaven."

"But what was Hoffmann really looking for – the Tesla machine?"

"No – at least I don't think so," Ryan said. "There is no mention in any of his papers about classified military projects or anything like that, neither did he ever talk about anything like it in his many trips to *fora*."

Sophie smiled and playfully slapped his shoulder. "So what, then?"

"That's what I'm here for," he said, puffing his chest out. "But I haven't had much luck in that department yet. The only thing I can find is that aside from Hoffmann's obsession with Lei Gong and the thunder gods, he also spent a great deal of time looking into the concept of divine immortality."

"And I thought earthquake machines were going to be trouble..."

"Felix Hoffmann's fascination with Lei Gong seems to have led him to something called the Reichardt Papers."

"The what?"

"Good question. I can find next to nothing about them on the internet except for the most cursory of references, usually tied into Hoffmann's own research and enquiries. All I can gather is that they have something to do with the search for immortality."

Sophie was starting to hate that word. A few weeks ago it had meant nothing more to her than any other word. It simply described an unobtainable fantasy that had gripped men and women for millennia, but now it brought a new, terrible meaning to her mind whenever she heard it.

Now it conjured horrific images of her adventures in Greece, being trapped in an underwater cave system and nearly blown into a thousand pieces in a boat explosion. To Ryan, it all seemed like a game, but she knew better. Back when she had worked for the French Secret Service her life was full of violence and deceit, so she knew better than anyone what people were capable of – the lengths they would go to take what they desired. And things had gotten even worse after she left the DGSE and started in her new job, the one she had told no one about, but this was no time to contemplate the path her life had taken.

"What is it with all these men and immortality?" she asked. "It always seems to be men – have you noticed that?"

"What do you mean?" Ryan continued tapping information into the computer as he spoke.

"I mean, why can't men accept their fate in the way a woman can?"

"Ah!" Ryan exclaimed, not even hearing her last sentence. "Now this *is* interesting."

Sophie leaned closer to the computer screen and placed her hand gently on his shoulder. "What have you found?"

"Some cracking stuff about Lei Gong. According to this, there was some kind of prophecy attributed to the Thunder God."

Sophie watched Ryan as he flicked through page after page of text. He'd been on the case for several hours now but was still as alert and interested as the minute he'd turned on the computer. He'd been all over Chinese myths and legends, starting at Wikipedia and the occasional hacked document and digging his way down from there until hitting gold nearly every time.

Sophie looked at the latest screen he had found and started reading. There was very little about this prophecy Ryan had talked about – just a few references on the periphery of various texts in the form of endnotes, vague yet enticing. All she could gather was that there was some kind of prophecy attached to the Thunder God, largely unknown by modern academia, that referred in some way to immortality, the end of the world and some kind of glorious rebirth of humanity.

"It's not very specific," she said at last, and shrugged her shoulders.

"But it's a start!" Ryan said. He sipped his coffee, his eyes ablaze with excitement and anticipation. "And if you have a start, it's only a matter of time before you have an ending."

Sophie smirked and kissed him on the head. "So what now?"

"We carry on cutting our way through all this and keep on with the research – there's a reference to a missing manuscript I'm keen on looking into, for one thing. I'm going to need some more coffee."

Sophie stretched her arms and agreed. More coffee was always a good idea, especially at times like this. That was what her father always said, at any rate. She missed him, but his words were always with her.

She watched Ryan open a new window on the laptop and start his search for the Thunder God prophecy, then she crossed the room and picked up the phone to order some more coffee.

CHAPTER TWELVE

Lea turned in her seat and saw what Hawke was talking about – several of Sheng's men had piled into a stolen Nissan GTR and were accelerating after them, hard and fast. In the front, Lexi Zhang floored the F-Pace and it raced forward, every one of them feeling its 3 liter supercharged V6 kick in with a startling lack of modesty.

"So this is *nice*," Lea said. "You finally got your arses into gear, then?"

Scarlet gave her a cool but relieved look. "Glad you could make it, darling."

Lea smiled and looked at Hawke. "What about you, Joe Hawke? Are you glad I could make it?"

Scarlet rolled her eyes and took a cigarette from her packet as Lexi accelerated the SUV.

Hawke smiled. "I was starting to think you'd gone AWOL," he said, turning on the back seat and kissing her. "What the hell happened?"

"I was trailing Hoffmann but lost him on his way to the airport when those goons back there ambushed the cab. Don't know much about why – they kept me blindfolded and never said much, but I do know I was being delivered as a kind of payment for something."

"It was for a stolen portrait," Hawke said. He couldn't stop looking at her – the shape of her lips, the way her hair blew in the open window. He hadn't felt this way about a woman since the day he stood on that windy platform in London and met the love of his life. The girl they murdered in Vietnam when they were trying to kill him instead. But this time he wouldn't let that happen. This time he was going to make sure no one hurt the woman he loved. "I'm glad you're safe."

"Me too..."

"You could be a little more grateful," Scarlet said.

"I'm sorry?"

"For us rescuing you. You haven't even said thank you."

"You never rescued me! I had the situation completely under control. I was going to play it like a lamb for that Chan guy and then after lulling him into a false sense of security I was going to blow his head off and fly back to London. Simples. All you did was expedite the situation, as Richard might say."

Scarlet snorted. "Should have left you there."

Hawke smiled.

Lexi pushed the SUV faster and harder.

"Maybe you should have," Lea said. "At least there were no megalomaniacs, cold-hearted bitches, no SBS sergeants with an attitude problem, no nerds and absolutely no ancient Doomsday weapons."

"Ah, about that..." Hawke said.

"What?"

"As far as Doomsday weapons and megalomaniacs go we might have another situation developing," he said.

"Oh, you're *kidding*! And here I was coming to China for the restaurants."

Hawke looked at her for a second, still excited she was back in his life. "I forgot, you already had this briefing from Richard, of course."

She nodded and smiled. "Why the hell do you think I'd come all the way over here? I want to get me some shooting and hunting!"

"Then you're in the right place," Lexi said. "Because they're gaining." She checked the rearview mirror.

"Almost on top of us, in fact."

Lea turned again and this time saw the smooth, cat-like grille of the silver GTR almost upon them now. Either side of them the suburbs of Shanghai were growing into much higher skyscrapers and commercial buildings, and the traffic was getting denser as a result. "Damn thing's much faster than this," she said.

"But you can make it slow down with your gun, right?" Lexi said, her words dripping with sarcasm.

"I could make you slow down with my gun, I know that," Lea mumbled under breath.

"What?" Lexi said.

"I said steady this car so I can take a shot."

Lea fired several shots but they all missed.

Hawke sighed and pulled out the Sig he had retrieved from one of Chan's bodyguards. "If you want a job doing..."

"I'd slap him if I were you," Scarlet said, and turned in the front passenger seat. She put the window down and began to fire some shots at the GTR.

Lea glared at Hawke. "If you even think about finishing that sentence then you can book another hotel room for tonight, you got that Action Man?"

"Hey – I was just joking!"

"Well I wasn't."

Hawke took the point, and began to fire a series of carefully aimed shots from the rear side window, just behind Lexi, while Lea covered the other side. For a few moments they were making headway, blowing out the GTR's headlights and cracking its windshield, but then Sheng's men took evasive action and began to swerve the powerful Nissan violently from side to side, ending any chance of another successful hit, especially on the tires.

Then, the man in the passenger seat opened fire with

what looked like a pretty old submachine gun. Hawke ducked behind the seat, and the rear window of the F-Pace was blown out in seconds. Then, the bullets struck the release mechanism on the tailgate and sent the rear door flying open.

"Oh, that is just arsing fantastic!" Lea said.

Seconds later another line of bullets ripped through the rear seat and thudded into the F-Pace's dashboard.

"Holy crap that was close!" Lexi screamed. "You gotta close that back door, Joe!"

"The thought had crossed my mind, thank you Lexi!"

Hawke knew he had to act fast. With the rear door open they were totally vulnerable to attack from the GTR and the next shots could easily kill them. He clambered over the back seat and gripped on to the handle inside the trunk as he leaned out, stretching his arm up to the handle on the rear door.

Then, the GTR roared to life and weaved through a short stretch of traffic until it was once again right behind them. Hawke could see the grinning faces of the men inside as the man in the passenger seat casually leaned out the window again and aimed his gun dead-straight at Hawke's chest. To add insult to injury, the man waved a sarcastic goodbye to him as he squeezed the trigger.

Hawke screamed. "Lexi, evasive action!"

Without asking why, Lexi Zhang skidded the SUV heavily to the right and pulled in tight behind a white van. With the violence of the maneuver she got them away from the GTR – for now – but also sent Joe Hawke flying out the back of the F-Pace.

*

Sophie Durand was watching the traffic far below in the busy streets of Shanghai, and contemplating what Hawke and the others were doing when she heard Ryan sigh loudly. She turned to see him leaning back in his chair and putting his hands behind his head.

"You've given up?" she said, surprised,

"Hardly, Soph. Ryan Bale doesn't give up."

"You know, only real jerks refer to themselves in the third person."

"Point taken. *I* never give up, if that makes you feel any better."

"It does."

"Good, take a look at his – my brilliance lives and breathes before us."

She rolled her eyes and returned to the computer, shifting some of the coffee cups out of the way so she could slide up onto the desk. "What am I looking at, *genius* – more about this prophecy?"

"No, unfortunately – there's basically nothing about it at all on the internet. It seems to exist only in the work of these Reichardt and Hoffman guys. We'll have to keep researching that one. The only thing I could find was a translation of some ancient Chinese poetry that referred to the prophecy being about the return of the Thunder God and the rebirth of humanity, but no specifics."

"But that sounds pretty bad, no?"

"Yeah, you could say that. After watching Hugo Zaugg trying to bury an entire town in millions of tons of snow and what he wanted to do with Poseidon's trident, any talk of a rebirth of humanity doesn't exactly have positive connotations in my mind."

Sophie nodded. She knew what he meant and she agreed. They knew so little, but the facts they had gotten hold of so far weren't looking good – the return of this Thunder God, a missing earthquake machine of unknown power and now a vague prophecy about a new start for humanity. All of this was starting to make her very nervous.

"So if it's not about the prophecy, then what has your magnificent brilliance uncovered?"

Ryan looked up at her and smiled, but spoke without acknowledging her sarcastic tone. "I hacked into this particular website – the one with the most references to the prophecy – and I used a simple piece of web tracking software to see who else has been looking at the site."

"You can do that?"

"Of course. Most website developers put some simple code into their sites that gets executed whenever anyone visits them, and that code then reveals and tracks various pieces of information about the visitor – simple stuff like operating system or browser but also the IP address."

"No, I meant *you* can do that?"

"Very funny…"

"But seriously, I like where this is going."

"Thought you might."

"So whose footprints have we got?"

"Not too many, which is hardly surprising given the esoteric and archaic nature of the content, and that made it much easier. In the past few weeks it's received less than twenty visits, mostly from Germany and the UK, but here's the interesting part – several IP addresses all from one location made a series of visits all in one burst just a few days ago."

"And what's the location?"

"Langley, Virginia."

Sophie's eyes widened. "Langley? You mean the..."

"The headquarters of the CIA, exactly."

"Now, that is very interesting."

Ryan nodded, smiling. "Uh-huh. Surprised they didn't mask that to be honest, but then whatever they were looking at on the site, why would they think anyone else would ever be looking for them? No one ever visits the site."

"I'm starting to believe that maybe you are in fact a genius..." she said, and turned to him, her expression peaceful, but serious. "Did you think any more about what we talked about?" She was thinking of her suggestion that the two of them drop off the grid together, maybe permanently. She'd had enough of living life in top gear, and had seen a farmhouse in the Loire to renovate, maybe even start a vineyard. Ryan seemed like the perfect man to do it with.

"I have, and... yes, I'd love to."

She smiled and they kissed. "I'm so pleased."

"Not sure what Hawke's going to do without me though..."

"A genius..." she repeated, "albeit one with a serious ego problem."

"That's the nicest thing anyone's ever said to me, although Joe does call me 'mate' from time to time, which is high praise from a man like that."

"Speaking of Hawke, do you think he's all right?" Sophie asked.

Ryan shrugged his shoulders. "Sure. Hawke's always all right. If he was in a hurricane, bet against the hurricane. I expect he's kicking someone's arse right now as we speak."

"You think?"

Ryan nodded absent-mindedly. "Definitely. Whatever he's doing, he'll be totally in control of it, rest assured."

*

For a moment, Hawke felt like he was totally out of control. Then he reacted in a split-second, and whipped his arms around, grabbing hold of the low lip that ran around the bottom of the open trunk door. He'd had better days.

"Lexi – slow down!"

He clung to the back of the F-Pace for all his life was worth, digging his fingers into the padded sill of the tailgate's interior as hard as he could. Lexi slowed in an effort to allow him to climb back inside the SUV more easily but this acted as an invitation to Sheng's goons who took advantage and accelerated towards them.

"Bloody well speed up, Lexi!" Hawke shouted, his words barely audible with the rush of the air and the hum of the Shanghai traffic all around them. Other drivers pointed in amazement and one child took a picture of him with his phone.

He turned to look over his shoulder and saw Sheng's men gaining on them again. His boots scraped along the tarmac and he knew letting go of the tailgate meant instant death under the wheels of the growling GTR.

Lexi sighed and shook her head. "Slow down, Lexi! Speed up, Lexi! Make your mind up Joe!"

The GTR once again roared forward. Hawke had been dreading this moment, and for half a second thought he was about get both his legs crushed between the fenders of the two speeding vehicles.

But instead he heard gunfire and the GTR suddenly braked and swerved into the next lane.

Then he heard Lea's voice calling from inside the SUV. "That's the sound of me saving your arse yet again, Joe! You can thank me later."

"That's very kind of you – but talking of arses, maybe you could drag yours over here and help me get back inside this bloody Jag!"

"I'll cover you, Lea!" Scarlet shouted.

A second later Lea was leaning over the rear seats and extending her hand to Hawke. "Can you reach it?" In the background he heard the sound of Scarlet's gun firing rapidly as she covered the rescue attempt.

"Does it look like I can bloody well reach it?!"

Hawke thrust one hand up while clinging to the back of the car with the other.

The GTR swerved back out behind them.

Lexi accelerated the Jag but tried to keep it steady. Hawke missed and nearly slipped off the back again.

Lea tried once more, and this time Hawke managed to grab hold of her hand. At the same time she aimed her gun and unleashed a brutal burst of bullets across the front grille of the GTR, striking the radiator and sending a shower of steam into the air.

Hawke clambered inside and yanked the trunk door down, securing it with a rear seatbelt to the internal handle.

Lea fired again, this time through the smashed rear window of the Jag. She struck the front right tire and it exploded in a burst of shredded black rubber. It sent the GTR squealing like a trapped pig off the road where it skidded uncontrollably down an embankment and smashed headfirst into the base of an enormous digital billboard advertising Rolex watches.

"Looks their time finally came," Hawke said. He wiped the sweat from his brow as he watched the GTR end its days in a savage explosion of sparks and smoke down at the side of the road. Slowly, the carnage receded into the Shanghai twilight as Lexi powered the F-Pace toward the city.

"You okay?" Lea said, ignoring his pathetic attempt at humor.

"Sure, but I'm not going to thank you later for saving

my arse like you just said."

"No?"

"No. I'm going to thank you now."

Hawke took Lea by the shoulders and kissed her.

"Oh get a room," Lexi said.

Scarlet sighed. "I'll second that."

"We've already got one," said Lea.

"And talking of which," Hawke said, "It's about time we got this sodding portrait back to the hotel. Something in this picture is the key that's going to unlock this whole mystery."

CHAPTER THIRTEEN

The portrait of Xi Shi that had once graced the walls of ancient palaces was now on a bed in the Ritz-Carlton hotel in central Shanghai. Hawke and the others stared at it in silence for a few moments.

Ryan leaned over the modest, faded picture. "So this is what all the hubbub is about?"

Hawke glanced at him and nodded his head. "Yup. This little baby right here is what our mate Sheng hired Johnny Chan to steal from the museum in Hong Kong."

"Just a few hours after Felix Hoffmann was killed by an unknown assassin in the Paris Métro," Lea added. "And then those bastards ambushed me."

"And only a few hours after that the Tesla device was taken from a US Navy transport vessel," Hawke said. "And somehow it all ties together."

"Somehow..." Lea said.

Lexi took her hair-tie out and shook her hair loose. "And, if what just happened back on the Henshang Road is anything to go by, it's pretty obvious Sheng will do anything to get his hands on it."

Scarlet frowned. "But what does he want with it?" She lit a cigarette and crashed into chair on the balcony. She crossed her long, slim legs and tipped her head back. "If he already has the earthquake machine then what does he want with a simple portrait like this?"

Hawke ran his hands through his hair and took a deep breath. Yes, it was true Sheng was prepared not only to deploy a small army to get the portrait, but was also more than happy to kill anyone who got in his way. But now, staring at the tiny picture on the bed he was at a loss to explain what its value was and why anyone would go to the lengths that Sheng had gone to in order to get their hands on such a harmless picture.

He turned once again to Ryan. "You think you can make any sense of it, mate?"

Ryan picked up the portrait and studied it for a few seconds before turning it over carefully in his hands. "I don't know... there's nothing on the back, and the front offers us no clues at all other than a simple image of a woman sitting on a riverbank beside what looks to me like a peach tree. That's our obvious starting point."

"Why is the tree an obvious starting point?" said Lea.

"The peach is an ancient symbol of immortality in Chinese folklore," Ryan said, repeating to the others what he had already told Sophie. "Seems to me that when Sheng had his men spray the name Lei Gong – the immortal God of Thunder – on the side of the ship carrying the Tesla device, he kind of showed his hand to the world. Whatever he's up to it's probably a lot worse than just causing an earthquake somewhere."

Scarlet blew a cloud of cigarette smoke into the air. "A lot worse than killing millions of innocent people?"

"You can't mean another fruit-loop like Zaugg?" Lea asked.

"I think so, yes," Ryan said. "Only much worse."

A knock at the door.

"Who the hell is that?" Lea said.

Hawke shrugged his shoulders and cautiously checked the spy hole. He laughed loudly and swung open the door. Moments later he and Olivia Hart were hugging in the hall of the plush hotel suite.

"The Return of the Commodore Heroes," Ryan said.

"Eh?" Hawke said.

"Forget it."

"You weren't sent by Richard Eden?" Lea asked, suspicious.

"Of course not!" Hart said. "Hawke called me."

The senior naval officer settled in and took a long look at the portrait.

"This is all we have to go on," Hawke said, and then gave her the full briefing on what had happened since their arrival in the Far East.

Ryan cracked open a beer from the minibar. "We now think this Sheng nutcase has bigger ideas than just triggering an earthquake somewhere."

"Then you'd be right," Hart said. "After you called me, Joe, I spoke with a contact in the Ministry of Defence. There's a lot of confusion there at the moment, but they've got hold of some chatter linking Sheng with Hugo Zaugg – for sure, no speculation this time."

"Zaugg?" Hawke said, stunned. "What the hell has he got to do with anything? The last time I saw him he was falling to his death from a Swiss cable car."

Lea shuddered. "And Amen to that."

"We're not sure," Hart said, "but we think maybe Zaugg was either working with Sheng or even for him. Sheng has considerably more wealth and power than even Zaugg had, and he would have been able to finance a much more expansive project in terms of searching for..."

"Searching for the secret to eternal life?" Hawke said.

Hart nodded grimly. "I think so, but that's all we have so far."

"It's all we need," Scarlet said, rejoining them from the balcony and sliding the door shut.

"What do you mean?" Lexi asked.

"I mean, who cares about the details? We know Sheng Fang is a very unpleasant individual who traffics vulnerable people around the world and hides it behind his telecom company. We now know he was pulling Zaugg's strings in search of the vault of Poseidon and the real treasure that was supposed to be inside it – the map."

"The map!" Ryan said. 'Exactly! Sheng is looking for the map!"

"And he needs this portrait to find it," Lea said, staring at the enigmatic little picture. "But the question is – why?"

Hawke thought that was a very good question indeed. He recalled Sir Richard Eden's debriefing back in Sion when he and the tight-lipped British Foreign Secretary Matheson had told them it was possible Zaugg was working for another agency. Could it be possible that agency was Sheng Fang, one of China's richest men? It seemed as plausible as any other explanation in this new mad world he had found himself thrown into. "Why, indeed," he finally said, staring at the voiceless Xi Shi. She stared back at him, coy, prudish almost, sitting there beside her peach tree and the gently flowing river, all those thousands of years ago.

Scarlet gently nodded and scowled at the portrait. "Come on, everyone! We must be able to work this out. There's five intelligent people in here – six if you count Lexi."

Lexi gave her a sideways glance but made no reply. The look she gave her was worth a thousand words.

Sophie rubbed her eyes – she too had nothing to offer.

"Give me a minute," Ryan said, and got his laptop fired up. "Let's get stuck into some hard research."

"I love it when the *boy* talks dirty," Scarlet said.

Hawke watched Ryan as his fingers tapped furiously on the keyboard. "You have an idea?"

"It's a long shot, but I remember reading something about Pliny the Elder back in Hoffmann's research."

"And how's that going to help us, Ryan?" Lea said. The frustration in her voice was rising.

"If anyone in here spent their spare time reading grown-up books instead of playing Mission Impossible video games someone might have already worked out what I was talking about, but as it is, you don't, so you'll just have to wait while I check something out."

Hawke kept tight-lipped, not wanting to fall out with Ryan at such a critical time. He didn't fancy having to beg him to continue with his research. And he happened to like Mission Impossible video games. To Hawke, reading about ancient language noun declensions was the truly suspect pastime, not kicking ass on cool video games, but it was a wide world.

"Ah ha!" Ryan shouted, suddenly energized by something he had read on the laptop screen.

"What is it, Ryan?" Lea asked.

"Pliny the Elder – I knew it all along! It's been bothering me since I first read a reference Hoffmann had made to him, which to me seemed incongruous in light of the main body of his research."

Lea sighed with frustration. "Bring it back to the moment, Ryan."

"Oh, sure. Sorry." Ryan pushed his glasses up on the bridge of his nose and carried on with his explanation. "Pliny the Elder wrote about hiding secret messages back in the ancient world. Long before digital encryption people still wanted to conceal messages in plain sight – lemon juice is a somewhat hackneyed example of this."

"Exactly what I've always thought," Lea said, rolling her eyes.

"And what does lemon juice have to do with Sheng Fang stealing a portrait?"

"That is the central question!" Ryan said. "And it is the key to everything."

"So could we have the key please, boy?" said Scarlet.

"As I said, lemon juice is rather a rudimentary method of concealing a message, and not that great, but there were other, cleverer methods."

"Like what?" Hawke said. This was why Ryan was on the payroll.

"This is where Pliny the Elder comes in. Way back in the mists of time when Pliny was writing, he wrote about the use of milk of tithymalus."

"The milk of *what*?" Lexi said.

"Tithymalus," Ryan said. "It's part of the euphorbia genus – a spurge."

Hawke smiled. "Still not with you, mate."

"It's a very diverse genus of plants covering everything from Madagascan cacti to your average Christmas poinsettia."

Lea glared at her former husband. "Sure, but what's it got to do with this sodding picture, Ryan?"

"Ah! I thought that would be the next question." Ryan got up from the laptop and asked Scarlet for one of her cigarettes.

"You're not finally starting to become fun, are you *boy*?"

Ryan looked from Scarlet to the cigarette and back to Scarlet. "This? You have to be joking! You take three minutes off your life with every suck."

Scarlet opened her mouth to reply but Hawke hushed her with his hand.

"I'm sure you have a witty retort on the tip of your tongue, Cairo, but let's just see what Ryan's up to, shall we?"

"If you say so," Scarlet said. "But if you're going to light it then do it on the balcony or you'll set the bloody smoke alarms off."

Ryan walked on the balcony and lit the cigarette. Far

below, the streets of Shanghai buzzed as the day wore on into dusk. Boats cruised up the Huangpu and slowly the neon city began to offer its nightlife to anyone who cared.

"What Pliny discovered was that if you wrote on parchment with milk of tithymalus, it dried until it was totally invisible." He flicked the ash over the side of the balcony with casual proficiency.

"And you said you never smoked before," Scarlet said, smirking.

"I never said *that*," he said. "I said I wouldn't smoke *these*. Now, Pliny the Elder – real name Gaius Plinius Secundus, for those taking notes – was a Roman naturalist, and he worked out that after you had written with the milk, all you had to was..." he paused for dramatic effect. "Soph – could you grab the portrait?"

Sophie emerged a few seconds later with the Xi Shi portrait.

"Hey!" Hawke said. "Be careful with that! One gust of wind and it's gone forever."

"I had grasped that fact, Joe," Sophie said. She handed the picture to Ryan. He placed it on the table and pinned it down with a coffee cup and Scarlet's Zippo lighter.

"Such respect for ancient art," Lea said.

"Needs must when the devil drives," he said. "So, what our man Pliny worked out was that all you had to do to reveal the hidden message was simply apply a little post-combustion residue powder of some description."

Lexi looked confused.

"He means ash," Lea said. "That's how Ryan says ash."

"Ah – ash!" Lexi said.

"So drop hot ash all over an ancient parchment?" Scarlet said. "What could possibly go wrong?"

"Let him finish," Hart said firmly. "I for one am

intrigued."

Hawke stepped forward. "I agree – do your best, mate."

Ryan flicked some of the ash in his hands and handed Scarlet the cigarette. He rubbed his hands gently together and then smeared them slowly over the back of the portrait.

And there it was, slowly emerging from the past into the present.

"It's a message!" Lea said.

Hawke laughed loudly. "You clever, smug bastard!"

"What does it say?" asked Hart.

They all peered in and looked at the message, barely legible, the milk weak after so many centuries. They were looking at a series of Chinese characters.

"Lexi?" Hawke asked.

Lexi Zhang looked hard at the characters. "It says..." she said, almost in a whisper, "it says, *The Great Khan's Secret is in His Thirteenth Chapter.*

"That's good to know," Scarlet said, turning to face the city and taking a long, deep drag on the cigarette Ryan had handed her. She shook her head in disappointment and leaned over the balcony to look at the street below.

"What does it mean?" Hawke asked Ryan, who for once looked lost for words.

"Not entirely certain. As hard as this might be for you all to understand I do not actually know *everything*." He went back to his laptop and typed a few words into Google. "But my best guess at this point is that our next stop is going to be Ulan Bator."

CHAPTER FOURTEEN

Later that night Hawke was cruising in a private jet arranged by Sir Richard Eden's London office. He watched the lights of China gradually fade away as the plane ascended to forty thousand feet and crossed over into the empty plains which stretched into Mongolia to the north. It hadn't taken Ryan long to work out that anything involving Genghis Khan meant going to Ulan Bator, and they were packed and on the plane within three hours.

But now, his mind raced with problems, worries and deceits. What was Sheng Fang really up to? Yes, he was a dangerous criminal, and his status as one of the richest men in the world made that danger positively lethal. Could he really be diverting millions of dollars into the search for a map that might not even exist?

He was struggling to keep things together. He'd asked Ryan and Sophie to stay at the hotel with Commodore Hart with a view to maintaining the safe HQ they'd established – somewhere they could work on the research undisturbed. It was Lea's idea, and Sophie in particular had objected at first, keen to get in on the action in Mongolia, but the team decided it was the right thing to do.

That at least was progress, but Hawke's mind still buzzed with confusion. He still didn't know who he could trust. Lea Donovan had tried to tell him something about the elusive Sir Richard Eden when she thought they were about to die back in the Greek cave system, but she had backed away from it when she realized Cairo

Sloane could hear what she was saying. He thought about that and what Eden himself had told him back on the phone in London. He wondered how close he was to learning the truth.

To make matters worse, he thought he was falling in love with Lea, but she would have to be honest with him if she wanted him to take her seriously and make any kind of commitment. After Hanoi, it hadn't been easy for Hawke to get close to anyone else, and this was as far as he had gone. And yet... what she was keeping from him was on his mind all the time and he resented the control Eden seemed to have over her.

Then there was the fact that both Cairo and Sophie were lying about their involvement in MI5 and the DGSE. That was another little wrinkle he had to iron out before he could really trust either of them. He wondered once again if Sophie had spoken to Ryan about her true story, and decided he would ask him about it next time there was a moment when they could speak privately. If Ryan could ever pry himself off of his new French lover, that is.

His mind snapped back to the mission. The last thing Ryan had told them was to start at the Genghis Khan Statue Complex just east of the capital. It was a long shot, but there was so little left of the ancient Mongolian Empire it was all he could think of. They kept a small collection of materials relating to the Khanate and it was the best shot they had to get to the bottom of anything to do with the Great Khan.

Now, Cairo was sleeping and Lexi was up front talking with the pilots, no doubt regaling them with tales from her colorful and sordid past. He watched her drape an arm over the first officer. Beside him, Lea's eyes were closed but he knew she was awake.

He poured a shot of vodka and sank it down in one.

He wished it were whisky, but it was all he could find in the on-board drinks cabinet. He looked at Lea again and decided now was as good a time as any to ask her what was really going on.

"What were you going to tell me about Richard Eden, Lea?"

She didn't flinch and kept her eyes closed.

"When was that?"

"Don't play games," he said. "Back in Kefalonia, in the cave system – we were watching the now dearly departed Hugo Zaugg pumping water from the defensive tunnel leading into the vault of Poseidon. You said there was something important you had to tell me about Eden, but then you glanced at Cairo and something made you stop. I'm sure you remember."

"Of course, but..."

She opened her eyes and faced him for a second before turning away and studying the digital readout that gave the passengers flight information: forty thousand feet, one thousand kilometers per hour.

"What is it you wanted to tell me. Lea? Don't tell me it's nothing because Eden's confirmed to me that something's up. He says he'll tell me when all this is over."

Hawke studied her expression, but she knew better than to give anything away. She kept calm and somehow even managed to yawn.

Finally she spoke. "I shouldn't have mentioned it back in Greece, and if Eden says he'll talk to you then so be it."

"You can't leave it at that, Lea. This is the second time I've risked my life for this guy. I respect you – you know that – and maybe..." he paused. He couldn't bring himself to say the words *I love you* to her, not yet. "It's just that I think I deserve some respect on this."

Lea looked at him and kissed him. "Joe, it's not for me to say. It wasn't back in Kefalonia and it's not now. Back then when I started to speak with you I thought I was going to die and I wanted you to know something, but it's not for me to tell you. It's much bigger than that. I promise you this, when the time's right Sir Richard will tell you just as he said he would, but please believe me when I tell you it's nothing you need to worry about."

"That's not good enough, Lea..."

Her face tightened, her old Rangers training kicking in. "It's going to have to be, Joe, because it's all you're getting."

Hawke saw something in her eyes change. She looked harder, like she had done the first time he'd met her back in London. Sometimes she was a beautiful woman, and other times she was a soldier again. He could forgive her that because once Liz had accused him of something similar – a great bloke one minute and a commando the next, she had said. Yet still the frustration grew in his heart, but he knew he had to trust her. It was all he could do.

"I just thought we had something," he said. "And that's not something I ever thought I would say again. Not after Hanoi."

Lea turned in the sumptuous leather seat and brushed his arm with her hand. "We do have something, Joe. I want it too, but..."

Then Lexi returned from the cabin. "Bad news," she said. "They just got a radio message from Jason Lao in Hong Kong. Apparently Johnny Chan was found dead in a shikumen lane about an hour ago. He'd been tortured for information and was missing several fingers. He'd been strangled to death. Jason says we should presume he told them everything about us taking the picture."

"Great," Lea said. "Sounds like they really went to

town on the bastard."

Lexi raised an eyebrow.

"What?" Lea said. "Did I say something funny?"

"It sounds like they went easy on him if you ask me. You obviously don't know Sheng's thug Luk if you think getting strangled to death is as bad as it gets."

"However dangerous he is," Hawke said firmly, his voice hardened by the vodka. "He's up against the SBS now, and I'm in a very bad mood."

"And the SAS and MI5," said Scarlet from the back. She had woken up and joined them at the front of the small jet. "That should make up for the SBS, at least."

Hawke smiled. He appreciated her support but her reference to MI5 only reminded him that she too was lying to him about her involvement with the Secret Intelligence Services.

"How is it that us SBS guys do everything you guys do, and then extra maritime training, and yet you still think you're harder?"

"Glorified frogmen," Scarlet said.

Hawke laughed. "Don't forget the SBS went into World War Two first, with you guys finally joining in five months later…"

Lea changed the subject. "Either way it looks like we're going to have a real war on our hands if we're not careful. Remember, no one in the world knows what happened with Zaugg and just how close that nutcase got to the map."

"Or experimenting with that damned trident," Hawke said. He wondered where the trident was – maybe in some US underground facility surrounded by men in white coats and a shroud of secrecy.

Lea shuddered. "There was something very weird about that thing."

Hawke nodded grimly and poured another vodka for

himself. He offered some to Lexi who took it and drank straight from the bottle. She wiped her mouth and passed the bottle back to Hawke. "Thanks."

"You're... *welcome*," he said, glancing at the amount of vodka she had taken without any apparent effect.

"So is this a problem?" Lea said.

"Not at all," Lexi said. "I learned to drink in the Chinese Navy."

"I meant Chan," said Lea, rolling her eyes.

"It's nothing to worry about," said Hawke. "Chan didn't know who we were, our names or anything about us. He couldn't have given them any information that would put us in jeopardy, not for the time being, anyway – no matter how much they tortured him."

"If I get my hands on this Luk character he'll wish he'd never been born," Scarlet said, and took the bottle from Hawke. "Anyone have a glass? It's terribly uncouth to drink straight from the bottle, don't you think, Lexi?"

Lexi made no reply, other than looking daggers at her.

"Certainly sounds like this Sheng character is serious about getting hold of that map," Lea said.

"Sheng Fang is serious about everything," said Lexi. "I told you that back in Shanghai. You should always listen to Lexi Zhang. That's what *I* say."

CHAPTER FIFTEEN

Ryan finished his coffee and walked to the minibar for something stronger. Years ago he'd filled his late night computer hacking with cannabis and super strength lager, but these days he was more sophisticated. He passed Sophie a cold bottle – Hart declined with a frown – and they settled back into the research. They all knew Hawke and the others were depending on them, maybe even placing their lives in their hands.

Hart stepped up. "So where are we, Ryan?"

"Apparently Anton Reichardt was Hoffmann's doctoral supervisor, and he spent his entire life searching for the secret of eternal life until he died around twenty years ago, according to this he burned himself out in the search."

"Talk about irony," Hart said.

Ryan ignored her. "Reichardt had worked out that all of this revolves around something called the Secret History of the Mongols."

"The *what*?"

"The Secret History of the Mongols. It looks like everything we're dealing with here in China goes back to it," Ryan said, his fingers flying over the keyboard as he unlocked more and more of Hoffmann's most confidential research.

"Keep talking."

"The Secret History has twelve chapters and famously disappeared hundreds of years ago, but Reichardt seems to have worked out that not only does it still exist but that there are thirteen chapters in it – the missing final chapter being the key to our puzzle."

"How so?"

"There was a translation made and the secret message written on the back of the Xi Shi portrait in milk of tithymalus was actually put there by the monk who had been asked to make a translation into Chinese by the Mongolians, so the existence of the thirteenth chapter wasn't lost forever."

"Why would a monk do that?"

"This is where old Reichardt really hots up! As I say, the original Secret History of the Mongols is twelve chapters long, but according to this there was a thirteenth chapter, but the Mongolians forbade the monk from making a translation of it because..."

"Because it contained the part of Genghis Khan's life when he was searching for the secret of eternal life?" said Sophie.

"Exactly! At some point the Mongolians must have made some kind of discovery with reference to the hunt for immortality and recorded it within the Secret History, but when they had the translations made they stopped the final chapter from being told to the rest of the world."

"So where is this original?" Hart said. She set her coffee cup on the desk and ran her fingers though her hair. It was late and she hadn't slept since London.

"Not worked that out yet, but we know it's in Mongolia, of course."

"We need more than that."

"Thanks to our mysterious monk and his hidden message on the back of the Xi Shi portrait we know they're linked. Although the reference to the 'Great Khan' could mean either Kublai or Genghis, but I don't think it matters. Either way, this is getting *very* interesting!" Ryan rubbed his hands together. Outside far below in the streets of Shanghai a cacophony of car horns drifted up to their open balcony.

"So what do we know about Khan, honey?" Sophie said. He'd never told her, but he liked it when she called him that. It sounded pretty damned great in her French accent. He knew that much.

"Okay – let's start at the beginning. We all know that Genghis Khan was obsessed with immortality, right?"

Sophie and Hart looked at each other for a second with vacant expressions.

"I don't know the first thing about Genghis Khan," Hart said first.

"He had red hair and green eyes!" said Sophie proudly. "I know that!"

Ryan sighed. "Maybe I should start *before* the beginning... Anyway, Genghis Khan was obsessed with immortality, as I just said, and..."

"And you think that's where all this nightmare begins," Sophie said. "With Khan?"

"No, I don't think so at all. Poseidon predates Genghis Khan by a long way – thousands of years. I think Genghis Khan was really just like us – he was on the trail of something far more ancient and mysterious, and that Hoffman and this Reichardt guy were trying to work out what that was."

"Okay," Hart said, sipping her coffee. "I'm listening."

"You sound just like a senior naval officer sometimes," Ryan said.

Hart replied: "Funny... but we have to move faster than this. We can't let Sheng get ahead now we've got the advantage. If Genghis Khan or his grandson knew something about this missing manuscript – and I guess we're all thinking it's something along the lines of where this bloody map is – then we've got to do everything we can to stop Sheng Fang getting hold of it. We have some phone calls to make."

Under Hart's direction, Sophie Durand ordered some coffee from room service and the three of them set about the almost impossible task of organizing what had quickly become a mission now totally out of control.

Hours later, after Hart had taken a shower and Sophie had grabbed some sleep, Ryan was still hammering away at the keyboard.

"So what have you got now?" Hart asked him, drying her hair.

Ryan scratched his head and pushed his glasses up the bridge of his nose. "The hidden message on the back of the Xi Shi portrait was clear enough – it's a simple whisper from the ancient past about Genghis Khan knowing a secret – some kind of ancient truth, and we've already worked out this somehow involved a previously unknown chapter of the Secret History. The real question is, what's that manuscript hiding? We'll need to work this out."

"That's supposing we find it."

Hart laughed. "If there's anyone in this world who can find it, his name is Joe Hawke. That man could rescue an astronaut stranded on Mars if he had to, believe me."

"We'll leave the heroics to Hawke then," Ryan said. "But we've got a job to do as well. We need a lot more knowledge on this subject if we're going to beat this Sheng Fang. I just hope Joe knows what he's getting himself into up there."

"Don't worry about the Major, he'll be all right."

Ryan looked over his shoulder at Hart. "The Major? Who the hell's that?"

"Hawke, who'd you think I was talking about?"

"No one, just that Lea told me Hawke was a sergeant before he left the Special Boat Service."

"He was," Hart said. "Hawke was busted down from

Major a long time ago but I can't break the habit of referring to his old title."

"Hawke was busted down to a non-commissioned officer?" Ryan leaned forward in his chair, enthralled. "I had no idea."

"I thought everyone knew," Hart said. "It's one of the reasons he hates officers so much."

"What was he demoted to sergeant for?"

Hart sighed. "If you don't know that then I'm certainly not going to tell you. That's Joe Hawke's business and no one else's. Let's move on, please."

CHAPTER SIXTEEN

Ulan Bator

They landed at Chinggis Khaan International Airport and immediately hired a Nissan Qashqai. Moments later they were driving into the city on their way to the Genghis Khan Statue Complex.

The highway from the airport to Ulan Bator was dusty and bleak and the sky overhead was an enormous harsh blue canvas the likes of which Hawke hadn't seen since the time he had trained in Australia.

The journey wasn't long, but halfway into the city as they were passing through an ugly industrial zone full of smoking chimneys and pretty ancient-looking cooling towers they realized they were being followed.

"You're thinking what I'm thinking?" Scarlet said.

"Pretty much," replied Hawke, checking his mirror. "If you're talking about the Rav 4 then it's been trying to pretend it's not tailing us since the airport. Damn!" Hawke banged the dash. "But who the hell knew we were here?"

"No one," said Scarlet. "Except Lexi Zhang of course."

Hawke checked the back seat, where Lexi was dozing, her head lolled against the headrest. Lea was also asleep. He was glad she was safe now. "I don't think so. I wouldn't trust Lexi as far as I could throw her with both hands tied behind my back, but not this level of deceit. Not her. She would stab you in the back if it meant her own survival, but I can't believe she would tip-off Sheng so he could follow us to the map."

"You're too trusting, Joe. Face it – she could easily have killed Felix Hoffmann and now we're being followed out of an airport no one in the world knew we were even at. It's not looking good for Madam Mao, is all I'm saying."

Hawke checked Lexi once again in the mirror and shook his head gently. "No, it's not her, Cairo. If that's one of Sheng's men behind us then they found out some other way. It's just an instinct."

"Oh God – not the famous Hawke instinct that nearly got us killed in Afghanistan?"

"No, a better one than that. A new and improved one, so just relax about Lexi."

Lea had begun to stir and leaned over the front seats. "Well whoever the fuck it is, shouldn't we doing more about it that just waffling?"

Hawke smiled – she had been listening. "Yes, we should," he said. "So hang on."

And with that Hawke spun the Qashqai around in a one-eighty on the highway and in a hail of grit and stone chips he floored the throttle and began racing towards the vehicle pursuing them.

"What are you doing?" Lea screamed. "Please don't tell me your medication has run out yet again."

"We're going to find out who's been following us from the airport and I think the best way to do that is to be up-front about it, don't you agree?"

Scarlet rolled her eyes. "At last, he grows a pair."

Lexi woke up and mumbled something about what was going on.

The way Hawke saw things, the Rav 4 had only three options. Either carry on driving and lose the vehicle they had been told to follow, wait until they passed them and then turn around to follow them in the other direction, or spin around and flee back to their base in the knowledge they had been rumbled.

The pursuers went for option three.

While Hawke and the rest of his team in the Qashqai were still several hundred yards away from them, the Rav 4 spun around and accelerated away in the other direction.

"*Awww*," Scarlet said. "They don't want to play any more..." Hawke heard her loading her Beretta Storm as she spoke.

"The little bastards want to get back to HQ," Lea said.

Hawke narrowed his eyes and clenched his jaw. "And I want to know just who the hell they are and how they found out we were here."

"Let's give them something to think about," Scarlet said. She leaned out her window and fired a couple of shots from the Storm. Each hit its target, smacking two neat little puncture holes in the rear panel.

In the distance they watched as the Rav 4 momentarily left the road and struck a metal barrier. A shower of sparks flashed into the air before they regained control and accelerated along the highway.

"Not bad," Lea said.

"Thank you, darling."

Hawke stamped his foot down on the throttle and watched the needle on the rev counter fly around the dial. He accelerated the Qashqai to one hundred kilometers per hour, more than twenty over the limit in this built-up industrial zone. Ahead, the Rav 4 was now exiting the highway.

"He's going back into the city," Lea said.

Hawke smacked the steering wheel. "Trying to lose us in the back streets. I guess that means he's a local. Brace yourselves!"

Hawke spun the Qashqai hard to the right and just

caught the off-ramp in time, racing down at a tremendous speed which was far too fast for the road. He slammed down on the brakes and after a few moments of skidding and burning rubber the vehicle was back under his control again.

He looked ahead through the dusty windshield and saw that the Rav 4 was now speeding across a bridge and disappearing into the southern quarter of the city. Soviet-era tower blocks loomed either side of them as they crossed the bridge in pursuit, but the Rav 4 was getting away, turning to the right now and entering a slipstream of cars driving into the city center. A second later the lights changed to red.

Hawke cursed but made the decision to jump the lights. It was now or never and if they lost this guy he would be gone for good.

As he approached the lights, he speeded up just as everyone else was slowing down. A cacophony of angry car horns filled the air as he skidded and weaved through the traffic, tearing off a bus's wing mirror just one second before he ripped across the junction and narrowly avoided getting hit side-on by a Toyota Land Cruiser.

"Where the hell did he go?" Lea asked.

"You haven't lost him, have you, Joe?" said Scarlet, disappointed. "I only got two shots off."

"No – the little bastard's just over there."

He pointed to a narrow exit from the road running parallel to the Telecom Mongolia headquarters. Momentarily blocked by traffic the Rav 4 slowed and blasted the horn for the other cars to clear out the way.

Hawke took advantage and after driving the wrong way down a few hundred yards of Peace Avenue and causing the most terrific congestion and two small pile-ups, he managed to navigate the Qashqai right behind the Rav 4.

"Now he's all ours," Lexi said. She too pulled a gun from her holster and got ready for action. Behind them they heard police sirens, and they sounded like they were getting closer.

"That's just great," Hawke said, seeing the flashing blue lights in the rearview.

"Maybe if you hadn't driven the wrong way down one of the main streets in the city they wouldn't have been able to find us so easily," Scarlet said. "You couldn't have drawn any more attention to us if you'd sent them an embossed invitation delivered by a trumpeting herald."

"Nice one," Lea said, laughing.

"Yeah, funny," Lexi added.

Hawke glared at her. "Hey, I did my best..."

"Yes... you're only a man, after all," Scarlet said.

"So I guess that *was* your best," Lexi said.

"I'm outnumbered three to one," Hawke said. "I never thought I'd say this but where the hell is Ryan Bale when you need him?"

"Then you'd be outnumbered four to one," Scarlet said, smirking.

"Ouch," Hawke said.

"Hey! I was married to him," said Lea. "So leave him alone, Ice Maiden, all right?"

"Or what?" Scarlet said.

"Or I'll box your bloody head off, that's what."

"Ladies, please!" Hawke said.

"No, I want to watch them fight!" Lexi said.

"If it hadn't escaped your attention," Hawke said, "we're in the middle of a pursuit right now, so can we just leave the handbags-at-dawn stuff for later?"

"The *what* stuff?!" Lea said.

"What a sexist pig!" Lexi said, tutting.

"You think you know someone..." Scarlet said gently,

shaking her head.

Hawke felt like giving up, but a second later the Rav 4 was through a gap and driving down a narrow side street on the west side of the telecoms business. A couple of swift right turns later and he was heading back in the opposite direction, trying desperately to shake them from his tail.

Now, they were emerging into an expansive outside space surrounded by impressively grand buildings.

"Ladies and gentleman, I present to you Genghis Khan Square," Lea said, reading off her mobile. "Previously known as Sükhbaatar Square, this is the centerpiece of the entire city and generally regarded as the key landmark."

"Excellent," Hawke said. "Then they won't mind if we take a closer look because our man's getting away."

Ahead, the Rav 4 was turning right and driving east behind the imposing Government Palace, so Hawke made the split-second decision to drive across the square to cut him off.

He spun the wheel to the right and launched the Qashqai over the curb and into Genghis Khan Square. The engine growled as the tires slammed back down on the pavement with a chunky squeal. Tourists screamed and desperately charged out of the way as he accelerated the massive Nissan across the public landmark.

"You do realize, darling, that is a pedestrian zone?"

"Yes, thanks, Cairo, I did work that out all for myself."

"Oh good. It's just that a moment ago I thought we had a nice little chat about how only total idiots draw attention to themselves and it does occur to me that driving a large SUV at great speed through an area designed for ambling tourists would certainly fall into that category."

Hawke sighed. "As I said... I thank you for your concern." Below them, the wide tires rumbled as they raced across the square.

Lea was still looking at her iPhone. "Joe, things are going to get really difficult up ahead. From what I can tell the Rav's about to head into a pretty built-up part of the city. I think we need to get on him right now."

"Or why not just wait for the police to catch us both?" Scarlet said. "Because they're right behind us."

Hawke had been preoccupied with keeping tourists from bouncing off the Qashqai's hood, but now he checked the rearview and found to his dismay that Cairo Sloane was right yet again.

"That's all we need."

"I did tell you, dear... would you like me to ask them to go away?"

"I guess we have no choice," Hawke said.

Scarlet and Lexi both leaned out their windows and began to unload their magazines into the Kia Rio following them at great speed, lights flashing and sirens blaring.

"They're insane," Lea said.

"They're in competition," Hawke said quietly. "And that can only be good for us right now."

A second later he watched the Kia skid off to the left, out of control – its front tires blown out.

"Good shooting," Hawke said.

"Thanks," Scarlet and Lexi both said at the same time.

"Hey!" Lexi said. "That was *my* kill, not yours."

"I don't think so, darling. It was the left front which was blown out first – look at the direction it pulled off in. All mine."

"I shot at the left as well."

"Hush now," Lea said. "Mum and Dad are very proud of you both."

"He's stuck in traffic!" Hawke said, racing towards the Rav.

"And he's getting out of the sodding car!" Lea said.

Scarlet smirked and reloaded the Storm. "Two can play at that game."

A second later and they were sprinting from the deserted Qashqai and giving chase through the backstreets of Ulan Bator. It was cold now, winter in the north and getting late in the day. The sun was pale against the concrete government buildings and residential tower blocks as they pursued the fleeing man.

Hawke watched the man as he desperately ran for his life. Then, Scarlet fired a couple of shots over his head, the sounds of her bullets were two thin cracks in the bustling city air. Pedestrians turned to see what was happening, a man in a taxi pulled up and began to film them on his phone.

"This guy's really beginning to piss me off," Hawke said.

"Why isn't he shooting back?" said Lea.

Lexi smiled. "Maybe he has no weapon!"

"Or maybe he's under orders not to harm us," said Scarlet.

Hawke said: "Either way, we need a chat with him."

A few minutes later the man stumbled over a curb and flew to the floor like a rag doll. He cartwheeled uncontrollably before tumbling into a heap in the gutter. Before he could move an inch Hawke was on him, and grabbed him tightly by the throat.

"Please!" said the man. "Don't kill me! I meant you no harm... I just..."

"What is it?" Hawke said. He squeezed his throat a little, just to add a small incentive to cooperate.

"Please... I can't breathe!"

"That's sort of the point," Scarlet said, and kicked the

man hard in the balls.

Instinctively he tried to double-up in pain, but Hawke's hand around his throat made this almost impossible.

"Is there a man alive you won't do that too?" Hawke asked.

Scarlet shrugged and Hawke returned his attention to the pleading man.

"Who are you?"

"My name's Altan. I'm just a local private investigator, that's all."

"A likely story."

"It's true! Look me up on the internet – my card's in my top pocket – please just take it."

Lea leaned in and took a small business card from his pocket.

"Anyone here speak Russian?" she said.

"It's not Russian," Lexi said. "It's Mongolian. It's just written in Russian Cyrillic. Don't they teach you people *anything*?" She took the card and glanced at it for a second. "It says he's a private investigator, but that's an easy cover to give yourself with a two dollar business card."

"Why were you following us?" Lea said coolly, ignoring Lexi's jibe.

"I was just told to keep an eye on you, that's all. No harm. I was never going to hurt you, I swear it!"

"I'd like to see you try," Scarlet purred.

"And who told you to watch us?" Hawke said.

"An American, that's all I know."

"I think you know more than that," Scarlet said, pulling her foot back and readying for a second kick. A warped smile spread across her face.

"No! Please, no! All right, I'll tell you. I was hired by an American man named Bradley Karlsson. That's is all

I know, I promise you! I don't know anything else about him."

"Come come, Altan," Scarlet said. "I'm sure you can be more helpful than that. Remember what's at stake." She pulled her boot back and squinted one eye as she aimed in between his legs.

"Okay – but this really is all I know. Bradley Karlsson flew into Ulan Bator yesterday and hired me to follow you. That's all I know. He said he was with the US Government. Please," Altan strained through Hawke's iron grip, his eyes crawling from his groin up to Scarlet's boot, "*please*, that is the truth."

"We'll see about that," said Hawke, and knocked him out. They dragged his body off the road and propped him up against a building. Now Hawke was starting to lose patience. Every time he thought he was making progress something happened to confuse him even more. Now, there was a rogue American agent by the name of Karlsson on the scene, but how the hell he knew about what they were doing and where they should be, he had no idea.

"So what now?" Scarlet asked.

"A tough call," Hawke said, "but I say we get to the Khan museum as fast as possible. Whoever this Karlsson is he obviously knows a lot more about us than we do about him, and for all we know he could be one step ahead of us as well. All we can do is stick to the plan and hope for the best."

"The classic SBS strategy," Scarlet said, smirking.

Then Lea's phone rang.

"Hold on, guys!" she said. "It's Ryan."

She answered her phone and spoke with him for a few moments.

"What's up?" Hawke said when she hung up.

"He says that the thirteenth chapter reference on the

back of the portrait is referring to something called the Secret History of the Mongols. Apparently it was an ancient manuscript written when Genghis Khan died and it's been lost for centuries."

"This day just gets better," Scarlet said.

Hawke agreed with Scarlet and tipped his head back to look at the sky. He took a deep breath in and a few seconds out. As if things weren't bad enough, they now wanted him to track down a manuscript that had been missing for hundreds of years.

CHAPTER SEVENTEEN

Hawke looked out over the enormous plains as they made the journey to the Genghis Khan Complex, easily imagining the vast armies of Genghis and later Kublai Khan crossing this country on horseback as they expanded their mighty empire. It was here, on these plains that Genghis Khan built the greatest empire ever known by man.

They pulled up in the car park outside the complex and got out the car.

"This is actually the middle of nowhere," Scarlet said. "I mean I've heard the expression before but now I actually know where it is physically located on the globe."

"No, I don't think so," Lea said. "I went to Edinburgh once."

"No, darling," purred Scarlet smugly. "You're confusing middle of nowhere with arse-end of nowhere."

Hawke stared at the massive statue of the Great Khan. It was at the end of an enormous series of giant stone steps which swept up a grassy hill ahead of them. A few tourists ambled here and there, many taking pictures of themselves with the statue in the background. A light breeze, cold and sharp, blew off the plains and cut into them as they made their way inside.

"More Westerners than I expected," Lexi said.

At the top of the steps were two massive bronze statues of Khan-era Mongol soldiers, sparkling in the brilliant, clear sun.

"They look like they mean business," Lea said.

"Those were the days," Scarlet said, stroking a bicep. "When men were men."

Hawke rolled his eyes and pressed onwards.

Inside was larger than he had expected, and he wondered where to start.

They split up and made a tour of the complex, keeping their eyes out for anything referring to the Secret History of the Mongols, but found nothing. Moments later, Scarlet returned with a smile on her face. She noted with amusement that if you walked through Genghis Khan's crotch you could go outside and climb up his horse's neck and look out across the plains.

"Anything of interest?" Hawke asked.

"Grass."

They moved on.

"Ask that guy," Lexi said, pointing to an old man with wispy white hair and a baggy jacket. "He looks promising."

"He looks like he's a hundred and forty years old," Scarlet said. "Maybe he knew Khan personally."

"Keep your voice down you tool," Lea said. "He'll hear us."

"We're looking for Professor Bayar," said Hawke.

"Then you're in luck," said the old man. He shuffled forward and held out his hand. "I am Bayar. May I help you?"

"We hope so," Hawke said, smiling warmly. "We're here to talk about the Secret History of the Mongols."

The professor smiled. "I'm afraid we're closing shortly. If you can come back tomorrow I'll be happy to show you around and..."

"We want to talk about the Thirteenth Chapter, professor, and a man named Sheng Fang."

Bayar narrowed his eyes and evaluated the group of foreigners for a few moments.

"The Thirteenth Chapter, you say? Perhaps I might have five minutes to spare. Please follow me."

Moments later, the professor was gently closing the door of his office and shuffling slowly back to his desk.

"You will know, I am sure," he began, "that Genghis Khan was obsessed with immortality."

"As a matter of fact," Hawke said, "we're just learning that today."

"He had who was essentially a Taoist monk by the name of Changchun summoned to his court in order to help him locate the secret elixir of eternal life. However, when Changchun arrived he patiently explained to his leader that there was no such thing, and that talk of immortality had always been metaphorical, referring not to actual physical longevity but the immortality of the soul."

"And is that what you believe?" Hawke asked.

Professor Bayar ignored the question. "Changchun told Khan that he could achieve immortality by purifying his soul, and in return Khan gave the monk the official title Spirit Immortal, but..."

"But what?"

"It's possible that the monk was lying. Giving a man like Genghis Khan the power of immortality would have proved to be one of the most dangerous and reckless acts in human history – any man would be bad enough, but Khan was one of the biggest killers in the world – he even killed his brother when he was just a child."

"Nice," Lea said.

"You must remember that Genghis Khan believed he was the son of the sun – that he was divine and that his destiny was pre-ordained by the heavens themselves. He was a very determined man, and as I say, he killed his own brother when he was a child to secure his own future."

"Sounds like a great guy," Lea said.

"Then I will tell you an old Mongolian proverb favored by Khan himself - *return what people give to you*."

"At least the monk never told him the truth."

"Exactly. The monk would obviously have been very wise and well-read. I think it's pretty unlikely he would offer the secret of eternal life to a man like Genghis Khan, and that if he knew of a way to achieve immortality he would probably have lied to Khan about it to stop him from getting that power."

"I can see the logic in that," Scarlet said. "It would be like giving a man like Hitler immortality."

"Precisely," Bayar said. "A deeply religious man like Changchun was hardly likely to give up such a power to Khan."

"But where does this leave us?" Lexi asked.

Hawke said: "Was there a thirteenth chapter to the Secret History, Professor Bayar? I saw your eyes when I mentioned it to you – I know that you know something."

Bayar shifted uneasily in his seat. His fingers drummed against the edge of the desk and time seemed to slow down. "For a long time I thought I would take this information to the grave with me, but now I can see it is more important to speak the truth. You mentioned the name Sheng Fang – I know what kind of a man Sheng is and if he were to succeed..."

He got up and looked out of his little window.

"Professor, we're kind of pressed for time," Scarlet said as patiently as she could.

"I can confirm that the Secret History of the Mongols has thirteen chapters, not twelve as history has recorded for the last eight hundred years. The last chapter contains the truth about the Great Khan's quest for the Philosopher's Stone – the secret of eternal life!"

Hawke wondered if he could really be hearing these words. "And where do you keep this document?"

Bayar spun around, faster than any of them would have thought he was capable of. "Where do *I* keep it?" He laughed until he had to sit back down at his desk again.

"Why do I have a bad feeling about this?" Lexi said.

Hawke's heart began to sink. "It's not in your possession, professor?"

"Of course not! You're talking about a manuscript which the entire world considers has been missing since the thirteenth century! It's not something I could keep here in a drawer or even behind a glass case. The Secret History of the Mongols is not here, no... it is with the two Keepers of the Truth..."

"Who are they?"

"Two people who pass the secret along to the next generation. One guards the manuscript, and the other can read it."

"But it's not here?"

"Of course not, and I'm not certain I should tell you where it is."

"But you've already admitted that it exists and wasn't lost all those centuries ago like the history books tell us," Lea said. "So where the f..."

"Lea..."

"Sorry – where on earth is it?"

Bayar thought for a long time before replying. "You will find the truth where it has been since the Great Khan died eight hundred years ago, at Genghis Khan's tomb."

Hawke narrowed his eyes. "Hold on, I might not know very much about Genghis Khan, but I do know that people have been trying to find his tomb since the day he died."

"That is correct!" Bayar exclaimed.

"Even I know this one," Lea said. "This is the legend about how everyone who saw Khan's body as they took him to his grave was killed, right?"

Bayar nodded. "All of them! And those who buried him were also killed, and those who killed the men who buried him were then killed themselves."

"Must have been a hell of wake," Scarlet muttered.

"But the tomb of Genghis Khan has been missing for eight hundred years," Hawke said. "Not even brand new satellite technology has been able to find it. No one knows where it is!"

"That," Bayar said confidentially, "is where you are most certainly wrong."

"You've got to be kidding me..." Scarlet said. "First Poseidon's tomb now Genghis Khan's lost grave. We should go into the tomb recovery business, Joe."

"Do you know where it is, professor?" Hawke asked, lowering his voice.

"I do not know precisely. But I do know it is in a temple high in the mountains of northern Mongolia."

"Ryan's going to wet his pants when he hears about this," Scarlet said. "I do hope he has a fresh nappy on when you tell him."

"What I tell you now," Bayar continued, "is of the most confidential nature. The tomb of Genghis Khan has been a secret for eight hundred years, maintained and guarded by a tiny number of people, mostly Taoist and Shaolin monks. There is an ancient, sacred order known as the Temple of the Golden Light. They are few in number, today mostly Shaolin."

"Aren't those the best martial arts fighters in the world?" Lea asked.

"Yes," Lexi said coolly.

"They are sworn to keep the unmarked grave a complete secret from the world, and I know they have killed in the past to meet their vows. You must tread very carefully from now on."

Hawke suddenly was all business. "Professor Bayar, you just told us you know what kind of a man Sheng is, and now you know he is doing everything he can to track down that missing chapter. If you care about anything or anyone at all, you have to tell us where the temple is."

Bayar studied them for a long while, thinking through the options. After several minutes he leaned over his desk and slid a piece of paper over to himself and began writing. "You have honest eyes, Mr Hawke," was all he said.

After watching Bayar leave the complex and drive away, Hawke and the others made their way toward the exit. They now had the location of the Temple of the Golden Light in their hands, but it was a long way and they had no time to waste.

Then, as they made their way to the exit in the near-empty complex, they heard a voice.

"Just hold it right there!"

The voice was behind them, but before Hawke had a chance to turn around, he heard the familiar sound of a safety catch being flicked off an automatic pistol.

CHAPTER EIGHTEEN

The man stepped out of the shadows, a gleaming Sig Sauer P226 in his right hand. He had suspicious eyes, a wide jaw, and a crooked smiled which spread to reveal a gold tooth.

"And who the hell are you?" Scarlet said, sighing.

The man held up his hand to signal they should keep away from him. "The name's Bradley Karlsson and I've been watching you since Hong Kong – and don't even think about getting any of those shooting irons out."

Hawke placed his accent as American, probably California. He was well over six feet tall and built like an industrial refrigeration unit. His hair was cropped low but looked dark blonde. He looked like he'd have made a pretty solid nose guard back on the college football team.

"Since Hong Kong?" Scarlet said. "Impressive."

Karlsson nodded. "Gee, thanks *honey*."

Scarlet raised an eyebrow.

"You lie!" Lexi said.

Hawke stepped forward. "Whoever you are, tell us what you want and why you're pointing a gun at us."

"I'm happy with that. I'm CIA, originally a Navy SEAL. These days I work for a small covert unit run by a man named Eddie Kosinski. I know you've heard of him."

Hawke's eyes narrowed with suspicion. The last time he'd seen Kosinski was on the side of a mountain in Switzerland when he flew away with the contents of Poseidon's tomb. "I know Kosinski, but how the hell did he know where we were?"

125

"Not hard for a man like Kosinski. He tapped Eden's office with a laser and that's how we worked out you were going to Hong Kong. From there it was a piece of cake to tail you to the airport."

"But how did you know we were in Ulan Bator?" Lea asked. "I know no one followed us to the private airfield."

"We didn't follow you to the airfield. In fact, I was waiting for you in Ulan Bator before you even landed. That's when I hired Altan – you broke his jaw by the way and he says hi."

Scarlet took a step closer to Karlsson. Hawke noticed she appeared to be evaluating his biceps. "You're not a magician, darling. So out with it – how did you know we were coming here?"

"The answer is simple, but I'm not at liberty to tell you at this time. Perhaps when we know each other better."

"Dream on, *suntan*," Scarlet said flatly.

Karlsson smiled. "All I can tell is you is that we have assets all over the place and you're not alone in the fight against Sheng."

"So we were betrayed by someone, then?" Lea cast a derogatory glance at Lexi Zhang.

"You were not betrayed, and you were not followed, but that's all I'm saying right now. We have work to do."

"We?" Hawke asked. "How'd you work that out?"

"Look, Kosinski isn't the villain you think he is. He's serious about bringing Sheng down and has been ever since he got hold of your little Greek treasure trove..."

"Yeah, about that..." Scarlet said. "When do we get our cut?"

Karlsson laughed, but dodged the question. "Certain elements within the US Government are now of the opinion that what you located in Greece is only half the

126

story, and that the other half is in real danger of being secured and controlled by Sheng Fang."

"We'd worked that out a long time ago," Lea said. "Good to see you guys finally caught up."

Lexi flicked her hair back. "But if you think we're going to trust you, then you're even more stupid than you look."

Karlsson scratched his jaw. "Now that's not playing nice, honey. I can bring a lot of influence into this situation, not to mention some pretty impressive gear."

"We've got what we need," Hawke said flatly.

"Maybe, but don't forget I was a SEAL for over ten years. I have skills."

Hawke nodded. He happened to rate the US Navy SEALS. They were almost as good as the SBS, but not *quite*, he thought.

"Then you won't mind if I do this," Lea said, and snapped his picture with her phone. "We'll see if that face of yours turns up on any of our databases."

Hawke watched her send the picture while Karlsson kept everyone covered with his pistol. Moments later her phone buzzed and she read a short text. 'He's good – as far as we can tell. His story checks out with Eden, anyway."

"For whatever *that's* worth," Hawke said.

Lea looked at him sharply. "What's that supposed to mean?"

"Nothing," said Hawke. "Let's get on with our job." He walked slowly to Karlsson and squared up to him, ignoring the gun. They were about the same size, but Hawke had confronted enough SEALS to know he would get the final word in any disagreement. "Listen, Karlsson. For now, I'm going to trust you, but any funny business and we'll have words, got it?"

"I think he likes me!" Karlsson said to the others, laughing.

*

Sheng Fang held the candle in his hands while he lowered himself to the floor. He smiled as he considered how close he was to achieving his destiny and finally fulfilling the prophecy of the Thunder God. No one understood what it meant except him, and he alone would pursue it until he brought the world to its knees.

Now, sitting alone in the dim light, the room filling slowly with the scent of pungent incense, his mind was as clear as a mountain lake, and his focus sharper than ever. Things were going well. It was true the Lotus had disobeyed him in Paris, and perhaps she would pay for that, but now was not the time to dwell on such things.

Neither was it the time to let his mind wander to Mr Luk, his right-hand man. It was also true that Luk sometimes frightened even him, and that was not an easy thing to do. Luk was unpredictable and dangerous, but Sheng was certain he could control the monster hiding behind the man. All men had such a monster, he considered, but Luk's was fiercer than most.

He thought about the Russian, now on his way from his dacha on the outskirts of Moscow. Could he be relied upon to deliver the awesome destruction he had planned? Yes, he was confident he could. He could be very persuasive when the occasion called for it. When the Russian completed his mission, the people of the target city would be the first to pay, and they would pay a very heavy price, Sheng thought, smiling in the candlelight.

A quiet knock on the door.

Sheng's eyes narrowed, and he cursed under his breath.

"Who?"

"The professor is here."

It was the Lotus's voice. She had brought him news.

"He may enter."

The Lotus opened the heavy door and an overweight, middle-aged Western man stepped nervously inside the darkened room.

"You have something to tell me?"

The man nodded. "Yes, sir. I have finished translating the Reichardt Papers."

Sheng studied the man as if he were watching a praying mantis.

"And?"

"They confirm that there was an additional chapter that was kept from the world."

Sheng felt his heartbeat quicken.

"Continue, professor."

"Reichardt even claims to have organized an exploration before the war, and writes that it was guarded for centuries by monks. He says it was written in code."

"Then we must take possession of it immediately."

The Lotus stepped forward. "It's too late. The Englishman and his team are ahead of us. They are already there."

"Where?"

"According to your contact in the Ministry, they are now in the mountains north of Ulan Bator."

Sheng considered the situation for a moment. "Then you must fly to Beijing."

The Lotus looked confused. "But Ulan Bator is in Mongolia."

"I know where Ulan Bator is, but you are flying to Beijing."

"I don't understand," she said. "Hawke and the missing chapter are in Ulan Bator right now!"

"Yes, but they will be in Beijing before the dawn."

CHAPTER NINETEEN

The journey from Ulan Bator to the Temple of the Golden Light took them through the Gorkhi Terelj National Park and high into the mountains far to the north of the city. It was late now, and the sun was almost below the horizon.

They drove for another hour after dark until emerging from woodland into a broad valley cloaked above by a grove of bright, white stars. Then they saw it, nestled in a corner of the valley, with a view taking in most of the western sky.

Hawke was speechless when the temple finally came into view.

Lit by the full moon, it rose into the night, its Tang dynasty hip-gable roofs elegantly perched above the various buildings that made up the isolated little complex.

They emerged from the car and walked across the gravel courtyard to the main entrance.

Scarlet looked up at a large statue in the center of the yard. "What the hell is that?"

Lexi laughed. "You're looking at Samantabhadra, a bodhisattva, or an enlightened being. He's riding an elephant out of respect for the Buddha's mother."

"Oh, one of *those*..."

They were met at the entrance by a thin, lean man with a shaved head who wore the traditional orange robes of the Shaolin.

Hawke stepped up. "We're here to..."

"You were sent by Nambaryn Bayar," said the man. "I know him well. He was a great friend of my father's many years ago." The man stepped forward and shook Hawke's hand firmly. A good sign, Hawke thought. "You may call me Han."

They walked through to a central skywell where a small fountain trickled gently in the cold night air. From there the monk took them into a small room looking out across the valley. A moment later another monk served green tea to everyone.

"I haven't seen so many orange clothes since Gitmo Bay," Scarlet said.

Karlsson laughed, but Hawke was less amused. "Enough, Cairo – keep your wit to yourself please."

Han gave her the subtlest of dismissive glances and returned his attention to Hawke. "I know why you are here."

"Then you're better informed than I am," Hawke said.

Han nearly smiled.

"You are here in search of the Thirteenth Chapter of the Secret History."

"Apparently... yes."

"The document you seek has been hidden from the world for eight hundred years by the monks of this temple. If it were not for Nambaryn's endorsement of your quest you would currently be on your way home empty-handed."

"I understand, but we need the manuscript to..."

"I know why you need it. You are not the first person in the world to search for the Great Khan's tomb, or any of its many treasures. The latest is a very wicked creature by the name of Sheng Fang. We know him and what he wants to do."

They sipped the green tea while Han spoke gently in the low light.

"This is about something very, very old, my friends. I wonder if you are truly ready for the journey to come."

Hawke was feeling a tortured blend of impatience, anger and fear.

"But we don't know what our journey is," Lea said.

Han smiled. "A long time ago, the Great Khan launched upon a quest to find the secret to immortality. To this end, he engaged several Tao and Buddhist monks to help him in his search, but they all told him that no such thing existed. He never believed them, and never stopped searching. Here, the subject of immortality is taken very seriously. You can imagine my reaction when I heard about the Swiss magnate Hugo Zaugg and his search for the vault of Poseidon."

"You know about that?" Lea said. "I thought there was a media blackout on it?"

"Only on the true meaning of his death," Han continued. "To the average man on the street his death was no more than a simple suicide induced by the worsening condition of his stock portfolio, but to those who know a little more, and who are able to use a greater context, the true meaning of his death was clear enough."

"I don't understand," Lexi said.

"He means he knew who Zaugg really was long before his death," Hawke said. "Am I right?"

Han nodded. "Let's just say it was in our interest to keep a man like Hugo Zaugg under observation. He sought something a man like him should never acquire, after all." He smiled broadly.

"Until I shot him," Hawke said flatly, no smile.

"Which is why I am speaking with you now, and why I told Nambaryn to expect you – yes, indeed. In ending the Zaugg threat you proved yourself a friend of the Golden Light, even though at the time you did not know it. This is why we know you can be trusted now in the fight against Sheng."

"Then you know why this Thirteenth Chapter is so

important?"

Hawke was finally feeling like they were making progress.

"No one knows the full importance of the Thirteenth Chapter, Mr Hawke."

"But I thought it was lost to history?" Scarlet said.

"Yes, and no. Five hundred years after it went missing, a Chinese copy was discovered in some private archives in Fujian."

"But the original manuscript was never found, right?"

Han sipped his tea and took a long time before answering. "The original manuscript did indeed disappear from the world, but disappearing is not the same as being lost."

"Go on."

"As I say, the original manuscript is here, in a manner of speaking, in the Temple of the Golden Light, including the thirteenth chapter detailing Khan's attempt to locate the source of immortality."

"But how did it get here?"

"The monk who copied the chapters of the Secret History was forbidden to translate the final chapter, so he made a covert reference to it on the back of a painting that was on the wall of the room he was in when he made the copy. It was a fifteenth century image of one of the Four Beauties."

"We know – it's the one that was stolen by Chan."

"Having told the world that the thirteenth chapter existed in the only way he could under such close guard, the original was then taken to the Temple where we have guarded it with our lives ever since. I am personally entrusted with guarding it, and with my life. It is an ancient and sacred privilege."

"But how did Reichardt work out the clue was on the painting in the first place?"

"There was a note that the monk who had made the translation had requested devil's milk to relieve pain in his hands from transcribing the Secret History. But Reichardt knew that devil's milk – the milk of tithymalus or spurge, had another use – to leave a hidden message. That is when he must have added it all up and realized the monk made a copy. He spent his life searching for the final chapter, but never found it. Please, walk with me."

They followed Han down a long corridor where he opened a narrow door and stepped outside into the moonlight. The walked through an ornamental garden, across a low bridge and finally made their way over a series of shiny stepping stones on a smooth gravel bed before arriving at small clearing.

Thirteen tall acer trees encircled a small area of smooth grass and in the dead center was a large boulder.

"This is all very wonderful," Scarlet said, "but we don't have much time."

"She's right, *for once...*" Lexi said. "Where is the missing chapter?"

"Is it in Khan's grave?" Hawke asked. "If so, we need to go there right now."

Han smiled. "You are already at Khan's grave – is it not obvious?"

Hawke looked at the pleasant clearing. "This is Genghis Khan's grave?"

Han nodded. "Yes. Buried beneath here is one of the greatest treasure hordes in all of human history."

Scarlet's eyes widened as the monk lit a candle and lifted the boulder to reveal a hole in the ground. As they descended into the tomb, Hawke saw the boulder was artificial and fixed on a hinge system to act as a kind of trap door.

It didn't take them long to reach an underground

chamber, much smaller than any of them had expected, and as Han slowly moved around the tomb, slowly lighting more candles, the vast array of treasure gradually began to glow before their very eyes.

"There must be fifty million dollars' worth of gold in here..." Scarlet said, reaching out to touch an enormous gold plate.

Karlsson whistled loud and long. "Oh *my*."

Lexi pointed in one of the corners. "And look at that heap of diamonds! That has to be *impossible*. Imagine how good they would look on my fingers."

"It's not impossible," Han said. "This is one of the largest collections in the world. You are looking at some of the finest stolen gold and precious stones ever collected by man, and over there is the great man himself."

He raised a candle to point at the far end where a small unmarked grave had rested silently for hundreds of years.

"That's it?" Hawke said.

Han nodded. "A modest final end for a man with so much, but he wasn't happy. He dedicated much of his life to trying to cheat death, and in the end died trying, the irony is obvious."

Hawke took a deep breath. "We're not interested in Khan's treasure, Han. We just need the missing chapter so we can locate the map and stop Sheng."

Han was silent for a long time, nodding his head gently and smiling to himself. He seemed to like what Hawke had just said.

Hawke repeated hs plea. "Han? We just need the map!"

"But you already have it," the monk said, smiling. "It is now time for us to fly to Beijing."

CHAPTER TWENTY

Eden's private jet continued its climb until it hit thirty-five thousand feet and leveled out for the duration of the flight. Joe Hawke stretched his arms and yawned loudly, and then glanced at Han who was sleeping peacefully on the other side of the aircraft, holding a small box he had insisted on bringing with him. Han had said they already had the missing chapter, but like all the others, Hawke had no idea what that meant.

Since Poseidon he had learned to put his trust in others, but to Hawke, none of it made any sense at all. The murdered man in Paris, the stolen Tesla machine in the Pacific, the cryptic Shaolin monk beside him. Sometimes he thought all of this might be just one long dream that could turn into his worst nightmare at any moment.

He thought about Zaugg and now Sheng, desperately seeking the chance to cheat death and live forever. It was in defiance of everything nature stood for, yet the idea of it had intoxicated great men like Khan and many others through history like a lethal poison, warping their minds and driving them insane.

Nothing would ever change man's capacity for evil, he thought, and it was up to the good people of the world to keep that evil at bay. How he had wound up at the center of it he didn't really know, but maybe it had something to do with his feelings for Lea Donovan. He knew they were the real thing when Eden's phone call woke him in the night and the old man had told him about her disappearance. He knew they were the real thing when he saw her again at Chan's villa.

He watched the darkness below the small jet as they skirted the eastern borders of the Gobi Desert and made their way across the plains of Inner Mongolia. If he knew one thing for certain, it was that there had to be many more people than just Sheng Fang searching for such an awesome power, and the arrival of Bradley Karlsson proved it.

Beside him, Scarlet sighed. "Just what the hell did that monk mean when he said we already have the missing chapter, Joe?"

"I know everything *you* know," he said and smiled. "I thought all you wanted to do was blast bollocks off? Don't tell me you're starting to actually care about other people?"

Scarlet ignored him. "Maybe it's in Beijing with this Jenny Tsao woman?" She was referring to the person Han had told them about on their way to the plane.

"Han says we have what we need, and I for one trust him."

She sighed again, long and deep. "When all this is over I think I want to retire."

"Retirement's for pussies."

They turned to see Karlsson walking toward them from the rear of the plane. He was gripping a can of beer which looked comically small in his bear-like paw of a hand. Hawke's instinct was to trust the man because he knew Eden had checked both him and his boss Kosinski out and given them the green light, but Karlsson's personality made trust very hard, and liking him almost impossible.

"Who asked you?" Scarlet said.

"Waiting to be asked is for..."

"We know," Lea said, rolling her eyes. "it's for *pussies*, right?"

137

Karlsson laughed. "Yeah, maybe I was going to say that, maybe not. Listen, I know you guys are suspicious of me, but there's no need."

"I'll be the judge of that," Hawke said.

Lexi interrupted them. "You guys really think it's possible to live forever?"

Scarlet shrugged her shoulders. "Don't ask me, Bumblebee, I'm just a hired gun."

"It's Dragonfly, but gee, *thanks* for your considered response."

"You're more than welcome, darling."

Lexi turned to Lea. "What about you?"

"Sure, I don't see why not. Some conversations with Ryan can last forever so I don't see why a person couldn't."

Hawke laughed and joined Karlsson by grabbing a cold beer from the fridge.

Lexi sidled up next him, causing Lea to raise an eyebrow. "And what about you, Joe? Do you really believe in all this or do you think something else is going on?"

"Like what?"

"Like we're just being used and all of this is just a distraction."

Hawke had considered that, but dismissed the thought. "No, I don't think anything else is going on here. It can't get any darker or crazier than the search for immortality, after all. When I started out on all this, back in London at the British Museum, my answer to your question would have been laughter and ridicule and a straight-forward no. But now, after all we've been through, I just can't believe men like Zaugg and now Sheng would go to so much effort and expense for no reason."

"Maybe they're just deluded nuts, ever considered that?" Karlsson cupped a handful of peanuts into his large mouth and began loudly crunching them up with his mouth half-open.

"Obviously they're insane," Lea said, "but that doesn't mean they're delusional, Professor Freud. Two different things."

"But what would you do if you could live forever?" asked Lexi. "If you could take a sip of magical water and never die?"

Bradley sat down and ran a hand over the stubble on his head. "Knowing Hawke here, he'd probably fall in the water and drown."

"Immortality gags, eh, Bradley?" Lea said. "They never get old, right?"

"Oh, you're a funny one," Karlsson said flatly. "I can see that now. I couldn't before, but I can see it now that you've had more time to be funny like that."

"The fact you make jokes about this tells me you are not ready for this fight," Han said, waking from his sleep. "This is no joking matter. I am entrusted with the most ancient of secrets, and I take it very seriously."

"Talking of which," Karlsson said, "What's in that little box – the manuscript? Is that what you're going to show your buddy in Beijing?"

"Dr Jenny Tsao is not my buddy, she is now the only person in the world who can read the code, and I am the only man in the world who knows how to access the code. It has always been this way – two Keepers of the Truth – for hundreds of years."

There was a long silence and then Hawke turned his head back to the window and closed his eyes. He had no idea when he might get the next chance to grab a few minutes of sleep.

*

139

Ryan Bale was in his element, knee-deep in earthquake research and anything else he could find on Tesla and the various conspiracy theories attached to him. Now he was going through a file of documents General McShain had emailed over to him on the subject. They were heavily encrypted but McShain had given Ryan access to the decryption matrix.

"Not that I needed it," Ryan boasted.

"Yeah, right..." Sophie said as she studied the Tesla research for a moment.

Ryan smiled. "For all its beauty I don't think this is a particularly complex code."

Sophie smiled. She could fall in love with this man. "That's what I was thinking. If you look here at the first line it's pretty obvious they're using a rudimentary substitution system."

"Yes, exactly, and... you're messing with me, right?"

She nodded. "It's just so easy. I don't know why you can't admit that you needed McShain's matrix to read the files, c'est tout..."

"And... wait – what have we here?"

"What is it?"

"It's Victor Li in Hong Kong – he's making a phone call, and thanks to when I put the tracking software in his phone we're about to hear every word."

"You can do that?" Hart asked.

Sophie shrugged casually. "Sure, there are hundreds of well-documented security holes in the Apple operating system. It's easily done."

"No, I meant *you* can do that, Ryan?"

Ryan ignored her and opened up the app on his laptop which he was using to track Victor Li's phone calls. "I'm sure McShain's files are very fascinating, but something tells me we'll get more juice out of this."

Seconds later they were listening to the gentle trill of

a ringing cell phone.

"You think he's calling Sheng?"

"Doubtful, but maybe one of this goons."

Then two men began speaking in rapid Chinese.

"That's about as helpful as a chocolate teacup, Ryan," Hart said. "How are we supposed to know what's going on. They could be talking about their favourite bloody noodle bar for all we know."

"Oh, ye of little faith," he said, and activated a real-time translator. Moments later they were reading English subtitles running along the bottom of the app, translating Li's words from Chinese into English in real-time.

"I don't know who they are..." Li said in answer to a question. "But they're trouble. Big trouble. They humiliated me in my club and really went to town on me, and if I ever get my hands on any of them..."

"He's not happy with you," said a woman's voice. "I would leave China if I were you."

"For how long?"

"Until you die."

"Is that a threat? If that's a threat maybe I'll go to the embassy and tell them all about your plans with the stolen American hardware."

"Now it sounds like you are threatening us. A big mistake. You heard about what happened to Johnny Chan?"

A long silence. "I'm sorry. I can be trusted to keep silent, of course. Is the Russian in China yet?"

"What do you know about the Russian?"

"Nothing. I just thought I could show him some Chinese hospitality."

"I would concentrate more on staying alive. Don't call me again."

Then the line went dead.

"So what do we make of that?" Hart asked.

"Not much..." Ryan said, and sighed. "This Russian guy might be worth looking into, and then there's the reference to the embassy. I'm guessing that means the Tesla device is no longer in China and that they intend to destroy a foreign city with it."

"It could be anywhere!" Sophie said.

"Tell Hawke," was all Hart said. "I need to clear my head." She picked up her jacket and stepped out of the room.

Ryan emailed the information to Hawke and breathed a sigh of relief.

Sophie pulled her hair-tie out and unbuttoned her top. She began to massage Ryan's shoulders. "I think maybe we need some down-time after all that hard work. "C'est une bonne idée, non?"

In the mirror, Ryan saw her glance at the bed.

He grinned. "Now you're speaking my language!"

CHAPTER TWENTY-ONE

Beijing

After an extended and irritating period at Chinese customs during which Scarlet nearly head-butted an immigration official, they finally got out of the airport and back into the city. On the way, Hawke picked up the email Ryan had sent about Li's intercepted phone call to the mysterious woman and briefed the others.

It didn't take them long to track down Dr Jenny Tsao. Her home was on the outskirts of Beijing, in one of the more salubrious districts. Hawke, Lea and Han climbed the steps to the house while Scarlet, Lexi and Bradley Karlsson waited outside in their hired Mercedes SUV.

Dr Tsao turned out to be in her early seventies, and opened the door with a cup of tea in her hand and vintage jazz playing on a radio behind her. Steam rose from a pot on the stove in the kitchen behind her and Hawke smelled pork and star anise. He couldn't remember the last time he had eaten a proper meal. Tsao saw Han and nodded sagely, gesturing for them to come in without saying a word. She spoke only when they were all gathered in the front room.

"I have waited for this moment all my life," she said.

"I felt like that about iPhones," said Lea.

Luckily, Tsao appeared not to have heard her, and instead approached Han. "So, you are younger than I thought you would be. I thought the Guardian of the Truth would be much older."

"You are thinking of Wei Zheng. He died a year ago."

Han handed the small box to Jenny Tsao with both hands and she opened it with great care. Inside was a gold ring. "A gift for you, Dr Tsao, from the Temple."

"You are very kind." She nodded again, a thin smile on her face. "Now, let me see the missing chapter."

Slowly, Han turned and began to remove his shirt.

"Steady on!" Lea said, but before she could make another comment both she and Hawke realized what was happening. There, on the monk's back, hundreds of tattooed Chinese characters glistened in the flickering candlelight.

"I don't believe it!" Lea said.

"I know..." Hawke's voice trailed away. "It's amazing – that's the missing chapter."

"No, I meant you were actually speechless for the first time in your life."

"Oh, that's very droll, Donovan..."

Han spoke up. "What you are looking at is the thirteenth chapter. It is the only place it exists in the entire world. Only Dr Tsao, the current Reader of the Truth can understand its code. I decided you were worthy to see it back in Khan's tomb. Surrounded by some of the greatest treasure in the world, you told me you were not interested in the gold and gems, but only stopping Sheng. That is when I knew I could show you the tattoo."

Jenny Tsao smiled and a tear came to her eye. "I have spent my life studying the ancient code, but never before have I seen the missing chapter. This is priceless."

Lea moved into the light of the candle on her desk. "It's beyond priceless."

"You're quite right, of course," she muttered. "What we are looking at could lead the way to the secret of eternal life."

Hawke noticed Tsao's hands were shaking. "So you

really believe in immortality?"

"Of course, young man," she said, almost in a whisper. "I am old... I think about immortality much more than you do. Do you not believe in it?"

Hawke rubbed his face and sighed. This again. "If you'd asked me that a few weeks ago I would have laughed in your face and called you an idiot – no disrespect – but after what we've been through recently I just don't know any more. I never got a chance to find out if Poseidon's trident could live up to its reputation or not – not yet, anyway, and we never got close to the map back in Europe, so for me it's all still just myths and legends, and yet being so close to it all like this is turning me into a convert."

Tsao smiled. "As Lao Tzu once said, to the mind that is still, the whole universe surrenders."

Hawke raised an eyebrow and was on the verge of offering a skeptical reply when Lea stopped him. Tsao walked forward and began to read the encoded characters on Han's back. She ran her leathery fingers respectfully across the symbols tattooed on the young monk's muscles. She stopped to take off her glasses and rub her tired eyes and then returned to her analysis.

"It's written by a different writer than the person who wrote the other twelve chapters. That's obvious at once. It's absolutely beautiful prose... look here at the description of the sunset on the last night of Khan's life." She ran her fingers over the monk's back once again as she gazed at the characters.

"I'm sorry, Dr Tsao," Lea said, "but we have so little time..."

Jenny Tsao didn't even hear Lea's words. She was too engrossed in the process of decoding the final chapter of the Secret History. "This part here describes Khan's search for the Philosopher's Stone – his desperation for its discovery before he died, but of course death took him before he could find it."

"Where was he searching for it?" Hawke asked.

"The court poet describes something here about a traveler from the west – a man with fiery hair who traded information for gold. He told Khan about an ancient map which led its bearer to the source of eternal life."

They both leaned in closer to Jenny Tsao and said in unison: "Yes?"

"Apparently, there was a tomb in the west – the tomb of the Sea God, which contained the map, but it was raided by a party of foreigners and the map was stolen. He notes that they must have known the map was in the tomb because they left the rest of the treasure untouched."

"I can vouch for that..." mumbled Hawke.

"But who were these foreigners?" Lea asked.

Tsao looked up at her, amazed. "They were the Chinese, of course."

"What?" Lea said, amazed. "You mean to say that old bastard Zaugg was on a wild goose chase from the very beginning?"

Jenny Tsao tutted when she heard the bad language, but nodded in agreement all the same. "The map was stolen by the Chinese when they raided the tomb thousands of years ago."

"Who raided the tomb?" Hawke asked. "Does it give a name?"

Dr Tsao nodded again, and squinted through her thick glasses as she re-read the tattooed text to make sure of what she was translating. "It does! The map was stolen by a party of tomb raiders working for the Emperor Qin Shi Huang."

"Ying Zheng?" Lea asked.

Jenny looked up at her and smiled with unfeigned

146

admiration. "You know Chinese history? I'm impressed."

"It's more like I know someone who knows Chinese history. Who was Ying Zheng?" she asked.

"He was the king of the Qin State, a territory in China over two thousand years ago," said Han, speaking up again. "He was eventually the first ruler in China to use the title emperor instead of king and he was responsible for a massive expansion of Chinese power, especially to the south. You might know him as the man who unified the Great Wall of China."

"Ah, I know *that* one," Lea said.

"Anyway, Emperor Qin spent a large amount of his reign – and therefore his life – in a fruitless quest for the secret of immortality."

"I just love it when all this shit comes together," Lea said, beaming. "It's like the A-Team."

"The *what*?" said Han.

"Never mind. You had to be there."

"Han is right," Tsao said quietly. She seemed suddenly anxious. "Qin was so obsessed with the elixir that he even started calling himself "The Immortal". Many charlatans came to his court to sell him various potions which they claimed would make him live forever and in his desperation he tried them all."

"He'd have got along like a house on fire with Hugo Zaugg," Lea said.

"Qin travelled to Zhifu Island many times in search of the elixir because of a simple legend about a mountain there."

"He left inscriptions..." Han said.

"Yes, he did!" said Tsao nodding and peering over the top of her glasses at the inked symbols. "Tourists can still see them today."

"But he never found his elixir?" Hawke said.

147

Han shook his head. "No. He died eating mercury in the belief it would help him live forever, and anyone who knows about mercury knows that's pretty much the last thing you want to do if you want to live forever. Or even for a few hours."

"He ate mercury?" Lea said, horrified.

"He did," Han replied. "It wasn't so crazy in those days. Even today in fact, some people think eating gold leaf will extend their life. There's no accounting for crazy, as you Westerners say..."

"But how does all this fit into today?" Hawke asked.

Tsao whispered the reply, still enthralled by the chapter. "Genghis Khan found out that Qin's men had stolen the map from the vault of Poseidon and had it brought back to their emperor. But this is where the story takes a turn for the worse – at least if you're Qin Shi Huang. Apparently he...ah!"

"What is it?" Hawke asked.

Han turned his head. "Yes, what is it? What have you read?"

"We have found the most precious hidden gem of all! It is all true... there was a map from the West, brought into China by Qin's tomb raiders and... *he buried it with him in his tomb at Xian!*"

"His tomb?"

"Yes, Khan knew this to be the truth and that is why he tried to invade China so many times... the Map of Immortality is in the Emperor Qin's tomb."

"Then we have what we need!" Lea said.

"Not so fast," Tsao said. "It says the map is located in the real tomb, deep beneath the one we all know...and it says he who wishes to hold the map must complete the five trials..."

"The five trials?" Hawke asked, his mind instantly going back to the cave system in Kefalonia where they

148

nearly all died. "What are they?"

Over the next half an hour or so, Jenny Tsao told them everything she could about Khan and Qin and their quest for immortality, both from her own research and from the new text on the monk's back.

But then without warning she was stopped by the sound of shooting coming from the street.

"What the hell is that?" Lea said.

"I don't know," Hawke said calmly. "But I don't like the sound of it."

He looked outside and saw their SUV under heavy fire. He watched as Cairo, Lexi and Karlsson tried to defend themselves from inside, but they were the definitive fish in a barrel. "Get out of here, you fools!" he shouted instinctively, knowing they couldn't hear him. Then a loud explosion signaled their attackers had opened a second front on the house and the next thing they knew they were under attack themselves.

Hawke pulled his gun and fired back through the open door. Jenny Tsao staggered back in horror, clamping her hands over her ears to block the tinny report of the pistol, deafening at such a range, but it was too late for her. She was struck in the back and knocked dead in seconds. She collapsed to the floor and Hawke took cover behind her old sofa, while Lea and Han ducked down behind an antique drinks cabinet in the corner.

"How are the others?" Hawke shouted. "I can't see them from here."

Lea fired a few shots through the door to keep their attackers at bay for a second while she flicked her head up and looked over the cabinet and scanned quickly outside the window.

"They're burning rubber, Joe!"

"That's something, at least."

"I'm sending Richard an alert!" Lea screamed. "Just

in case these bastards get my phone."

From his position behind the sofa, Hawke could see the now-dead Dr Jenny Tsao sprawled over the floor beneath her desk, and outside in the hall at least three heavily armed men were trying to enter the room.

"They're here for Han!" Hawke shouted. "And they'll want Tsao's computer as well!"

"We can't let them get it."

Hawke agreed. He aimed his Sig at the laptop and fired two shots at it, totally obliterating it into a thousand tiny pieces.

"Good work!" Lea shouted.

"We have to get Han out of here!"

Hawke and Lea covered the door with a ferocious burst of gunfire to enable Han to get through the window. He watched the monk begin to climb through it, but it was too late. He turned around to see Lea standing in the door with a gun to her head. The weapon was being held by a woman the same size as her, with a shaved head.

"Wrong, Mr Hawke," the woman said, pushing the gun's cold steel muzzle hard into Lea's temple. "It's time for you to come with us."

*

"I told you not to drive away!" Scarlet shouted at Lexi.

"It was either that or get killed, you idiot!" Lexi said.

"You never desert your unit!"

"Ladies, please," Karlsson drawled.

"Shut up!" They both said to him at once.

Bradley Karlsson sunk into his seat and decided to enjoy the rest of the ride in silence as Lexi cruised the Merc through the backstreets of Beijing.

"It was the right thing to do," Lexi insisted. "I don't know about your SAS but I was taught to leave the wounded behind."

"And the SEALs too," Karlsson added helpfully with a casual shrug of his broad shoulders.

Scarlet had to fight hard not to punch them both. "The SAS teach the same thing, but they weren't wounded. They were under attack and we drove away."

"Same thing," Lexi said. "Now we live to fight another day, and to rescue your friends."

"If Sheng's men don't kill them first, yes."

"Your problem is that you're too negative," Lexi said. "I think you need more Feng Shui in your life."

"And your problem is that no one trusts you, including me."

No one said anything else after that. Scarlet contacted Eden and told him what had happened. Moments later she received instructions to drive to Beijing airport where the private jet was waiting to bring them back to Shanghai. They were to regroup with the others and then meet with Lao. She felt like a total failure, but knew there was one person she could rely on to help her claw things back. She picked up her phone and flicked through the speed dial.

151

CHAPTER TWENTY-TWO

Hawke stared hard at the man in the white suit. His eyes were obscured by a pair of Persol sunglasses but he didn't need to see behind them to know who he was looking at.

The man grinned. "You are a very difficult man to get hold of, Mr Hawke."

Hawke never broke eye contact with him. He was older than he had expected, with silver in his temples and an ominous snarl that seemed to be a permanent feature on his lean, clean-shaven face.

"My name is Sheng Fang, perhaps you have heard of me?"

Hawke made no reply. His eyes crawled over the room as he assessed the situation for a potential egress point. That seemed unlikely. The only door was behind him, and guarded by two men wearing shoulder-holsters, and behind Sheng was nothing but an enormous window offering an impressive view of downtown Beijing, but too high to use as an escape route. Beside him, Lea said nothing, and Han stood in silence too, measuring his fate.

"And you are even more elusive, monk. You and your secret."

Sheng lit a cigarette and blew the smoke at the ceiling. "Where are my manners?" He clicked his fingers and an armed man immediately pushed the silver box of cigarettes to Hawke.

"I'm trying to cut back," he said. "What do you want?"

"Ah – this I think you already know, and if you do not

152

give me what I want, then I will kill you all, starting with the lady." He fixed his eyes on Lea. "How nice of you to rejoin us, by the way. I was most disappointed with you in Shanghai. You were supposed to be payment for a portrait I desired."

"You bastard, Sheng!" Hawke moved forward to attack him – an involuntary impulse caused by the thought of Lea being kidnapped and used as common currency, but a second later he felt a heavy blow in between his shoulder blades and collapsed to the floor in a wheezing heap.

"Please, Mr Hawke, I must ask you to refrain from using bad language in the presence of a lady."

Hawke got to his feet and saw the person who had struck him was the woman with the shaved head who had held a gun to Lea's head back in Jenny Tsao's house. She was dressed from head to toe in black. She was smiling sadistically at him as he tried to get his breath back.

"Meet my personal assistant. She calls herself the Lotus."

Hawke struggled to get the air in his lungs. "She needs work on her interpersonal skills, Sheng."

"A joke, how British of you... but I thought you would be more interested in her – she is after all the person who killed Felix Hoffmann."

Hawke finally got his breath back and looked hard at the woman... so she was where all this had started back in Paris.

"I thought," continued Sheng smugly, "that framing the traitor Dragonfly was a particularly nice touch of hers, but then that's the Lotus, always thinking outside of the box. Please don't underestimate her diminutive stature, Mr Hawke. That was Hoffmann's mistake. The Lotus is an expert in Jeet Kun Do, Jiu Jitsu and Muy Thai."

"Thank you, but I've already eaten today."

Sheng was expressionless. "I'm glad you have a sense of humor, Mr Hawke. You will need it a great deal over the next few hours."

Hawke ignored the threat. "Why are you doing this?" he asked.

"Because I can, is the simple answer. The pursuit of the elixir is a venerable Chinese tradition going all the way back to our very first emperor, Qin Shi Huang, Mr Hawke, as I hope you are aware. I am merely following in a long line of brilliant leaders who desired the ultimate power for themselves."

"Like Hugo Zaugg, you mean?"

Sheng laughed loudly. "Mr Hawke, please don't make me laugh. Hugo Zaugg was a small-time amateur compared with me. In fact, as you may know, he was in my employ. Leading a man with his particular psychology to believe he was searching for the map for himself was very easy. Only when he discovered that it was not in Poseidon's tomb did I redirect my studies elsewhere."

"And that's when you found out about Qin?"

"Indeed. I have known about his brave search for the elixir almost all of my life, but it was only when we realized the map was not in the Greek tomb that it became apparent that someone had raided the tomb and removed it. With a little help from Professor Felix Hoffman and the Reichardt Papers we were able to work out that the Secret History of the Mongols had a previously unknown thirteenth chapter, and that in that document we would find the final piece of our puzzle."

"Only we got there first."

"Too bad for you, but yes. Now we know that the legends were right, and that the map was raided by men working on the instructions of Emperor Qin himself, and brought back here to Chinese civilization."

"How did you know we would go to Dr Tsao in Beijing?"

"A simple deduction. Tsao is a world-renowned scholar of ancient Chinese and Mongolian studies, and an acknowledged expert on deciphering linguistic codes. As soon as we cracked the Reichardt Papers we knew we would need Tsao, but as you say, you got there first. We would have beaten you to it had the Lotus brought Hoffman to me alive, as were her instructions, but she has always been very difficult to control and is not the most reliable assassin."

"You just can't get the staff these days."

Sheng was silent for a long time, and then he spoke. "Won't you please join me?"

Before he could answer, Hawke felt another hefty whack delivered by the Lotus, this time in the small of his back. It was her way of hinting that he should walk with Sheng Fang.

With Lea back in the office, they led Hawke and Han along a plush corridor and into a large chrome elevator. Seconds later they emerged on the roof of the skyscraper. It was a vast area of satellite dishes, industrial-sized water pipes and humming air-conditioning vents. Above the city of Beijing hovered an ominous brown smog.

Sheng wandered casually to the edge of the roof, hands in pockets. He glanced down over the side for a few moments and stepped back. "You see before you the rise of the dragon, Mr Hawke. For hundreds of years your Western nations pillaged us, and humiliated us. Your imperial power took everything from us and left us a burned-out husk, but now all of that is changing."

"If you say so."

"We are now the most powerful economy on earth, Mr Hawke, overtaking even the United States. Soon we will dwarf that country, and then we will expand. Our military has the fastest growing blue-water navy in the world, and we launch a new submarine every few months. Soon we will make the Pacific Ocean our private playground."

"You're as mad a box of frogs, Sheng."

"You will find out what insanity is only when your country is humiliated like mine was. What man doesn't desire that kind of revenge?"

"To be honest, all I want these days is a quiet night in front of the TV."

"Always with the jokes... but life is more serious than you admit. Your Western ideas have dominated our world because of your military and economic power, but now we are overtaking your military and economic power the ideas will soon change too. The world will have our values, not yours."

Hawke laughed. "And how do you plan to make all this happen?"

"I am the Thunder God, Mr Hawke! Reincarnated and ready to take my destiny in my own hands. What I make happen will happen. It is preordained."

"Better make that five boxes of frogs!"

"Ah – you think it is insanity to talk of being a god... of course you do! You have such an ordinary mind. You should ask yourself what makes a god?"

Sheng clicked his fingers and the Lotus and another guard dragged a woman from the elevator. She was unconscious, so he had the Lotus kick her in the stomach. Seconds later she was awake and gasping for breath.

Hawke saw Han's eyes widen in horror. "What is it, Han?"

"That's my sister! They have my sister!"

"A god is a god because he is immortal, Mr Hawke," Sheng continued, watching the poor woman with relish in his eyes. "A god may give life and take life."

"A few assumptions there, but do go on... I haven't had a good sleep in a long time."

Sheng ignored him. "And so if a mortal man could become immortal then would he not be a god?"

Sheng spoke in rapid Mandarin to the Lotus and she dragged the woman to the edge of the skyscraper. She made no effort to escape and a look of total despair spread across her face like a hideous shadow.

"The God of Thunder, Mr Hawke – Lei Gong! A genius! A powerful and divine ruler who used his omnipotence to punish sinners – but he was once a mortal man, just like me. A mortal man who tasted the peach of immortality... and I too will drink of the elixir that gives eternal life, and have the total power and knowledge that comes with it!"

"I've heard it all before, Sheng," Hawke said, thinking of Switzerland. He knew he had to stand up to this maniac and not show any sign of weakness. "Zaugg had the same look in his eyes as you do now – until I killed him, that is."

"As I have said, poor Hugo had no real fight in him. He was obsessed with his father's Nazi legacy and allowed too much of the past to cloud his mind. Also, he made the fundamental mistake of surrounding himself with idiots, which I have not done."

As he said these words, the elevator doors opened to reveal a stocky man with a long pony tail and wispy black beard. He stalked across the roof of the building and approached Sheng. They exchanged a few quick words, and then Sheng turned to Hawke.

"This is the indispensable Mr Luk, from Hong Kong. He has certain unique talents which are hard to come by, but so necessary in my line of work."

Luk's face was expressionless, his eyes cold as sharpened steel.

The Lotus held Han's sister on the edge, where one nudge meant a fall of hundreds of feet to her certain death. Luk joined her and grabbed Han's sister by the neck.

"Where is the final chapter of the Secret History?" Sheng demanded, staring expressionless at Han.

"I... I don't know," Han said, glancing from his terrified sister to Hawke.

"An unfortunate lack of knowledge on your part," Sheng said, and ordered Lynn Han an inch closer to the edge. Luk and the Lotus pushed her almost over the side, holding on to her by her arms.

"Please!" Han screamed. "Don't hurt her. She knows nothing."

"Don't tell them, Qiao!" his sister screamed.

"I assure you I am not bluffing, monk," Sheng said firmly. "In less than a minute your sister is about to commit a terrifying and extremely painful suicide. The location of Khan's manuscript, now!"

"I... I..." Han shut his eyes tight and shook his head in disbelief. Hawke had been to the same place in his mind, but knew it wouldn't help Han change the reality of the situation no matter how much he wanted it to.

"You'll pay for your life with this, Sheng," Hawke shouted. "I'll see to that personally."

Sheng was calm and undeterred. "I think not, Englishman." He stepped closer to Han, almost face to face now, and lowered his voice to a whisper, icy cold and emotionless. "Last chance – the location of the missing manuscript or she dies, right now."

Hawke saw Han wrestling with his terrible situation. On one hand, his very own sister, her life in his hands, and on the other, a lifelong vow of the most grave import.

"I..., Lynn... I'm...*sorry*..." He lowered his head and began to sob.

Sheng raised his chin and looked at Han with something that might have resembled respect in a man with any humanity. Then, with no further thought he snapped his fingers a final time and Luk and the Lotus launched Lynn Han over the side of the building. They all heard her screams recede into the busy Beijing bustle. Moments later the sound of car horns and sirens.

Han collapsed and screamed with rage on the concrete roof of the skyscraper. Hawke clenched his jaw and fixed his eyes on the monster who had ordered an innocent woman's death right in front of him.

"I can see your psychological training is indomitable, monk," Sheng said. "But if I cannot break the mind, I will break the body."

He ordered Luk and the Lotus over to Han, where they roughly hauled him to his feet and Hawke saw the monk's tear-streaked face in the bright sunshine. His neck muscles were bulging with rage as he began screaming at Sheng in Mandarin, but Hawke needed no translation to understand what was being said.

Before Han could finish his threat, Luk punched him in the back of his head and knocked him out. Moments later they were tying him to the side of an industrial air-conditioning unit. Then, Luk tore the shirt from the monk's back as the Lotus pulled a horsewhip from her belt and prepared to whip him until he gave the location of the missing text.

A wave of crushing disappointment and anger rushed over Hawke as he watched the eyes of Sheng, Luk and the Lotus settle on the monk's back for the first time and behold the elaborate tattoo. Sheng smirked. They had what they wanted, and when Han awoke from his unconsciousness, he would know he had lost his sister for nothing.

CHAPTER TWENTY-THREE

Shanghai

Jason Lao had turned the top floor of an abandoned office building into a temporary HQ and Scarlet was silently impressed as she watched a group of men in boiler suits add the finishing touches to the office – wifi routers – telephones and laptops.

They had landed back in Shanghai less than one hour ago and after a rendezvous with Ryan, Sophie and Commodore Hart they travelled across the city in a private SUV to meet Lao. Scarlet was used to working fast and moving even faster, but even she had found a moment on the plane to think about what fate might have dealt Hawke, Lea and Han since their kidnapping back in the capital.

Now, somewhere in the distance she recognized General Frank McShain as he stood among a small group of American and Chinese military personnel. She considered how big and real a threat had to be to bring the American and Chinese military top brass together like this, and the conclusion was an unsettling one.

Lao and Lexi shared a few words of Mandarin before they were all invited to sit down for the briefing, which would be delivered by General McShain in English first. Scarlet took a seat at the back – an old habit – and Hart joined her, along with Ryan and Sophie. She watched Bradley Karlsson with more than a little suspicion as he took a seat at the front alongside Lexi Zhang and Jason Lao.

"As you know," McShain began. "We are here to neutralize a serious threat that is jeopardizing both our nations and many others. That threat is the billionaire telecoms magnate and people trafficker Sheng Fang."

Scarlet watched a ripple of excitement, tinged with apprehension go around the office. Something told her she was about to get the fight of her life.

"It has come to our attention that Sheng Fang is seeking a very ancient power the likes of which no one on Earth has experienced for millennia. We don't know exactly what form this power will come in, but we do know..." McShain took a breath and looked anxiously around the room. All eyes were on him, hanging on his every word.

"He can hardly believe he's about to say it," Scarlet said.

McShain cleared his throat. "But we do know it more than likely contains the power to greatly extend a man's life, possibly infinitely."

The room erupted with agitation when the general delivered these words, with American and Chinese intelligence operatives and military personnel hardly able to believe their own ears.

"Everyone calm down!" McShain said firmly. "That's enough!"

The room settled.

"I know what it sounds like, but there it is. We have very good intel on this, part of which came from a recent attempt to secure the...ah... *power* that I just described by a man named Hugo Zaugg, who thanks to British intelligence we now believe was being used as a sort of puppet by Sheng."

"And what about the burning sky reference?" Scarlet called out from the back.

McShain looked at her with irritation as another wave

161

of concern rippled through the room.

"That is nothing to be concerned about."

"What does she mean?" shouted a man in the front row.

"It's nothing, like I said," the general repeated. "There is a peripheral reference to the sky setting on fire if the source of eternal life is ever manipulated by mortal man, but that is not our concern right now. We don't know what it means, if it means anything at all – and it's just another reason for us to redouble our efforts to stop Sheng from getting his hands on the map that leads to this power, at all costs."

Ryan smirked. "Nice work. You really put him on the spot."

"Yeah, but I bet he's not going to mention the Tesla device," Scarlet said with a palpable lack of surprise in her voice.

"Hardly a *shocker*," Hart said.

"Very funny," Sophie said.

Scarlet remembered that only she, Hawke and Lexi had been at that meeting back in Hong Kong. "But Lao knows. I was in the office when McShain told us about someone swiping it from the American transport vessel. We now know that was Sheng."

McShain ran through a raft of tactical details about Sheng's retreat on Dragon Island, most of it garnered by on-going satellite surveillance, others gathered by spies posing as fishermen or tourists in the water park. He explained how Sir Richard Eden had confirmed that Lea's tracker showed they were in the air, and sat-surveillance showed the airfield on Dragon Island was being readied for the flight so the inference was they would land on the island, not Shanghai.

"Another thing we all need to be aware of is that a few hours ago Sheng took two of our people and a third man hostage. They are Joe Hawke, a former British Special Forces man with considerable experience, and Lea Donovan, a former Ranger with the Irish Army. Both are very capable people who are able to look after themselves in grim situations like this but at this moment in time we have no idea if they are alive or not. The same goes for the monk. All personnel need to be aware of these three friendlies during the assault. The last thing I want to hear about is their deaths from friendly fire."

Upon hearing McShain's terse words and grim analysis, Scarlet thought about Hawke and Lea and whether Sheng had killed them or not. She thought not, because they would be good to barter if things got really sticky during a firefight and he was backed into a corner. But then second-guessing the logic of egomaniacs was never a great idea.

She wondered how Hawke would react if anything happened to Lea, knowing the terrible impact that Liz's death in Hanoi had made on him all that time ago. She had heard about the murder when she returned from a joint SAS-SBS operation to rescue two kidnapped journalists in Iraq.

That was a good mission. They arrived by helicopter and marched for six hours in order to conduct a surprise attack on a compound near the Jabal Kumar mountain. They rescued both the hostages and killed all fourteen of the kidnappers in less than four minutes. Scarlet was disappointed. She had made a bet it could be done in less than three.

But when she was on the transport back to England, one of Hawke's colleagues in the SBS had gotten wind of the murder and told everyone on the plane. She phoned Hawke when she landed but he had dropped off the radar. When he resurfaced weeks later she tracked him down to his house, sitting in a darkened room with his hands wrapped around a bottle of cheap Scotch.

She hoped nothing like that ever happened to him again, and she put the whole thing behind her and focused. All those years in the SAS had to add up to something other than a reputation, after all, and she returned her attention to McShain's briefing, which, she hoped, might at some point get interesting enough to pay attention to.

*

Later, after the briefing, Ryan and Sophie made use of one of the laptops to get deeper into their research of Sheng and the Tesla threat. Scarlet walked over with Olivia Hart while Lao and McShain finalized details with their teams in preparation for the assault.

"I noticed McToughnuts over there never mentioned the Tesla device," Scarlet said, gesturing at McShain. "Anything about that?"

Ryan nodded grimly. Scarlet had only known him a short time, but lately he seemed to have aged a lot. She could see rings around his eyes from the lack of sleep and he seemed to spend a lot of time drinking coffee and Coke to keep himself going.

"Yes, but not a lot," he said in reply. "As you can guess, to say a device like that would be classified is a ludicrous understatement and I've been trying to look at stuff away from what McShain's already given me, just to make sure we're getting the whole picture."

"But what have you got?" Scarlet asked, sighing.

"Hey! He's doing his best!" said Sophie. "I'd like to see what you could come up with."

"I'd like to see my fist in your face, but..."

"Enough, the two of you!" Ryan snapped. He rubbed his eyes in an attempt to energize himself. "As a matter of fact I was able to find a few buzzwords relating to the project on conspiracy theory websites."

"Oh *God*," Scarlet said. "Not the tin-foil hat brigade, Ryan! This is serious."

"It's a very reliable forum, actually," he said patiently, as if explaining to an infant why putting your hand in a fire is a bad idea. "From there, I was able to get some kind of idea about what we're talking about and managed to hack some intercepts between the US Navy and an American professor of physics in California."

"You see now what good work he does, no?" Sophie said.

Ryan reached out and touched Sophie's hand. She smiled and rubbed his shoulder.

"All right, all right," Scarlet said, seeing the contact. "Either get a room or get on with the briefing."

"It's not much more than we've already got. All I can say from reading the intercepts is that the device is definitely real, definitely works and was definitely stolen by Sheng. They also make it clear that if this thing is used it will annihilate an entire city and according to InsideMan, if it's anything like..."

"Sorry?" Scarlet said. "But who the hell is InsideMan?"

"One of my hacking colleagues."

"One of your nerd friends?"

"He's an expert hacker and one of the finest conspiracy theorists in the world," Ryan said with pride.

"You mean he sits at his computer desk in his underpants surrounded by empty takeaway cartons and wishing for a girlfriend?"

"I mean," Ryan said with exaggerated slowness as if talking to a young child again, "that he has a very good track record on predicting *natural* disasters, for one thing."

"Explain."

"I mean that not all natural disasters are what they seem, despite McShain's protests, and that's why when this came up I contacted him. It seems right up his street."

"Have you ever met this guy, Ryan?" Scarlet said.

"Of course not. We're all anonymous."

"He could be bloody anyone then!"

"And?"

"And he could be giving you disinformation!"

"Maybe, but our lives don't depend on what he gives me. All he tells me is that if a big global city has a major earthquake in the next few days then the authorities will simply tell the public it was a natural disaster while in the background they're racing around trying to find and either kill or bribe the perpetrator."

"Not sure how this helps us."

"Well for one thing, it tells us we can't trust McShain, because in Hong Kong he told Hawke outright that the US has never used the machine to artificially trigger quakes."

Scarlet raised her eyes from Ryan's laptop screen and glanced at McShain, now talking in animated fashion with Jason Lao. "You can't trust anyone, Ryan, didn't you know that?"

CHAPTER TWENTY-FOUR

Dragon Island

Lea Donovan's mind was burning with questions and fears as Sheng's private jet roared south along the Chinese coast. She had just woken up from the chloroform dished out to the three of them by Luk back in Beijing, and she had the headache to prove it. Sheng himself, with Luk and the Lotus were up front, talking quietly in rapid Mandarin. She didn't understand a word of it. Either side of her were Hawke and Han, both still out cold.

The gentle hum of the luxury cabin and the softness of the leather seat almost made her forget she was a prisoner of these people, and as she watched the clouds flick past below her, occasionally revealing a snatched-glance of a yet another Chinese city, she was almost enjoying the flight.

Until she remembered why all this was happening. Until the hideous black ghosts of the past like Hugo Zaugg and Heinrich Baumann crept into her imagination like poisonous shadows. She shuddered when she thought of Baumann, on fire in the wine cellar, and when she closed her eyes she could sometimes feel Zaugg's hands around her throat as the gondola swung in the snowstorm.

From what she had heard from Sir Richard Eden and Lexi Zhang, these people were even more dangerous, and now she and Hawke were disarmed and in their power. Would they kill them before they had a chance to escape or fight back? Would Hawke die before he knew the truth about what she had been concealing from him?

Lea was more sure than ever that Hawke deserved to know the truth, but she knew it wasn't her place to tell him. As she looked at him, knocked unconscious by a brutal pistol-whipping delivered courtesy of Mr Luk, she began to wonder if he could be more than a lover.

Since their first night together in the Swiss Alps, Lea Donovan knew he was the kind of man she could really fall in love with – maybe even spend the rest of her life with, but there was always the issue of what she had kept from him. The way he had dismissed her concerns over what had happened in Syria had meant a lot to her, but this was different once again. This was out of her hands. How would he react to yet more deceit?

Slowly, Hawke began to moan and come back to life.

Lea leaned forward and hushed him.

"Don't let them know you're awake, Joe," she said in a gentle whisper.

"Where the hell are we?" he said, confused. He tried to rub his head and then realized his hands were tied behind his back with plastic cable ties. "Damn it!"

"We're in Sheng's jet. That Luk bastard knocked you out back at the airport – do you remember any of that?"

"Yes... it's coming back to me. Another private jet, eh?" He hauled himself up a little and stretched his neck to relax the muscles. His eye was swollen and bruised from the beating Luk had given him earlier, while he was held back by some of Sheng's men, and it felt like at least one of his ribs was broken. "I'm starting to feel like a rock star."

"Sure," Lea said, "rock stars on their way to an execution. Real glamorous."

Despite the pain, Hawke chuckled.

"So where are we going?" Hawke asked. "Shanghai?"

Lea shook her head. "No, we're going to his island

just off the coast of Shanghai – Dragon Island."

Hawke frowned. "The place where he tortures his victims to death?"

"So he says."

"I heard they're having trouble getting tourists there," said Hawke. "Something about the screams putting people off their crispy duck."

"Is that another one of your jokes?"

"I'm sorry. Just have a headache right now and really starting to hate flying. What about him?" Hawke nodded over at Han. "I wouldn't want to be Sheng if he ever gets loose."

"Out cold the whole flight."

"You think your buddy Richard knows where we are?"

"Finally he asks an intelligent tactical question!"

"Well?"

She shrugged. "No way to tell, but I think so. The emergency alert I texted him back at Jenny Tsao's place would have triggered a protocol response and the tracker I have in my boot means he could well know where we are if it's all working right."

"That's great news. Hopefully Eden and Lao can get some kind of a force together and get to the island. We're going to need to get away from these idiots and make the assault on Sheng's fortress by Lao's men as easy as possible."

"Plus we have to work out where Sheng is going to deploy that damned Tesla thingy as well, and so we'll need to divide our forces into two, right?"

"Finally she gives me an intelligent tactical answer."

The Lotus stepped toward Hawke and gave him a twisted grin. "Any more talking and I'll gag you both – got it, action man?" She took hold of his hair and yanked his head back, kissing him roughly on the mouth.

Lea recoiled in disgust. "Hey! That's my boyfriend and you're not his type!"

Hawke stared at the Lotus hard. "She's right, you're not really my type at all. I've always preferred my women a little less psychopathic."

"Too bad." The Lotus flicked a quick glance at Lea, then scowled as she powered her boot into Hawke's stomach.

Hawke doubled over, wheezing in pain as he struggled to suck the air back into his winded lungs.

The Lotus turned to Lea, who was watching Hawke squirming in agony on the soft carpet of the jet, helpless to comfort him with her hands tied behind her back. "Maybe I should have kissed you instead?"

"Maybe you should just fuck off and jump out this plane instead?"

The Lotus took a step forward and grabbed Lea's hair with her hand. She leaned in close, as if to kiss her, but instead spat in her face. Laughing, she roughly released Lea from her grip and turned on her heel. "If you knew what was in store for you, you'd beg me to throw *you* out the plane, believe me."

The Lotus smirked and strutted back to the front of the jet.

Hawke tried to snap the cable ties with brute force, but with no luck. "I wonder what she means by that?"

"Oh, I expect she means they have a night of Karaoke planned for us." Lea gave him a sarcastic half-smile and rolled her eyes. "And by the way, you didn't exactly object to that absolutely *disgusting* example of sexual harassment in the workplace a minute ago."

"I couldn't do anything about it!" he protested. "My hands were literally tied behind my back."

"Oh yeah, sure. How many times have I heard *that* one before?"

"Eh?" Hawke looked confused. "I'm guessing absolutely zero times, am I right?"

Lea made no reply other than to close her eyes and turn her head away from Hawke.

"I'll take that as an admission of defeat."

A long silence.

"I said," Hawke repeated, "that I'll take that as an..."

"Well don't, because it isn't. *Eejit*."

"I cannot believe you're actually jealous because one of Sheng's nutcase minions forced a kiss on me." Hawke tried to suppress a cynical laugh.

"I am not jealous."

"What are you then?"

Lea sighed. "Oh... I would say disappointed, but that would imply I expected more of you, so let's just go with I'm *disgusted* with you, Joe Hawke."

"Uh-oh!"

"What?" Lea craned her neck down the aisle expecting to see the Lotus on her way back to them.

"You used both by names," he said smugly. "That always means at least half an hour of nagging and whining."

Lea sighed. "If my hands weren't tied behind my back right now..."

"What?"

"I'd beat your arse, that's what, Joe Hawke."

"I'd like to see you try, Donovan."

"Uh-oh!"

"What?" Hawke tried to lift himself up to see if anyone was approaching them.

"You just called me by my surname. That always means at least an hour and a half of bullshit and bravado."

Hawke smiled. Lea was a keeper, as his mother used to say.

171

*

Sheng's private jet began to descend just as it passed the Shanghai metropolis outside the starboard windows. Hawke felt the pain from Luk's earlier beating thud through his upper body as the plane banked heavily to port. He knew that somewhere ahead of them lay the infamous private island that Nightingale had warned him about.

His hands were tied behind his back with several cable ties so tight they were restricting the blood flow. They had done the same to Lea and Han. Now, as the plane prepared to land, the Lotus rejoined them and sat opposite them with a smirking face.

She aimed the muzzle of an automatic pistol at them and directed some fast Mandarin to the front of the aircraft. She glanced at Han and pulled a second gun out to cover him when he awoke from his blackout. Hawke could see trust wasn't a big commodity in the world of Sheng Fang.

"When are you pricks going to bring around the peanuts!" Lea said. "We're almost landing and not one sodding Coke! I'm going to complain, you know!"

He smiled.

The Lotus did not, but instead got up and kicked Lea in the stomach. She doubled over in agony.

"We're landing now," the Lotus said flatly. "I want you where I can see you all."

"But I don't think she has a first class ticket," Hawke said.

"You don't want to be mixing with steerage trash like me, you mean?" Lea said with an honest smile.

The Lotus was unmoved by the banter. "You sure do talk a lot of shit for two people who are about to die in the most horrible of ways."

A thin smile danced on her mouth, all crooked and black lipstick. Her cold hate-filled eyes watched Hawke and Lea as if they were a couple of insects.

"What are you talking about, you bitch?" said Lea.

She made no reply, but turned to watch Han as he began to come back to life.

"Where...am...I?"

"You're on Psycho Airways," Lea said, nodding in the direction of the Lotus. Han craned his neck and watched her sitting a few feet in front of him. His face reddened with rage and thoughts of revenge. "I swear I will gut you like a fish, and all the others who murdered my sister will suffer the same fate!"

"Get in line, boyo," said Lea.

The Lotus laughed and scratched her leg with the muzzle of one of the pistols.

"I know how you feel, Han, believe me," Hawke said. "But this isn't the time. We need to keep our heads clear for the fight to come. When we get to Dragon Island we're going to need all of our wits about us just to survive, never mind getting revenge."

Han's eyes narrowed with hatred. As the plane banked and began to descend, neither Lea nor Hawke thought they would have much luck stopping Han from avenging his sister's brutal murder.

CHAPTER TWENTY-FIVE

On their way out to the Jeeps, Scarlet, Hart and Karlsson were a few paces ahead of Lexi, Ryan and Sophie when a familiar face stepped into view at the end of the corridor.

It was Vincent Reno, known to the wider world as Reaper.

Scarlet frowned and put her hands on her hips. "About time you turned up, you lazy French bastard."

"Better a lazy French bastard than a cold English cow."

For a second they stared at each other, and then laughed and embraced for a few moments before the former French Foreign Legion paratrooper pushed her away and pulled a cigarette from a crumpled packet in his back pocket. "Don't get too close to me, I'm easily turned on. Who is this?"

"Brad Karlsson, CIA."

They shook hands and Reaper struck a match on his belt, ready to light the cigarette.

A man in Chinese military fatigues stepped up to the bear-like Frenchman. "Hey! No smoking here!" He took the cigarette from Reaper's mouth with a scowl and took it away.

Reaper pinned the man to the wall by his neck and slowly retrieved the cigarette, put it in his mouth and lit it up. "Lucky I'm in a good mood today, oui?"

Scarlet and Karlsson laughed, but Reaper was still scowling as they took their seats in the vehicles. "So your message said Hawke had been captured?"

"Yes, in Beijing." Scarlet's voice was low, and measured. She was in control again. "A surprise attack in a house they were in. It belonged to a professor who was translating the secret chapter for us. She was killed in the attack."

Reaper sighed. "Too bad. At least he'll owe me one when I save him though."

Scarlet smirked at the thought. "I was thinking the same thing. Not like him to get caught out like that. He's been out of the game for too long. Maybe time to get him back inside."

"What do you mean?"

"Forget it," Scarlet said. "Let's get going." She turned to Ryan as the Jeeps raced toward the airport.

After a few moment of contemplation, Reaper turned to Ryan. "I hear this Sheng guy is looking for the same thing Zaugg wanted?"

Ryan nodded. "Pretty much, only he's getting much closer than Zaugg ever did. He's playing with fire..."

"What do you mean?"

"Why would anyone with immortal power feel the need to create a map that leads to the location of their power? If such a thing ever fell into the wrong hands then you could lose access to that source and die, or any number of terrible things. So at the moment there are still more questions than answers."

"Which is always the way," Sophie said, tying her hair back. "Always the way..."

*

When Hawke landed, a host of serious men and women were on the tarmac to meet Sheng Fang, some of them in business suits and others in military fatigues. Han was dragged out first and taken away by two men in fatigues and the Lotus. She looked like she was relishing her work, and looking forward to torturing the monk for as much information as she could get.

Hawke and Lea's welcoming committee consisted of a dozen men in camos with assault rifles.

"I see our reputation precedes us," Lea said, frowning.

"I'm more worried about Han. Now they have him, they not only have the missing chapter that's tattooed on his back but all the knowledge Jenny Tsao gave him before they killed her in the raid. I know I can take whatever interrogation shit they throw at me, and maybe you too, but Han... he's a monk for God's sake."

"I wouldn't bet on him cracking," Lea said. "He seems pretty tough to me – look at the way you told me he let his own sister die before breaking his sacred vows not to reveal the location of the missing chapter. Don't get much tougher than that, Joe. Could *you* do it?"

Hawke made no reply. He knew he couldn't answer without disappointing her. If he said yes he would look like a cold-hearted robot, and if he said no he would look weak, the kind of guy you couldn't trust in a combat situation, or at a time like this.

He felt a heavy whack in between his shoulder blades – the universal signal to get moving, he thought, and trudged slowly down the steps of the small jet. He had no idea what Sheng had in store for him, but if it involved Mr Luk it wasn't going to be pretty.

*

Scarlet saw the airport first as the Jeep raced along the highway to its west. Moments later they were being ushered inside a single-story building guarded at the door by two men with guns.

"They must be expecting you, Scarlet," Reaper said.

176

"That's good. I like to be expected. It gives them time to get frightened."

Reaper laughed and shook his head. "What planet are you really from, Sloane?"

"Planet Nutbar," Ryan said.

"Don't be like that, *boy*. We both know you'd still strip for me if I snapped my fingers."

"In your wildest dreams, crackerjack."

"Exactly my thoughts," Sophie said, glaring at Scarlet and moving closer to Ryan. "You should learn to treat Ryan with more respect. He only gets naked when *I* snap *my* fingers, right, Rye?"

Ryan blushed a little and was saved by the bell when a grim man in military fatigues told them to wait inside until Jason Lao arrived, but that didn't stop Scarlet winking at him as she walked toward the water cooler.

CHAPTER TWENTY-SIX

The goons forced Hawke and Lea at gunpoint along the shore of the island toward a low-slung white building built into the sand dunes. Two of the men shouldered their rifles and swung open the large double doors at the front to reveal an industrial boatshed.

Inside, they found what looked at first like some kind of hideous Halloween prank – a corpse was hanging from an overhead beam. Its fingers and toes had been removed and there were burn marks on the face. Someone had pinned its lips into a macabre smile.

"That's just not right," Lea said, disgusted.

"The work of Mr Luk, I should think," Hawke said.

"Silence!" shouted one of the goons, and aimed his weapon at them. Hawke thought he looked nervous, but the sweat might have been caused by the humidity down by the water, it was hard to tell.

Lea nudged Hawke in the ribs. "Speak of the devil..."

A squat man entered the building from a rear door and approached them. He looked at the corpse and then shifted his eyes to their horrified faces. "Ah – please let me introduce Inspector Wu of the Shanghai Municipal Police."

Hawke and Lea said nothing as Luk appeared to study the shape of their bodies. A moment later he barked some orders in Cantonese and his men hauled Hawke and Lea over to two benches and tied them down with heavy anchor chains which they secured with padlocks.

Pleased with the work so far, Luk ordered the men to leave the boatshed and sighed deeply as Hawke struggled against the unbreakable chains.

Hawke watched Luk pull a long razor blade from a tool bag and begin to sharpen it on a leather strop. The sweat built slowly on Luk's forehead as he gently drew the blade back and forth along the strop, smiling as he worked.

Lea strained to see what was happening, but she couldn't lift her head high enough to see. "What the hell's going on, Joe? I can hear what sounds like a knife being sharpened."

"I'm not too sure, but I think Mr Luk here must be preparing us some dinner."

Luk began to speak, almost in a whisper. "Some have translated *lingchi* as death by a thousand cuts, Mr Hawke. Others translate is as the lingering death, but myself... I prefer *slow slicing*. For me, this most adequately expresses the nature of the process, as I am sure you will soon agree, wholeheartedly."

Hawke heard Lea struggling against her chains. "This doesn't sound too good, Joe. I hope you have a plan."

Luk set the leather strop down and turned to face Hawke, the freshly sharpened razor now glinting in the low light of the boatshed.

"Are you ready?"

"That's very kind but I already shaved today. Perhaps just a wash and blow dry instead?"

Luk stared at Hawke with dead, emotionless eyes.

"I think it's a little more serious than that, Mr Hawke."

"Please, don't tell me you're talking about full hair systems! Anything but that."

Luk looked confused.

"Yeah, maybe you are going a little thin on top," Lea said, straining her head up to see. "You only get away with it because you're so tall no one can see up there."

"I am *not* going thin on top!"

"Ah, save it you vain bastard."

Luk scraped the razor along the edge of the chains which held Hawke to the bench. "You see, tradition demands that first I must remove your eyes, Mr Hawke, followed by the tiniest of cuts until your ears and nose are removed, then the same method will be applied to your fingers, toes and even your manhood, if I can put it like that. You will of course be kept alive for the entire process." Luk erupted into a terrifying, hollow laughter and moved even closer to Hawke.

"Get away from him you animal!" Lea shouted.

"Ah, your turn will come, Miss Donovan. Mr Sheng wants you both to enjoy this treatment. You will be delighted to know," he licked his lips, "that I can make this last for three days, and my record number of cuts before losing a victim to bleed-out is just under four thousand."

Then a large man with his hair tied back in a pony tail entered the room and spoke rapid Cantonese with Luk, who sighed and put the razor back down on the bench.

"Unfortunately, I have been summoned, Mr Hawke. The agony of delay will be much prolonged for you, but there is no alternative. Please accept my sincere apologies."

Luk and the man left the room, shutting off the lights. Only a small beam of light came in through a thin crack at the bottom of the door.

Hawke heard Lea rustling her chains in the semi-darkness. "We have to get out of here, Joe!"

"No shit! I'm the one he wants to turn into a Christmas turkey!"

"And I guess I'm the dessert... and thanks very much by the way."

"For what?"

"For another amazing Joe Hawke rescue attempt. You bust me out of Johnny Chan's frigging clutches and drag me all over arsing *Mongolia* of all places only to bring me down here to Mr Slice n' Dice and his House of Horrors."

"Well... there's gratitude for you."

"I'm just *saying* is all."

"No, you're just annoyed you've had to be rescued not once, but *twice* by me now and your ego can't handle it."

"My ego? You have got to be *joking!* You're the one with the ego, Joe Hawke! Your ego is so damned big I'm surprised the frigging SAS don't use it to teach mountain climbing."

"SBS."

"Whatever."

"Listen, I hate to stop you in mid-flow, but don't you think our time would be better spent trying to get out of here while we still have the chance?"

"Oh – you just worked that out did you? I was wondering how long before that penny dropped."

"I bet you were..."

"I was, you pig! If you hate me that much then you're not going to want to know how I picked Luk's padlock."

"You what?" Hawke said, stunned as Lea began to free herself from the chains. They slipped to the floor with a metallic clunk. "How did you do that?"

"Hairpin, boyo. We Irish girls are very resourceful, you know."

She rushed to Hawke and clicked open his padlock. He stopped to pick up a knife from Luk's impressive collection of torture instruments and moments later they were fleeing the boatshed.

"I'm going to climb up on the roof for a better look at this hellhole," Hawke said. "We need to find Han before they kill him and then sabotage the place as much as possible for Lao's assault."

"Good plan."

He paused while he was climbing and turned to Lea. "It's not true, is it?"

Lea looked at his concerned expression. "What?"

"About me going thin on top?"

Lea said nothing for a second, then laughed and slapped him playfully on the back. "You are just such a fool."

*

From the roof Hawke was able to see just how much wealth Sheng Fang had accumulated over the years to build such an immense fortress on a private island as large as this. The main building itself was constructed to resemble a medieval Chinese palace the kind Hawke knew only from all the old martial arts films he'd watched.

A long balcony ran around each floor giving an impressive view over Hangzhou Bay. The island itself was a lovingly landscaped jumble of Zen gardens and tiny wooden bridges leading from one shade-dappled enclosure to the next. Hawke had a nasty feeling much of it had been constructed with slave labor.

"Just goes to show," Lea said, climbing up to join him. "If hard work isn't working out for you there's always people trafficking."

"Is that something your grandmother told you?"

"Hey now! My grandmother was a fine old Irishwoman and never once did any human trafficking."

"I'm glad to hear it."

"Although there was that time she tried to flood the village with her homemade poitín, but we don't like to talk about that."

"Funny."

Lea frowned. "Hey! That wasn't a joke!"

"We need to get forward to the house," Hawke said, and they climbed back down off the roof and made their way silently to the main compound.

Closer now, Lea nudged him and pointed to the main house. "Look!"

Two men with submachine guns casually slung over their shoulders walked slowly towards each other and took a moment out to light cigarettes. One of them told a joke and the other laughed loudly for a second or two.

Hawke scanned the area, keeping low and out of sight. "It looks like it's just these two guarding the outside, but then how many more are inside it's impossible to tell."

"When they find out we're AWOL all hell's going to break loose anyway," Lea said. "We'll count them up then."

"Hey – what have we here?" Hawke pointed out to the northwest where an enormous super yacht was moving into view from behind a cliff covered in trees.

"What the hell!" Lea exclaimed. "Tell me it's not the frigging ghost of Hugo Zaugg, please!"

"It's not – look carefully and you'll see it's got two helipads. Poor old Hugo only had one."

They watched as the yacht powered through the water and slowed its engines a few hundred yards offshore. A few minutes later a smaller tender craft sailed noisily from an opening at the back of the yacht and brought several unsmiling men to the jetty where they were met by the Lotus. They shook hands and then the Lotus led the men up to the main house.

"I think it's time we joined the party."

"Always with the bright ideas..."

They crab walked below the line of a magnolia hedge until they were right next to the main wall of Sheng's house.

"What now?" Lea said.

"Now, we climb that tree and get our arses inside."

They silently clambered up the gnarled trunk of the tree, looking around them as they went to make sure no one was about. There was the possibility of one of Sheng's guards seeing them from the courtyard, or even one of the men on the roof, but it was easy to time the operation to get inside the building before any of the men came back into their view.

Inside, they made their way along a plush corridor decorated with porcelain statues of tigers and elephants until they reached a kind of mezzanine boxed in by an ornate carved wooden screen. Beneath them was a plush executive suite – what could only be Sheng's study, a sumptuous affair of dark hardwood panels and an extensive art collection hanging on the walls.

A moment later Sheng Fang himself entered into the room and moved to his desk. He was wearing a white suit, no tie, and smoking a cigarette. He casually glanced through some papers and tapped his fingers on the side of his desk. Seconds later, Hawke and Lea watched in silence as the Lotus and Luk entered the study with the man from the super yacht. They bowed deeply in front of Sheng before stepping back and awaiting his next order.

"We have the device," Sheng told the man.

"Where is it?" the Russian replied.

Upstairs on the mezzanine, Lea whispered: "What's that accent?"

"Very heavy Russian," Hawke said. "Probably somewhere south of Moscow."

"The device is in a safe place," Sheng said. "All ready for the true enemy."

The Russian drummed his fingers on the arms of his chair and made no reply for several long, awkward moments. "I must see the device or I will not even consider moving on with our plan."

Now it was Sheng's time to think.

After another long silence, he spoke: "You know I cannot transport the device out of China. The Americans are closing in on me, and certain, shall we say, obstructive elements within my own government are also joining the chase. Therefore I need you. You know this."

The Russian nodded slowly before he replied. "I am happy to transport the device to the location we have agreed on, but before I do so I must make sure it is real, that it is what you say it is and not, for example, a nuclear device. When this is verified I will order my men to take it on board my yacht and transport it to the target destination."

High above, Lea whispered to Hawke. "What a shame we don't have a gun, Joe! We could take the whole fucking lot out right now and be home in time for tea."

"You should have become a poet."

"Why, thank you, sir! But seriously, we're going to need to communicate this stuff to the outside world in a hurry. If something happens to us then no one's going to know about the device being moved from psycho to psycho like this."

Sheng and the man spoke for several more moments and then reached an agreement. They left the study, and Hawke and Lea retraced their footsteps back outside the house and watch as the Russian's men loaded the device onto the tender and climbed aboard. Below them, the Russian spoke to another man in rapid Russian, but one word was mentioned several times – and that word was the same in Russian as it was in English – Tokyo.

"Oh my God," Lea said. "They're going to destroy Tokyo."

"That was what Sheng meant when he told the

Russian about the true enemy. I thought he meant the Americans, or the West in general, but I should have known better. The Chinese and Japanese have an ancient history of warfare between their two nations. Clearly Sheng wants to settle that once and for all by totally destroying the Japanese capital."

He listened again, and this time heard another word repeated several times *vody*, the word for water.

"How do you know that?" Lea asked.

"Same root as the word vodka... And just then he said St. Petersburg as well and that's the limit of my Russian, I swear. Either way, this bloke looks pretty serious about doing Sheng's bidding."

"But what the hell's in it for him?" She nodded her head at the Russian who was now making his way back to the tender with the Lotus at his side.

"I don't know, but whatever it is, it must be pretty big to try and kill twenty million people. And it looks like Sheng's sent the Lotus to oversee the job."

With everyone on board, the super yacht turned in the harbor, its massive engines now powering the vessel out of the small bay and away from the island. They watched in despair as it slipped effortlessly toward the hazy horizon and moved at great speed to the east where Tokyo bustled in total ignorance of the lethal threat to its existence now racing towards it.

CHAPTER TWENTY-SEVEN

Jason Lao met Scarlet and the rest of her team at Hongqiao International Airport and less than an hour later they were flying in a Chinese army helicopter south over the city and out over Hangzhou Bay on their way to Dragon Island. Below them in the water Scarlet saw a tiny armada of RIBs racing across the bay, filled with whatever forces Lao could put together with the smallest amount of fuss.

It seemed the self-styled Thunder God had finally rattled someone high enough up in the food chain to give Lao some extra muscle and the authority to go in and take him out. Scarlet Sloane was only too pleased to be heading up that operation with all of her SAS experience.

The thought of a whack-job like Sheng getting hold of the map and using it to locate the elixir of immortality was enough to freeze the blood in her veins, but what really enraged her was the thought of Joe Hawke and Lea Donovan, kidnapped and held at his mercy. That had happened once before in Greece when Zaugg took Lea, Ryan and Sophie, and she had sworn never again. Now was revenge time and Sheng would pay not only for his crimes, but for everything Zaugg had put them all through as well.

Now, sitting in the lead helicopter her mind was focused like never before, and the events of her turbulent past seemed to align in perfect clarity for the first time. She could finally begin to understand what was happening in the world. For men like Zaugg and Sheng, limitless wealth wasn't enough. They wanted more. They wanted the ultimate power – the power to live forever. *Men*, she thought... total idiots.

But these men were dangerous idiots. They knew the power existed somewhere in the world, but it was hidden by the ancients – maybe even the gods in the far distant past. But all that remained today was an ancient map, older than time itself for all anyone knew, and whose very creation was perhaps the biggest mystery of all.

Zaugg had tried to find it and failed in spectacular fashion, but only thanks to the bravery and determination of a handful of people from all walks of life. Even Joe Hawke had turned out to be an asset, something she was pretty skeptical about when he had walked back into her life in Geneva.

Perhaps one day he would know the truth about her – about everything – but that wasn't her call to make. For now she was focused on rescuing him and Lea and stopping Sheng and his insane henchmen from getting their hands on the map of immortality. Something told her that would be very bad news indeed, plus she thought of all the fun she could have taunting Hawke with the fact she had saved his life. Some things were beyond priceless.

A warm subtropical breeze blew in through the open door and brought her attention back to the moment. Opposite her, Bradley Karlsson was joking with one of Lao's soldiers, but most of the humor seemed to be lost in translation. Times like these had a way of bringing people together, no matter what languages they spoke – they all knew the way missions like these panned out. They all knew not everyone would be coming home after the battle.

At the front of the chopper Lexi was sharpening her combat knife. Something told Scarlet that Lexi and the Lotus had met before, and that Lexi Zhang had decided this time would be the last. Opposite her, Hart was sitting silently with her eyes closed.

Ryan and Sophie were sitting to her left at the rear of the helicopter, talking quietly with one another while Sophie checked her gun was fully loaded and ready for action. Ryan looked at the weapon in her hands with cautious eyes. Perhaps he should have stayed back in Shanghai at their makeshift headquarters, but he'd insisted on joining Sophie, probably just to impress her. Whether Ryan Bale really wanted to be there or not, it was too late to change his mind.

Now, the chopper raced away from the Chinese mainland, followed by several more behind it, and trailed further back by the RIBs as they crossed the choppy waters that separated Dragon Island from the rest of China.

Then the pilot communicated to them from the cockpit. "Two minutes!"

Scarlet checked her watch and made sure her HK subcompact was ready to go. She was also carrying her old SAS-issue combat knife and several grenades. This was going to be her last hurrah, she thought. She was getting too old for this lark. She needed to retire while she was still young enough to enjoy it.

Retirement, she had decided, was definitely wasted on the old. The only problem was she needed a lot more money that she had. For a moment her thoughts turned to all the gold and treasure she had seen in the vault of Poseidon in Kefalonia and now the enormous stash in Khan's tomb, hidden from the world in the Mongolian mountains. Why, she asked herself, was she still so poor when she seemed to have such a natural talent for tracking down stupid amounts of gold? Then, the sound of the blades whirring fast above her brought her back to reality once again.

Her own personal stash of treasure would have to wait, for now at least. She had an old friend's arse to pull out of the fire and she was looking forward to the challenge.

*

It didn't take long for Hawke and Lea to devise a plan to rescue Han and neutralize Sheng's island defenses. From the surveillance he had done on the roof of the boatshed, it was clear the island was not well protected, presumably because Sheng wasn't expecting a full-scale military assault any time soon.

There were two outposts on the wall surround the northwest part of the island – the part facing the Chinese mainland – but only one seemed to be manned. In that one he had counted two or three men acting in the capacity of guards. Sheng's paranoia seemed to run as far as a couple of general purpose machine guns but that was about it. It might not look like much but it was enough to cripple an advancing helicopter or rigid inflatable that wasn't expecting it.

Taking Luk's knife, Hawke climbed the wall of the outpost and when he was on the roof he gave Lea the signal. She moved forward and threw some stones at the door, and then ducked back down in the long grass.

A man opened the door and poked his head outside.

Hawke leaned over the edge of the roof and grabbed the man by his throat and lifted him a few inches off the ground until he passed out. Another man inside saw what was happening and began firing indiscriminately through the open doorway, but Hawke dropped down through the skylight behind him and struck him on the back of the head with the handle end of Luk's knife.

"All done!" he shouted, picking up the man's weapon.

"Less than a minute, Joe," Lea said. "I'm impressed,

but I hope you're not so fast in bed tonight."

"That's rather presumptuous, Donovan."

"Hey, all I meant was..."

She was stopped by the sound of two small jet engines whining from somewhere behind the complex.

"What the hell is that?"

"Sounds like Sheng's private jet," Hawke said. "They must have got the information out of Han quicker than we thought..."

Hawke and Lea climbed onto the roof of the outpost and looked over the complex wall to the eastern side of the island where the runway was located. There, on the tarmac, they saw the same shiny white jet they were brought to the island on, only this time Sheng was striding back out to it with Luk a few yards behind him.

"Any sign of Han?" Lea asked.

Hawke frowned. "Not at all, and that's what worries me. If Han told... wait – look there!" He pointed into the western sky where several helicopters were now rapidly approaching the island.

"Scarlet Sloane, if I'm not very much mistaken," Lea said.

"Yeah – that explains why Sheng's making a break for it as well. We have to get closer to the action."

CHAPTER TWENTY-EIGHT

Scarlet Sloane was certainly back in her element as the chopper she was in dropped out of the sky and hovered just over the tree line on the far side of the island from Sheng's palace. Immediately someone began firing on them with an assault rifle, but she fast-roped from the helicopter along with the rest of the unit in seconds and ran to some cover as the chopper flew the others across the island.

Her Heckler & Koch gripped tightly in her hands, she raced through the long grass, keeping low to avoid the tracer bullets which occasionally zipped over her head with a terrifying whistle. The sound of death, she thought. Behind her was Lexi Zhang and several of Lao's men. She heard through her headset that Hart, Ryan, Sophie and Karlsson were landing on the other side of the island and were now moving forward toward the main complex from the southeast creating a pincer movement.

A series of bullets slammed into the tree trunk she was hiding behind and two more flew past her at head height before whistling into some palm tree leaves just behind her. "Just like my honeymoon!" she said, and wished she had a CornerShot to take out whatever bastard was pinning her down. That was her idea of accessorizing.

Without warning, Lexi spun out from behind her tree and fired three shots in rapid succession. A second later a man in black fell from one of the watchtowers and crunched into the foliage below.

"That's fifteen love to me, Sloane."

"If that's the way you want to play it, then fine darling," Scarlet said coolly. "I happen to be an ace at tennis."

She flicked the H&K around her tree and fired a couple of rounds into the same watchtower. They struck the second man in the chest and sent him flying back into the compound behind the wall.

"Fifteen all, I think."

They now swept forward through the jungle with the rest of the assault team, taking out the occasional target as they presented themselves. The thought of fish in a barrel flashed through her mind but then she stopped herself being so smug when she realized they weren't even inside yet. Cockiness was a dangerous trait in wartime. She knew that from experience too.

Now, closer to the compound, Sheng's men were fighting more fiercely in an attempt to slow down the assault and give their boss time to retreat. One of Lao's men placed a simple charge on a service entrance but got killed running back for some cover before he could detonate it.

Lexi sprinted into the clearing and took the radio transmitter from him before being chased back into the jungle by at least two machine guns fired from somewhere high above her. Scarlet heard her screech with insane laughter for a second and then watched as she hit the button, blasting the heavy door off the front of the compound and sending a thick shower of wooden splinters and plaster out into the hot jungle air.

Scarlet sprinted forward now, with Lexi and the others right behind her. To the east she heard the sound of more machine gun fighting and two or three grenades. Clearly Hart and her unit were rattling some cages on the other side of the compound.

Scarlet's orders were officially to neutralize Sheng and find and secure the device, but as she ran forward and kicked her way through a small door into an internal courtyard, she knew she was really searching for Hawke and Lea. The rest she could finish later. She knew what Eden would say about that, but he wasn't here.

She scanned the courtyard and saw another small door on the other side of an ornamental bridge. Lexi was running up some stairs to her left and telling her over the headset that she was going forward to the upper levels.

Scarlet decided she wanted to try that door.

*

Hawke and Lea could still hear the sound of machine gun fire and grenades as they made their way to far side of the complex. It was about five hundred yards from their current location and they were desperate to get in on the action.

"Good job we knocked out that gun nest," Hawke said. "Sounds like Cairo's having a great time."

"Sure sounds like it," added Lea, "But what do we do now?"

"There's not much we can do – not while we're here. We have to get to the others, see if Han's still alive and somehow get after Sheng. We also have to inform Lao about the yacht and Tokyo."

"You really think Tokyo was the target?"

Hawke nodded. "I know we didn't hear much, but they said Tokyo several times and something tells me they weren't talking about their favourite baseball team. They'll be well on their way by now – and did you see the chopper on the helipad?"

Lea nodded.

"The smart money's got to be on them using that as

soon as they're in range of Tokyo."

They waited a few moments, and then made the final few yards of their journey to meet up with Scarlet and the others. The gunfire at the main house was heavy, and it sounded like the fighting had quickly become a ferocious, no-holds barred war for supremacy of the island and the airfield, at least until Sheng was safely airborne.

They were almost at their destination when just inside the main courtyard a man saw them approaching and raised his weapon, but the noise of a grenade explosion startled him. Hawke saw his chance and fired, hitting the man in the throat and bursting it open with savage accuracy. He fell back in a crumpled heap, and Lea snatched up some of his grenades. With the way now clear, they smashed their way into the compound's outer section and got one step closer to the rest of their team.

Now, inside the main yard, Hawke finally saw Scarlet Sloane and Lexi Zhang fighting a rear-guard action in the face of overwhelming force, delivered courtesy of some of Sheng's most determined fighters – what looked to Hawke like a team of heavily-trained mercs.

Hawke unleashed a burst of fire from a submachine gun in a bid to provide some cover and distract the men from closing in on Scarlet and Lexi.

Lea threw a grenade and five seconds later a terrific explosion ripped through their offensive position and blasted two of the men back through the air like dolls, killing them instantly.

Hawke and Lea leaped up and made their way across the yard to Scarlet before the enemy had a chance to regroup. A second later they crashed behind a wall beside Scarlet and her team. A round of friendly nods went around as the bullets traced over their heads, but now, at least, they were together again.

CHAPTER TWENTY-NINE

"I am so pleased you finally decided to show up," Lea said.

Scarlet smiled. "I knew you'd miss me, darling. You can thank me for rescuing you later. That's two nil, I believe..."

"It's so nice to see you, too," Lea said through clenched teeth.

Scarlet snorted. "I'm just grateful you never tried to hug me."

Hawke smiled. Same old wisecracking Cairo – that meant she was up for the fight.

"Hey..." Lea said in response to Scarlet's jibe, but Hawke hushed her to point out Hart's team who were joining them from the southeast. They took cover with them behind the wall and began a consolidated fight back. A few minutes later and most of Sheng's men had either been killed or were retreating.

With a lull in the fighting, and everyone grouped together at last, Hawke spoke up. "Okay, listen up everyone! This is the situation – Sheng and Luk are retreating from the island and almost certainly on their way to Xian to raid Qin's tomb – it looks like he got the final location by torturing Han."

Ryan's eyes widened. "The map's in Qin's tomb?"

"Yeah."

"How do we know that?" Ryan asked excitedly. "I know archaeologists recently found some kind of new annex there – it must be to do with that!"

"Before Sheng's goons killed Jenny Tsao, she told us

all she knew, and the rest came from the tattoo on Han's back."

"Tattoo?"

"We'll fill you in later. According to Tsao, the Emperor Qin couldn't translate the map and so it was useless to him. So enraged was he at his failure to crack the code that when he found out he was dying from the mercury poisoning he ordered that the map be buried with him in his tomb so that no other man could ever hope to use it to gain immortality for himself."

"And that's why he built the famous Terracotta Army...' Ryan said, his voice trailing away in wonder. "What a bastard."

"Exactly," Hawke said. "According to Tsao, Qin surrounded his tomb with thousands of soldiers with the basic idea of protecting him in the next world. It took over seventy thousand men to create the necropolis, and the whole place was booby-trapped with crossbows hidden in the walls. If that weren't enough, his son, Qin Er Shi, the second emperor, dictated that all his father's wives who had failed to bear any children for their husband should be buried alive with the dead emperor."

"Sounds like they were all crackers to me," Hart said.

"Not so crazy. Tsao told us it was probably to stop rival claims for the throne. To top it all off, it was decreed that all the men who had built the tomb and who knew what treasures it concealed – like the map, for example – couldn't be trusted to keep it secret, so they were sealed inside the tomb just before it was shut off for ever."

"Imagine what it was like if you were one of those men sealed inside, just after the last stone had blocked you in," said Ryan, his imagination running riot. "They probably ate each other."

"Thanks for that, Ryan," Lea said.

"That is the story of the first emperor's death," Hawke said, proudly.

"Now that's what I call a state funeral!" Scarlet said.

"But where does Khan tie into all of this?" asked Ryan.

"Genghis Khan found out about Qin's search for the map, and in his quest he managed to uncover the truth about the emperor's success in finding it in the west, and his failure in not being able to translate it. Khan obviously knew Qin had hidden the map in the tomb when he was buried, and set out to retrieve it, but according to the last few verses in the chapter he too died before he reached the tomb."

"So now we know that the map Zaugg was after..." Lea said.

"And Genghis Khan," Hawke said.

"And Qin Shi Huang," said Ryan.

"And don't forget Sheng Fang," Lexi said, scowling.

"What they were all after," Lea said, "was raided from Poseidon's vault by Qin and was in his tomb here in China the whole time."

"Where it's been for the last two thousand two hundred years," Ryan said.

Hawke nodded. "So our job is to get that map back and that means we have a date with a few thousand terracotta soldiers and one of the world's most famous tombs, but first we have the little problem of getting off this insane island – and you," he said, turning to Scarlet, "have a little date in Tokyo."

"Why's that, darling?"

"Because that's where the Lotus and her mysterious Russian friend are going to activate the Tesla machine."

As he spoke, Bradley Karlsson pulled a phone from his pocket and moved a few yards away to make a call, fast and quiet.

"Tokyo?" Ryan said, almost in a whisper. "That's one of the most geologically unstable cities in the world."

"And one of the most densely populated," said Scarlet.

"How do you know this?" Reaper asked Hawke.

"We overheard some of the Russians as they loaded the device onto the tender before going back to the yacht. They were speaking Russian but we clearly heard them mention Tokyo several times, and then laugh."

"That could mean nothing," Reaper again, casually pulling a cigarette from behind his ear and lighting it with his Zippo as a bullet traced over his head. "It could be where one of them is going on his honeymoon, no? Or maybe even they knew you were there and were playing you like a violin, is that how you say it?"

"Playing him for a fool is more appropriate in this case," Scarlet said.

Hawke frowned. "No, I don't think so. The yacht is sailing at top speed towards Japan as we speak. It's pretty clear to me that Tokyo is Sheng's target destination for the Tesla device. That's my call and I'm making it."

"In which case, this is no problem," Reaper said, shrugging his shoulders. "A yacht like that would not go faster than seventy knots, so..."

"And what's that in English?" Scarlet asked.

Hawke rolled his eyes. "*SAS*... it's eighty miles an hour. You'd know that if you didn't let us to all the hard work at sea."

"Don't get me started, Joe."

"Either way," Reaper interrupted, "Tokyo is over a thousand miles from Shanghai so sailing at top speed it's going to take them twelve hours to get there. We have plenty of time to organize an assault force to take them down. Nothing could be easier, and we will be enjoying a cold beer before sundown, no?"

"No," replied Hawke grimly. "There was a Sikorsky S-98 Scout on board. I saw it with my own eyes."

"Never heard of it," said the Frenchman dismissively.

"It's a gyrodyne."

"A what?" said Ryan.

"A very high-speed compound helicopter with an extra propeller at the rear to provide extra forward thrust. As far as the world is concerned it's still under development back at Sikorsky HQ, but somehow our mysterious Russian friend seems to have got hold of one, and it looked like it might have been modified."

"And how fast does this thing go?" Reaper asked, interested enough now to move his eyes from the tip of the cigarette to Hawke.

"It can go well over two hundred and fifty miles an hour, and has a range of over seven hundred and fifty miles. If the Russian takes his yacht out a couple of hundred miles – three hours' sailing – then they can launch the S-98 and be in Tokyo in less than four hours, and the water here is packed with similar vessels. They could easily hide out in busy water and it would take us all day to find them."

"So in other words Tokyo could have less than seven or eight hours until it's totally destroyed," Scarlet said. "Even less depending on how that gyrodyne has been modified, right?"

"Exactly," Hawke said. "But sadly for Sheng and the Russian, that's not going to happen because we're on it."

As he spoke, he saw the familiar outline of Sir Richard Eden's private Gulfstream as it descended onto the airfield. It had come to collect them now the fighting was under control.

"So what's the plan?" Reaper asked, flicking his cigarette over the wall.

"I'll take Lea, Lexi, Reaper and the Commodore and

finish this here. Cairo, you lead Karlsson, Sophie and Ryan to Tokyo and take out the Russian and our old friend the Lotus. We'll take Sheng down in Xian, secure the map and meet up with you later."

"Excellent," Scarlet said. "More shooting! But..."

"You need him, so don't even ask."

"Seriously, no one needs Ryan Bale, Joe."

"Hey!" Ryan protested.

"As it stands at this moment, Cairo, he knows more than any of us about the Tesla device and its capabilities. It could come down to your life in his hands as much as the other way round on this one, all right?"

"My life in his hands? That's the sort of traumatic thought you never forget, Joe."

"Ryan saved my life in Greece. I'll never forget that and neither should you. If you mess him about you'll have me to answer to."

"Easy tiger, I'm sure I can babysit Ryan Bale for a few hours in Tokyo."

"If that thing goes off in Tokyo it's going to be total carnage on an unprecedented scale," Ryan said.

"Right," Hawke said. "Which is why you're going to stop them before they do anything naughty, all right?"

Scarlet smiled at the prospect. "Ooh, this is *exciting!* I've never been to Japan before."

"It's not a bloody sightseeing trip, you fool," Lea said.

Hawke stopped Scarlet from replying and turned to face the group. "This is it, everyone. Right now it's up to us to save the world..."

"And that's a worrying thought," Scarlet said. "A very worrying thought."

With the Lotus and her team sailing off to the east in the super yacht and Sheng flying his team west to Xian and the temple, it was now time to kill two birds with one stone, and that mean breaking everyone up into two teams and finalizing their plans.

All around them Sheng's men were deserting the island, and now in the midst of the clearing smoke of the battle, they stood and listened to Hawke as he finished detailing the plans and gave everyone their final orders. These people had become his friends over the last few weeks, and in some of the toughest circumstances he had ever known.

Scarlet would lead the team going to Japan, backed up by Ryan, Sophie and Karlsson. Meanwhile, Hawke would lead Lea, Lexi, Hart and Reaper into the battle at Qin's tomb in Xian. But around twenty minutes later, as he was finishing the briefing, he suddenly stopped talking and pointed at the sky. "What the hell are they?"

The others turned to look at several F-15s racing toward the island from the northern horizon, armed to the teeth and ready for action.

CHAPTER THIRTY

Bradley Karlsson spoke first. "Look like Eagles to me. Must have come over from the new deployment on Okinawa."

"The Yanks have sent three F-15 Eagles to attack Dragon Island?" Lea said. "That's just plain arsing brilliant."

"Pretty much," Hawke said, shaking his head in disbelief. "It could start world war three! Must be McShain, but how did he find out?"

All of them turned to look at Bradley Karlsson.

"What?" Karlsson said. "Okay, I *might* have just told Eddie about your Tokyo discovery."

Scarlet rolled her eyes. "Oh, for *fuck's* sake. You tell Kosinski and now there's three bloody tactical bombers launching an attack on the People's Republic of China."

"The ambassadors are going to be busy tonight," Ryan said. "How the hell did they get here so fast?"

Above their heads the powerful jets screamed and roared and strafed the remaining soldiers of Sheng Fang as they scattered all over the island.

Karlsson shrugged. "Sixteen hundred miles per hour, Ryan, and only four hundred miles from Okinawa – you do the math."

"We can't waste time talking about this – we still have work to do!" Hawke shouted over the roar of the jets. As he spoke, a series of massive explosions from the main complex indicated the Eagles were already at work. "Let's move out!"

The groups split up and Hawke watched as Scarlet

and her crew moved down to the airfield and climbed into Eden's jet.

"What about us?" said Lea.

"We're not going anywhere until we rescue Han!"

They watched Eden's Gulfstream and after a few moments trundling along the runway it turned and roared up into the eastern sky. If they failed, Hawke knew the Lotus and her thugs would kill them in a heartbeat, or they would die in the earthquake. Either way he would never see any of them again. Thoughts like that could cripple a man, he knew. Thoughts like that projected images of ghosts into your mind. The ghost of Liz, dying in Vietnam was enough. He didn't want to add any more to that particular horror show.

He cleared his head and focused on the mission. It was true they hadn't stopped Sheng yet, but they had slowed him down, and now they had destroyed his headquarters and were only a few minutes behind both of his teams.

Now, Lea strained to see the compound through the smoke. The F-15 Eagles had unloaded a series of devastating ordnance on the island and surrounding outbuildings, including a GBU-15, a two thousand pound guided bomb which sailed down and landed smack on the main roof, destroying most of the palace.

The resulting explosion had started fierce fires which were now spreading all over the north part of the compound. White-hot flames flicked like devil-tongues from any remaining structures and the smoke grew thicker and billowed out of the broken building into the hot air outside. The Eagles turned to the east, presumably on a mission to track down the super yacht.

"Okay, it's time to stop Sheng," Hawke said. "We can't let them get to the tomb at Xian. One mistake there by us and the map's his." He checked his weapon and began to move out.

Hart moved closer to Hawke and held him by the arm to stop him moving forward. "Joe, I have something to tell you."

"What is it, Olivia? We don't have a lot of time."

"I know, but it's just that if I don't make it..."

"Sounds ominous, but you will make it. Tell me later, all right?"

Hart nodded, but didn't look very happy about it. "You need to know this, Joe, believe me."

"I need to know a lot of things," Hawke said, his honest face breaking into an almost childish smile. "But now we have to stop Sheng, yeah? Get on the blower and have Lao send some air transport down to us pronto, and in the meantime, you take Lea, Lexi and Reaper down to the airfield."

"What about you?"

"I've got a monk to save."

"I want to come with you!" Lea said, looking into his eyes.

"No, it's too dangerous." Hawke's face hardened. "I'm going to find Han alone. If he's still alive we can't leave him in a place like this, and if what he told me about Sheng's human trafficking activities is true then there might just be more people here to liberate. You go with Olivia and Lexi and make sure the airfield's safe and me and Han will be there before you know it."

Reluctant to leave him, Lea kissed Hawke and they held each other as the flames rose around them.

Hawke sprinted back into the complex and began a measured room-by-room clearance and search for Han and anyone else who might have fallen foul of Sheng Fang.

In the east wing of the complex he heard cries behind a large door.

He fired at the double doors and they splintered into thousands of pieces in a few seconds. A second later he was across the hall and kicking the remaining parts of the door down with his boot. He saw a stone staircase leading into darkness below, and began to make his way forward, gun raised.

Behind him a terrific explosion filled the air and he turned his head to see an enormous fireball out in the courtyard. Screams of pain and terror filled the air a second later, and for a moment he wondered if he'd heard any familiar voices, but shook the thought from his head. He knew better than anyone that you couldn't take doubt or fear into the front line or you'd be the next casualty.

He moved into the dark room and instantly heard Han crying out for help. He stepped forward and lowered himself to a crouching position, and could hardly believe what he saw. Han was there, in the dirt on the floor, doubled in agony, the tattoo on his back made unreadable by what had to be at least a hundred savage lashes, and worse, he was gripping his torn shirt around a stump where his left hand should have been.

"I told them... I'm sorry... I told them what Tsao told us. I told them where the map is buried." He broke down in a wave of desperate sobs. "They said they would bring my parents here and do the same to them, they said they would kill my whole family, Joe... and now Lynn died for *nothing!*"

"We'll balance our account with those scumbags, Han, don't worry about that. But you need emergency care on that arm or you're not going to make it, especially in this heat, and another thing, if we..." he stopped talking for a moment. "What was that?"

"What?" Han asked, confused.

"I thought I heard something – there, behind that wall."

Both men listened again, more attentively.

There it was again – a scratching noise, and a thumping sound – and was that people wailing? Hawke went to the wall and searched but found nothing, then he heard it again. "No – it's coming from below us! Look for a trap door!"

They searched for a few moments, kicking the mats and straw aside, and then Hawke found what he was looking for – a simple wooden trap door held in place by a bronze bolt. He slid the bolt open and aimed the gun at the door.

"Stand back, Han."

He flicked the trap door open with his boot and took a step back. "Whoever's in there, come out slowly with your hands raised."

For a moment nothing happened. It was quieter than when the trap door was shut. Then there was a shuffling sound followed by moaning and then Hawke heard the desperate pleas of broken people.

They both watched in horror and amazement as dozens of pale, emaciated people crawled through the trap door in the floor and emerged dazed and blinking in the low light of Sheng's dungeon.

Hawke shook his head in disbelief. "What the hell?! Are they Sheng's prisoners?"

"No," Han said grimly, gripping the bloody shirt over his arm. "They are Sheng's slaves. We're looking at the real victims of Sheng's sick trade – the people he trafficks around Asia and the world as slaves."

Less than five minutes later Hawke and Han were running toward the Chinese transport plane organized by Hart and Lao. Han saw the chance he had been looking for when he saw a line of burning grass alongside the runway.

Without pausing for thought he ripped the shirt from

his arm and plunged the bleeding stump into the white hot embers. His screams could be heard all over the island.

When he was finished sealing the wound, they sprinted over and jogged up the rear cargo door to see the rest of their team, plus Lao and a dozen more men in full military kit looking back at them. Lea was looking at Han, horrified at what she had just witnessed. As they strapped themselves in, at least a dozen other soldiers exited the aircraft.

"They're going to help the people you saved," Lao told Hawke. "Then we'll get them off the island and to a hospital on the mainland."

With everyone safely on board, the Shaanxi Y-8 whined as its four ageing turboprops pulled it up into the air. For a few seconds Hawke watched the smoke and flames engulfing Sheng's complex down on the annihilated Dragon Island, his former luxury retreat, and was pleased with his work, but the job was only half done.

Hawke took a deep breath and closed his eyes. They were finally on Sheng's tail, and almost close enough to stop him once and for all. He thought about Scarlet and the others who were racing towards Japan in Eden's Gulfstream IV, and the thought of her and the Lotus in a final face-off somewhere in Tokyo made him nervous. Cairo was the best, but her fatal flaw was how unpredictable she was, and it ran through her like a black thread in a complicated tapestry. The lives of twenty million people were in her hands now.

*

Scarlet Sloane tapped her cigarette gently against the solid silver case and raised it to her lips. Packing the tobacco down in the end of the cigarette in this way made it easier to light and burn faster. Smoking was not allowed on Sir Richard Eden's forty million dollar Gulfstream, but there wasn't a man or woman aboard who was going to object to Cairo Sloane lighting up, and she knew it.

Now, her mind wandered between the mission in Tokyo and the uncontrollable mess that was her life. But she had little problem living with all the lies and deceit the present circumstances had forced upon her, especially with Joe Hawke. Would he ever learn the truth? Maybe, she thought. That wasn't her decision.

All she really cared about was achieving her long-held dream of an early retirement somewhere warm. She had her eye on a small private island in the Caribbean but to say it was out of her price range was a gross understatement. To buy that little baby she would need millions of dollars, and she spent a lot of time thinking about how to get it.

But now, she turned her attention to Tokyo, and started to check her weapons for the imminent battle.

CHAPTER THIRTY-ONE

As the ancient transport aircraft cruised at twenty-eight thousand feet on its way to Xian, Hawke tried to get some sleep but he was kept awake by the same persistent thoughts that had been torturing his mind for so long. His final attempt to get some sleep was stopped when Olivia Hart sat beside him. She was holding half a bottle of *baijiu*.

"What the hell is that?" he asked.

"They call it Chinese vodka." She unscrewed the cap. "Do you regret leaving the service, Joe?" Hart asked. Good old Olivia, straight to business.

Hawke thought about how to answer for a few moments. "No," he said at last.

Hart laughed. "I waited a minute and half for that answer! Typical Joe Hawke."

"What?" he asked, smiling.

"Nothing.... but why don't you ever want to talk about yourself?"

"Just the way I am. I like to keep my thoughts to myself. That's why I make the jokes."

"You make jokes?" she said. "I hadn't noticed."

"Very *droll*, Commodore," he replied. "But no, I don't regret it. I did, when I was contemplating working in Civvy Street, but then I met Lea Donovan and Sir Richard Eden and my whole life changed."

"But that wasn't so long ago, Joe. It could all end in a heartbeat. What then?"

He shrugged his shoulders and sipped the vodka. He hated neat vodka. "I'll find something. I always do."

"Joe Hawke the eternal optimist," Hart said. "You think you're in love with Lea?"

"I don't like to talk about myself," he said, smirking. "Did I not just say that thirty seconds ago?"

"You did... you did, yes. Just be careful, Joe. She works a tough, dangerous job. She could get hurt, or worse. You have to remember about how you felt when Liz was murdered. You can't go through that again."

Hawke looked across the aircraft and watched Lea Donovan for a moment, sleeping peacefully as the plane cut through the air. "I won't let anything happen to Lea," he said, clenching his jaw. He gripped the vodka bottle hard. Hart had put the image of Liz back into his mind – her terrible death, the inability to avenge her, the permanent absence of closure that tore at his heart and mind every minute of every day.

"Believe it or not, Joe, there are some things in this world that are outside of your control."

"I know that!" he snapped. "I'm... sorry. It's just that I learned that lesson back in Vietnam."

For a long time Hart was silent. Then she spoke quietly: "I'm sorry, Joe. I didn't mean to upset you. You're right. I'll shut up now."

"I wish you would, thanks." He smiled. He'd known Olivia Hart for nearly twenty years. In many ways she was like a second sister – but unlike his younger sister, Emma, Olivia would definitely be of the older, more maternal variety. She was a friend, either way.

"Actually..." She started to speak again, but stopped herself.

"What *now*, Olivia?" Hawke said, trying to conceal a smile.

"Someone told me something a few days ago, Joe, and I didn't know how to react to it."

"Doesn't sound like the intrepid Commodore Hart

we've all come to know and slightly like."

"I'm serious, Joe. It was about Hanoi."

Hawke sat up in his chair and was suddenly all business. His eyes widened and he fixed them on Hart. She looked strangely nervous, and worse than that, hesitant.

"What is it, Olivia?" he asked. "Don't play around with me on this."

"First of all, it was nothing official. You understand what I mean by that, right?"

Hawke nodded. "Of course. Get on with it. Who was the contact?"

"No one you know."

"British or foreign?"

"British services, Joe. Army man, very senior and an old friend. He knew John before he died."

Hawke saw the look of pain in Hart's eyes when she referred to her former husband. "What's his name?"

Hart shook her head. "No way. If what he said has even the slightest grain of truth in it then this needs to be kept as tight as possible. If I tell you his name then his life could be at risk in the future. You can handle yourself, Joe, but my friend is retiring this year and has a life of sailing and hill-walking ahead of him. He can do without the particular brand of hell you seem to spend so much time fighting your way out of."

"Fair enough, all I need to know is if you consider him to be reliable."

"Absolutely reliable. As straight as they get. That's why he never got past brigadier."

"And what did the mysterious Brigadier X tell you about Hanoi, Olivia?"

Hart swallowed and for a long time kept her silence. She closed her eyes for a while, as if she were rehearsing what she was about to say, or maybe even reconsidering saying it at all.

Hawke spoke again. "If this is has anything to do with why they tried to kill me in Hanoi, then I need to know, and right now."

Hart was looking into his eyes now, and he could see something was troubling her a great deal. "That's just it, Joe, back on that terrible day in Hanoi it wasn't *you* they were trying to kill."

Hawke felt confusion wash over him like a tidal wave. "I don't understand what you're saying. You mean it was just a bungled robbery or something?"

"No, Joe. My contact told me that it was your wife, Liz, who was the target, not you."

Hawke's world came to a stop. It felt like everything had slowed to a standstill, from the jet racing across the sky to the very act of drawing his own breath. Liz was the target? He could hardly believe he'd even heard such a thing, and if those mad words hadn't come from the mouth of Olivia Hart he wouldn't have believed them at all.

"What the hell are you saying?" he asked.

"My contact told me that Liz was the target, and not you. He was very clear about this and told me the information was one hundred percent reliable. I'm so sorry, Joe, I really am. I don't know what to say."

His mind raced with the craziest of thoughts. He tried anything he could do to make sense of it, to try and think a way out of it that made sense to him, but nothing came. It felt like something was crushing his head.

"I still don't get it. It was easy for me to understand that I was the target. Back then I was a Special Forces operative in the most covert unit in the world. We'd been involved in some pretty dodgy stuff in North Korea and I presumed it was a professional government-sponsored hit on me in revenge for that, but..."

"But what?"

"Its just that one thing that always bothered me was how I was the only member of the unit who was targeted."

Hart nodded slowly. It looked as if she had more to say. Finally, she spoke. "So you had doubts?"

"Yes – but never that Liz was the target! She was just a translator in the MOD, Olivia! Why would anyone want to kill her? What possible reason could anyone in Hanoi have to put a professional hit on her?" He stared once again at Lea, snuggling into her seat beside the far window. Outside the morning sun was lighting the tops of the clouds purple and pink. It would have been beautiful except for the bombshell that had just been dropped on his life.

"Joe, I want you to promise me you're not going to go crazy when I tell you this."

He felt the crushing feeling once again, and gripped the armrest of his seat with all his strength. "What?"

"It had nothing to do with Hanoi. The kill order came from the UK."

Hawke almost felt dizzy. Now he had heard it all.

"From the UK?"

She nodded grimly. "The Brigadier told me that Liz was the target, that the order came out of London, and..."

"And what? Is there a name?"

"No, but... he told me that it was called Operation Swallowtail."

"It was an actual *operation*?" Hawke couldn't take it all in. A codenamed operation meant premeditation, planning, organization and money. It meant authority and reach. It meant trouble.

"Yes, but forget about researching Swallowtail. I've looked into it as far as you can go, and so did my army friend, and there's just nothing out there. We have no idea who was behind Swallowtail."

"You mean who was behind the murder of my wife."

"Yes... I'm sorry, I..."

"Forget it. If it wasn't for you I wouldn't know any of this. I'd still be in the dark, like the proverbial mushroom, being fed bullshit from above."

"Joe..."

"Swallowtail..." his voice seemed far away now. His mind was awash with fresh images of Liz – how they met, the jokes they shared, their wedding day on the coast and how excited they were when they boarded the plane to Vietnam. The way she looked at him when she first saw Vietnam. "Swallowtail... some bastard plotted my wife's death and had her gunned down right in front of me." He was silent for a long time.

"It was a long time ago, Joe."

"It was, but you know what the funny thing is?"

"No. Tell me the funny thing."

"That the piece of shit who ordered the kill thinks he got away with it."

"I know what you're going through – you know I do. But your mind has to be focused on Sheng now, Joe. You know that. Remember your training. I only told you now I case I don't make it. If there's revenge to be had over what happened to Liz then you'll have it, but now's not the time."

Hawke frowned and stared out the tiny porthole. He knocked back another swig of the baijiu. Yes, he thought, the Commodore was right as usual, and on both counts.

Yes, it was time to focus on Sheng.

And yes, he would get his revenge.

CHAPTER THIRTY-TWO

Xian

Sheng felt a wave of nervous energy cut through him as Mr. Luk led a small army of mercs into the lobby of the Mausoleum. A moment earlier they had invited themselves into the massive building with some plastic explosives and a Type 67 general purpose machine gun. Now he was closer than ever to the map and his loyal Lotus was waiting to annihilate Tokyo on his command. This was the meaning of the word *fate*.

"We are so close!" he said to Luk as they marched through the lobby toward the main part of the mausoleum. All around them were the dead bodies of the mausoleum's security detail.

Now, he and his men were surveying the vast aircraft-hangar sized enclosure that housed the terracotta soldiers. From where they had stood their silent vigil for so many centuries, thousands of them now stared back at Sheng but all he saw when he returned their gaze was his destiny.

"The main tomb is over there!" Luk pointed his submachine gun across the heads of some of the soldiers to their right.

Sheng didn't need Luk to tell him where the main tomb of the Emperor Qin had stood for the last two thousand years. No one had studied the great leader more than he had, and no one had more right to take what had been hidden from mankind within that tomb since antiquity.

Sheng turned to his men and gave them their next orders. "Move forward!" Soon the mausoleum would be crawling with police and PLA officials.

They moved forward through the ranks of silent terracotta statues until they reached the tomb, and it didn't take them long to find the sealed-up entrance so recently discovered by archaeologists. It was in the floor at the base of Qin's tomb, and they lifted it to find steps descending into darkness beneath the sarcophagus.

"This must be it," Luk said, kicking the Do Not Enter sign over with his foot. "Bring me the glow-sticks!"

Sheng looked on as Luk ordered some men into the darkness under the strictest instructions not to lose their nerve. They lit their way with the glow-sticks, which now cast a gentle amber light inside the narrow stone tunnel.

A moment later one of the men returned and told them the way looked clear. With a look of incipient triumph on his face, Sheng gently pushed Luk to one side and began his descent into the hidden tomb.

*

Hawke tried to focus his mind. This wasn't the kind of mission where you let your thoughts wander. If you did that not only would you get yourself killed, but you'd get those around you killed too – those who depended on you for leadership and guidance.

And yet his mind buzzed with everything Hart had told him about Liz.

Operation Swallowtail.

It was almost impossible for him to believe. It wasn't hard for him to accept that there existed in the world people who wanted him dead. He left a trail of embittered, defeated people behind him like a line of stale breadcrumbs, but the thought of anyone hiring a professional hit man to assassinate Liz was beyond comprehension.

Now, not only did he have to face the fact that the person who ordered her murder was still alive, but that she had been killed for a reason, and that the hit that day had nothing to do with him. The thought almost tore him in half.

It meant she had been lying to him.

She had told him she was a simple translator working in the Ministry of Defence, and that story had never evolved into anything else in all the time they shared together. Not like the day he decided to tell her the truth about his career – that he wasn't a simple sailor in the navy but in fact a former Royal Marines Commando and an elite Special Forces operative in the Special Boat Service.

She had never heard of it – or so she said. He explained they were like the SAS only more clandestine and tougher. He couldn't help saying this – it was part of the rivalry between the SAS and the SBS. But now he began to question everything that had passed between them, including when she told him she had never heard of them.

If she somehow merited a professional hit, hired from within the British Government, then she must have known about the SBS – it was one of the two most elite forces in the British Armed Forces.

So she had lied again.

And what else had she lied to him about?

He fought hard to push the thought away. The thought that his entire existence with her had been a lie, that she had been holding the truth back from him, in the way he knew Cairo Sloane and even Lea were doing to him right now.

What was her true story? He didn't know, but he was damned sure he was going to find out, and he didn't care how many dirty stones he had turn over to get to the truth.

"Wake up, dreamer."

It was Lexi. She smiled at him, and in a flash his mind was with her back in Zambia that night when they had first met. Like everyone else in his life, she seemed different now too.

He pushed the dark thoughts away and smiled back. "We're there?"

She nodded. "Uh-huh." He watched Lea and Hart checking their weapons, and sharing a laugh with Reaper.

The rickety transport plane thundered to a stop on the runway on Xian Airport and moments later they were all crossing the tarmac to an ageing Aérospatiale Super Frelon. They climbed aboard the chopper and strapped themselves in, in preparation for the short flight to the mausoleum.

He chatted with some of Lao's men for the duration of the flight, and then Lexi walked over to him once again, a Sig Sauer casually stuffed into the front of her jeans.

"That little bastard Sheng and his lapdog Luk are about to meet their makers. Wanna help me send them on their way?"

Hawke laughed and rose from his seat as the pilot reduced power to the engine and the chopper descended to the grounds at the front of the mausoleum.

They disembarked from the helicopter and jogged toward the building. They walked up the front steps and entered through the main doors, now hanging off their hinges after the devastation of Sheng's frontal assault on the mausoleum.

"Definitely Sheng's handiwork," Lea said.

"It's time to go to work!" Hawke shouted.

Lexi scoffed. "Work? This is what I call fun, not work."

Lea rolled her eyes and pulled her pistol from the holster. "Sure it is, and one screw-up and it's ten years in a Chinese gulag."

"You're not wrong," Hawke said. "This is one war we really have to win."

Then the sound of gunfire.

"Over there!" Hawke alerted the others to several men who had taken up defensive positions in the lobby.

"Looks like Sheng's serious about keeping us out," Lea said.

Hawke nodded. "Too bad we're just as serious about getting in. Olivia, you lead a group to the north and we'll go over here."

And with that the fight began.

*

Olivia Hart watched Hawke's unit as he advanced in the middle of an intense firefight, and ordered her team forward into the fray. She knew the dangers involved – this was not her first time in lethal combat. She cleared her mind of all doubt and pressed on, more determined than ever to crush Sheng and secure the map.

She moved forward too far in an act of over-confident bravado, and knew immediately that she had made a mistake. One of Sheng's goons saw her exposed position and raised his gun.

She raised her weapon, one of the old Chinese carbines Lao had supplied her with on the chopper, and took aim, but then her worst nightmare happened.

The gun jammed.

She looked down at the weapon, struggled with the

cocking handle for a second but no luck. She tried to find cover but it was too late.

She heard Sheng's man firing his weapon.

She saw the muzzle flashing as it fired the bullets at her, and then she felt them searing into her stomach and chest.

As the hot, burning pain raced through her body she collapsed on her knees and felt her blood rising inside of her and causing her to cough violently.

She began to feel dizzy and knew her blood pressure was dropping.

She saw Hawke and Reaper pushing forward with their unit, but they never saw her. She hoped with everything she had that he would survive and bring Sheng to account.

And then it was over.

*

Scarlet Sloane peered through the porthole of the Gulfstream IV as Tokyo loomed into view. It was vast, stretching out to the horizon but obscured by a thin layer of mist that made the whole mission seem even more sinister.

Today, a few thousand feet beneath her, millions of people were going about their daily business without the slightest thought that this could be the end of the city they called home, and the end of their lives.

Somewhere far below them she knew the Lotus and her crew were assembling the stolen Tesla machine and waiting for Sheng's orders to annihilate the entire city.

The jet banked hard to starboard and descended sharply as it made its final approach to Haneda International Airport. Minutes later two government officials whisked them through customs and drove them to a Japanese Air Force Black Hawke Sikorsky. Inside half a dozen men in black commando uniforms and face paint looked back in silence at Scarlet as she boarded the chopper and took her seat. They were from the Japanese Special Forces Group, an anti-terrorist unit.

"Can I help any of you?" she said coldly.

"We know who you are," said one of the men. "So I doubt it."

They shared a brief, low laugh and after Karlsson, Ryan and Sophie were aboard the chopper lifted off the tarmac. Seconds later the airport was behind them as they headed out into the city, then the man introduced himself as Sergeant Yakamoto.

"Who's the nerd?" said Yakamoto, nodding his head in the direction of Ryan Bale.

"He's about to change your world," Scarlet said. "We know your team was put together at the last minute, and you know next to nothing about this mission. There wasn't time for a proper briefing. So the nerd, as you put it, is going to tell you all what's what, so listen up."

"Thanks," Ryan said, and faced the men with surprising confidence. "Several years ago the US Department of Defense initiated a Top Secret program called Operation Poseidon. Ordinarily, none of us would ever be given knowledge of this, but desperate situations call for desperate measures, and you have been cleared by both the American and Japanese Governments to know this information."

The men looked unfazed. Typical Special Forces, thought Scarlet with respect.

Ryan continued. "Operation Poseidon involved the invention and construction of a radiant energy generator, or what is more commonly known as a Tesla Device. After many failed attempts, the program was finally successful and the device became a reality."

The sergeant scratched his stubble and nodded his head sagely. "Go on."

Ryan glanced back at Sophie and then to Scarlet, and then carried on with the makeshift briefing.

"In tests on an island in a secret location in the Western Pacific, the creators of the device were able to demonstrate to DoD officials that they could generate an earthquake of any magnitude between two and nine on the Richter Scale."

"But nine is a major earthquake!" the sergeant said.

"It is," Ryan said.

One of the others leaned forward, a mix of skepticism and anxiety on his young face. "They can artificially generate earthquakes?"

Ryan nodded. "Yes."

Yakamoto rubbed his eyes for a moment. "This is unbelievable. An earthquake of nine on the Richter Scale causes total destruction, and they only happen once in decades. If the Americans can cause such devastation at will then..."

Scarlet leaned forward. "Except the Americans no longer have the device."

"What?"

"The device my colleague has just described was stolen from an American transport vessel a few days ago by a man named Sheng Fang."

The men on the chopper shared a worried glance.

"We know Sheng. He's a joke here in Japan – a people smuggler masquerading as a businessman."

"Well, if he's a joke it isn't a very funny one," Scarlet said. "Sheng stole the device, and as I'm sure you've already figured out by now, he's moved it to Tokyo where he plans on destroying the entire city. We don't know why he chose Tokyo, but we think it might have something to do with an old war vendetta."

"You're certain?"

"Of course."

"So what's he waiting for?" snarled the sergeant.

"That's where it gets complicated," Ryan said.

"Or insane," said Scarlet. "Depending on how you look at it."

The soldiers looked confused.

Ryan stepped forward. "Sheng Fang believes he is the reincarnated spirit of Lei Gong, a Chinese mortal who became a deity, more specifically the God of Thunder. He thinks he has located the source of eternal life in the tomb of the Emperor Qin, and when he finds it he will fulfill some kind of ancient prophecy. We believe he is waiting until he has secured the map which leads to the elixir before he orders his people to destroy your capital city."

Silence, and then the men fell about laughing.

"Immortality? Now I've heard everything!"

The sergeant laughed for the longest, until the laughter finally subsided and he wiped the tears from his eyes. Only then when he saw the expression on Scarlet's face did he realize this was no joke.

"You're being serious?"

Scarlet nodded. "Of course, darling. I'm always very serious."

The sergeant was quiet for several minutes. "But I can't believe it. If Sheng is searching for this elixir, then who is setting the device up here in Tokyo?"

"We don't know his name, but the device was imported into Japan by an unknown Russian with some kind of connection to Sheng Fang. Our people are still looking into his identity, but we don't believe he's going to activate the device. We think that little job has been left to one of Sheng's underlings, in this case a psychotic assassin who calls herself the Lotus."

The sergeant shook his head in disbelief as he slowly came to terms with the madness he was hearing. "Then we have no choice but to kill all of them and deactivate this weapon."

"And that's the mission," Ryan said. "We only have until Sheng locates the map, and then you can kiss this whole city goodbye."

"And probably our lives as well," said Sophie.

Scarlet checked her gun and looked up at the soldiers. "And make no mistake about it – he *will* use the device to totally destroy Tokyo and kill millions of people."

"Not to mention devastating the Japanese economy for decades," Ryan added.

"And," Karlsson said, addressing everyone in his California drawl, "the only people in the world who can stop him are sitting on board this helicopter, especially the nerd here, because he's the only one who can figure out where this device is. At the moment we know only that it's in the central Tokyo area, the rest we have to figure out as we go."

Scarlet stared at the sergeant, her face deadly serious. "So not such a nerd after all, it turns out."

CHAPTER THIRTY-THREE

The first Hawke knew about Hart's terrible fate was when Lea alerted him to it. She had seen the Commodore's brutal murder and then called out to Joe. He looked back with horror at her body sprawled out on the marble floor of the lobby, but he knew he couldn't stop.

Having blasted through the men defending the entrance to the mausoleum, he stepped forward with caution. They moved silently along a corridor and emerged in the main part of the mausoleum where the terracotta soldiers were all lined up around the tomb. They entered into the tomb, using the same route Sheng and Luk had taken, and moments later they saw where the Thunder God and his minions had blasted a hole in the back wall of the newly discovered tomb, opening a new pathway into the hidden labyrinth deep beneath the public area.

They moved inside and soon found themselves in a narrow tunnel with sandstone walls and a dusty, sandy floor, illuminated by several fading glow-sticks. Hawke checked the safety was off his gun and calmly looked down the ancient corridor using the remnants of the glow-sticks to see.

He tried hard to settle his turbulent mind, but after all that had happened it was still almost impossible. Despite everything he told himself about focusing, he just couldn't stop thinking about the Commodore. Olivia Hart was one of his oldest friends in the armed forces, and seeing her lifeless body sprawled out on the floor like that had ignited something inside him he hadn't felt for a long time – pure hatred. The unfamiliar feeling was accompanied by a renewed burning sense of revenge that he hadn't felt since that day in Hanoi.

He knew Sheng would be made to pay in the most brutal way possible, and at his own hands if he had anything to do with it. It was weak of him, but it was primal, and couldn't be fought. But he also knew how to move on – how to use adrenalin surges to his advantage, and most of all he knew he couldn't avenge Hart's death if he lost his focus now and got himself killed.

Refocused now, he was back in the moment and ready for action. "Han, tell me more about the Five Trials that Jenny Tsao mentioned."

The Shaolin monk was only a few steps behind Hawke and armed with nothing more than his wits. He had refused point-blank to take a weapon back at the chopper when they landed at the tomb, and that made Hawke thought he might be a little crazy.

"Emperor Qin was a very intelligent man, but like all great, powerful men he was vain and paranoid. That is why he had himself buried among all this magnificence. He had the Map of Immortality buried with him because he never wanted another mortal man to find the source of the elixir..."

"It's that live and let live attitude I love so much," whispered Lea, her voice bouncing off the cold stone walls in the eerie silence.

"Not only that, but legend says he made extra sure that no other man would ever get his hands on the map by creating a series of trials based on *Wu Xing* or the Five Elements. Any man brave enough to enter his tomb would have to pass these trials to secure the map."

"I feel like I'm in a sodding Indiana Jones movie, Joe," Lea said.

Hawke smiled. "Fun isn't it!"

"Not really... if you set off a load of blow darts I'm going jump out of the way and let you handle it, okay?"

"Fine."

"But that's not going to happen, right?" Lexi asked, her voice unusually nervous.

"No," Han said calmly. "This not some stupid movie. The tests devised by the Emperor are dangerous and cunning, and *not* ridiculous."

"Hey," Lea said, "that was *not* a stupid movie! That was a freaking amazing movie."

Hawke saw that they were nearing the end of the tunnel and were now faced with a set of smooth steps which descended into almost complete darkness. He struck another glow-stick and tossed it down the stairs where it bounced a few times before settling at the bottom of the steps.

"Down we go again, I guess," Lea said, looking at Hawke for reassurance.

"We'll be fine," Reaper shouted from the rear, his voice rich and heavy in the damp silence. "I want my dinner, so if we hurry this along I would be most grateful, merci bien."

They descended the second set of steps and found themselves faced with another long corridor, this one at a sharp angle to the first.

"We keep going," Hawke said firmly, and ordered everyone forward with a hand signal. There was still no sound or sight of Sheng.

Hawke spoke quietly over his shoulder. "Carry on, Han."

"The Five Trials are what they say they are – five tests, and they are designed to kill you, not let you pass. In Chinese culture, *wu xing*, or the five elements – or as they are sometimes called the Five Stages – are very important. They are wood, fire, earth, metal, and water. Qin thought protecting himself with the five elements would be lucky – lucky for him, not for us. They are not fair, so don't be complacent."

"Well, I don't know about you guys," Lea said, "but that's just what *I* wanted to I hear."

They pressed on. Hawke had finally cleared his mind of his ghosts and was now focused on the mission. Ahead of them there was potentially the greatest discovery in the history not only of archaeology, but of all world history. For now, he knew they were sworn to secrecy, but how long could the discovery of immortality really be kept from the world?

As they moved forward through the tunnels, a dark new thought entered his mind. What if they weren't the first to find out about the map, and to track down the ancient hidden location of the elixir? How could something like that ever have been kept secret for so many millennia? His mind leaped from one conspiracy to the next like stepping stones across a rushing river, each one less stable than the last.

What if there were people who had always known about the elixir? Over so many centuries they would have formed into a society of men who held this most ancient of secrets and kept its benefits purely for themselves.

He imagined them greedily drinking the life-giving water while millions of people all around the world died before their time, but shook the thought from his mind. If there were such people as that, he wasn't sure he wanted to meet them, or discover the lengths they would go to in order to keep their secret from the rest of mankind.

"Look at this!" Han said, disturbing his thoughts. Hawke turned to see him gently rubbing his hand over the wall. "These carvings of dragons are similar to those on the cover of the Secret History. I think this is about to get very real."

Hawke and Lea shared a glance, both silently confiding in the other that this situation could easily get out of hand. Somewhere a few minutes ahead of them, one of the greatest secrets in the history of the world was about to fall into the hands of Sheng Fang and his army of psychopaths.

"We have to move faster," Hawke said at last. "Reaper, text Scarlet and give her an update – and find out what's going on in Japan."

"Got it."

Lea nodded, and the others stepped forward to join them. Han moved ahead of them, and a moment later he returned with a nervous smile on his face.

"What is it?" Hawke asked.

"I think we just found the first chamber."

*

As the Sikorsky thundered over Tokyo, Ryan Bale studied geographical maps of the city. Hawke had told him that he'd overheard the Russian talking about not only Tokyo but that he had mentioned the word for water a few times. For the first time the truth dawned on him like the rising sun.

"Oh no," he sighed. "I don't think they're planning an earthquake at all."

"What the hell are you talking about, boy?"

He turned to Scarlet, his mind awash with ideas and worry. "I've been studying the map again and I was thinking about the Russian's reference to water and St. Petersburg."

Scarlet's phone buzzed and she took it from her pocket. She read the message on the screen. "It's Reap.

He says Sheng is inside the hidden tomb and probably through at least the first of the tests. What were you going on about, Ryan?"

Ryan spoke up. "I think they were talking about the massive flooding of the city of St. Petersburg in 1824. It was a tremendous flood that killed tens of thousands of people. If Sheng were to position the device beneath Tokyo Bay, it would cause a tsunami of unimaginable proportions and flood the entire city."

Scarlet stared at him. "But Tokyo still gets destroyed and millions of people still die, Ryan."

"Yes, duh. The point is it changes the location of the device. If they wanted to cause an earthquake then they would choose a completely different location to trigger one than they would if they wanted to trigger a tsunami."

Scarlet sighed. "Bloody hell, Ryan! We haven't got time for this! You heard Reap's message – Sheng almost has the sodding map. We haven't got the luxury of going on a tour of Tokyo while you tick various places off your list. You need to tell us where to go and now, Ryan, and there's no room for error. The lives of twenty million people are in your hands."

"But... maybe we could split up?"

"Great idea," Scarlet said. "Which half of the helicopter do you want, the front or back?"

"Ah."

"Where's the device, Ryan?"

Ryan Bale cleared his mind and returned his attention to the map as the military chopper circled over the Tokyo skyline. Slowly, Ryan started to turn a strange greenish color.

"What's the matter, honey?" Sophie asked.

"Nothing... it's just that if I choose the wrong location it's all over for everyone in Tokyo, including us."

"Better hope you don't fuck up then, eh, *boy*?" Scarlet

underlined her point by tearing open a fresh box of ammo and sliding bullets into her assault rifle.

"I'm not used to the pressure the way you are, Scarlet..."

"That's Captain Sloane to you."

"Sorry, I..."

"I'm *kidding*, Ryan. Sodding hell..." Scarlet shook her head and smiled. "You really are a turnip, but your heart's in the right place."

"Thanks, I think."

Scarlet watched Ryan with a skeptical eye. It was true that the boy had stepped up to the plate and saved Hawke's backside back in Greece, but she wondered how much that was clouding the former SBS man's judgment of a young man who was essentially an easily distracted nerd. Not the best person to have around in a deadly combat situation.

Then Sophie turned to Ryan and said: "Maybe when all this is over we could spend a few days here – I mean restaurants and sightseeing rather than black-technology earthquake devices and maniacs with machine guns. That's not so romantic, you know?"

"You like romance, huh?" said Karlsson. He leaned forward in the chopper and snuggled up to Sophie.

"Yes, and I'm with Ryan, so why don't you go take a cold shower and leave me the fuck alone?"

Scarlet's laugh was involuntary and explosive. "Ouch!"

"Yeah," said Ryan with somewhat less authority. "She's with me, you ridiculous human protein-shake."

"Hey!" Karlsson said. "Don't blame a guy for trying. It was that accent of yours honey... enough to drive any red-blooded man crazy. And just imagining you two in bed together is all wrong."

"All right, that's enough," Scarlet said, taking back

command of things. "I'm running this unit and we're not getting personal. We have a job to do, so it's time everyone focused."

"She's right," Sophie said, scowling at Karlsson. And gripping Ryan's hand tighter.

Everyone nodded. It was clear, and suddenly the atmosphere in the helicopter had changed from excited levity to grim determination.

As an experienced SAS soldier, Scarlet had been on the receiving end of more than a few briefings like this, and so she had no problem gauging the correct tone to deliver one of her own. Not only were the lives of countless millions resting on a knife-edge that only she could rescue them from, but there was her reputation with Sir Richard Eden to consider as well, and it was not something she thought about lightly.

"So where are we going, Ryan?" Scarlet asked.

"Like I said, it's got to be in one of two places. Either in Akihabara if they're planning an earthquake – that's the city's shopping and entertainment district – also known as Electric Town, or..."

"What is it?" Sophie asked, leaning closer and resting her hand gently on his knee.

"Or, they're going to put it in the Tokyo Bay Aqua Line."

Yakamoto's eyes darted over to Ryan, a look of grim terror on his face. "If you are right, this will be totally catastrophic..."

"I am right," Ryan said with confidence. "It's the tsunami! They're planning a tsunami! Sergeant Yakamoto, tell the pilot to go to the Aqua Line straight away."

"But if you're wrong..." Scarlet said.

"If I'm wrong we're all dead."

CHAPTER THIRTY-FOUR

The first chamber was larger than they had expected and they detected a further subtle incline as they walked into it. Hawke led the others into the chamber and wondered how far ahead Sheng had managed to get since they'd arrived.

As they moved further into the chamber they realized it was actually an enormous natural cavern that Qin had cleverly used as part of his five trials. Below them the ground fell away to reveal a deep fissure in the earth around a hundred feet deep. At the bottom they were able to make out a sea of sharpened wooden spikes pointing up at them menacingly. The only way across was by an ancient wooden bridge that the word rickety barely managed to describe.

"Trial by Wood," Han said. "This is Qin's first test – based, as I say, on the Chinese philosophy of the five elements. The first step, or state is wood, as you can see."

"And what are the others again?" Hawke asked.

"The normal progression is described as the mutual generation, which is wood, fire, earth, metal and then water, but..."

"But what, Han?"

"There is another progression – the order of the mutual overcoming. This is wood, earth, water, fire and metal. I suspect we can expect Qin to have used this order."

"I could be at home right now, you realize," Lea sighed. "Instead I'm about to get sodding razor blades flung at me or some such arsing nightmare."

Han clenched his jaw. "We must have the nerve to cross this underground canyon on the bridge, Lea. After that, there are only four more... *arsing nightmares* between us and the map."

"And if we fall or the bridge gives way, then there's a few hundred razor-sharp punji stakes down there waiting for us to impale ourselves on," Hawke said, frowning. They looked down at the fresh corpse of one of Sheng's men, skewered on one of the stakes like a kebab.

"Just whose bloody idea was this again?" said Lea. "I could be watching a romance film with a box of flaming chocolates on my lap and instead I'm risking getting impaled on a sodding Punjabi stick."

Hawke rolled his eyes. "*Punji* stick, not Punjabi stick."

"Whatever."

"But you're not far off," Hawke said. "The name derives from the north of Burma when the British Army first discovered them in conflict with the Kachins."

"Thanks, Joe," Lea said. "At least I'll have that to think about when I'm slowly dying down in that pit with a six foot splinter up my ar..."

"What was that?" Lexi asked.

"What?" Lea said, her last sentence already forgotten.

"I heard something up ahead."

"Me too," Reaper said. "Maybe one of the tests has slowed Sheng down?"

Hawke hushed everyone and listened hard but there was no sound other than the wind howling through the chamber complex. "Maybe just the wind, or a falling rock," he said.

"Yes, a magic rock that just decided to fall over all by itself," Lea said. "Or maybe a little magic pebble that decided it was time to go on an adventure to the surface after two thousand years down in this shit hole?"

"Your concern is noted," Hawke said.

"It's not concern, Joe! How can a bloody rock just fall over – we're obviously closing in on Sheng!"

"Then we had better shut up and get on with it or he'll get away again, yeah?"

"If only Ryan were here," Lea said.

Hawke looked at her. "Eh?"

"We could send him across first."

Hawke smiled. "I'd be up for that. He could bore the trial to death."

Slowly, Hawke led the way across, and carefully worked out where to tread and where to avoid. After the final soldier had crossed the canyon, they made their way through the next tunnel, closing in on Sheng. After a few slow minutes moving through the long, twisting tunnel, Hawke and the others emerged into the next chamber.

They were staring at a broad expanse of what looked like a sandy-clay, submerged beneath a few inches of icy water. Around the outside of the chamber stood a dozen more terracotta soldiers like the ones from the public tomb above. Each one stared at them with dead, silent eyes, somehow beckoning them deeper into the tomb.

Han nodded and smiled. "This confirms the trials are in the order of mutual overcoming – the next will be water, with no doubt, and this is trial by earth."

"But it's underwater!" Lexi said.

"Wrong," said Han flatly. "It's the Trial by Earth."

"Otherwise known as quicksand," Hawke said, pushing the steel toecap of his heavy boot gently down into the water until it hit the squashy surface of the sand beneath. He frowned as he studied the wide expanse of sand. He knew from his SBS training the dangers of quicksand – a loose sand that has turned into liquefied soil due to the water being unable to escape from it.

"I read quicksand is not that dangerous, actually," Lea said. "It's just some crap they put in the movies to get rid of unwanted characters during the final act."

"True enough, if the sand is on a dry surface," Han said. "But underwater like this, it is utterly lethal. Trust me. The Emperor was not concerned with crap they put in the movies when he devised this defense, and that is why he put the sand beneath the water. That is what makes it dangerous. Now the earth beneath the water will test us as we must walk across this pool to reach the other side. There is no other way."

Hawke went first, bravely pushing out into the water and feeling tentatively with his boots as he went. There was an art to walking across quicksand. There was an art to getting yourself out of it as well, but he didn't even want to consider that at the moment.

Other than the quicksand, the path ahead of them was clear enough – the far bank was a shallow, smooth rock leading up to a door-sized hole hewn from the rock thousands of years ago by Qin's men. The very same men whom the Emperor had sealed up inside after the tomb was completed, Hawke thought with a shudder. Perhaps one of the many skeletons they had seen at the entrance once belonged to the man who had carved that hole, or created this fiendish quicksand trial.

As he moved slowly forward, the water slopped and splashed around his ankles, and behind him the others followed in his footsteps, taking care not to deviate from the path he was finding through the lakebed. He looked up to study the surface of the lakebed a little further ahead and caught another glimpse of one of the stone soldiers. It stared back at him in the silence – cold, dead, inanimate terracotta.

For a second he thought he saw it move ever so

slightly – just a quick flick of its eyelid – but rebuked himself for being so stupid. Flights of fancy like that got you killed fast on SBS missions, and if anything this was the most important mission he had ever been on.

Over the years he had fought more foreign soldiers and terrorists than he could remember and each time the security of the nation was at stake, or even the safety of the people. His superiors, including Hart, had told him whatever they'd had to in order to make him do the things he had to do for Queen and Country, but this was different. He closed his eyes for half a second... Hart – Sheng would pay for that.

Never before had he faced the prospect of a man as powerful as Sheng getting so close as this to something as powerful as the Map of Immortality. It made even Zaugg look like small fry. As for the lives of every man, woman and child in Tokyo now being in the hands of Cairo Sloane and the others, the weight of the responsibility he was holding felt heavier than ever.

"How's it going?" It was Reaper, calling from the back – his thick French accent boomed in the cavernous chamber.

"Not too bad," Hawke called back. "But it's almost impossible to tell where..."

A second later he felt himself tumbling over to the right. His right boot was rapidly disappearing beneath the sucking surface of the quicksand under the water. Lexi screamed but immediately reached out and grabbed Hawke's belt, almost toppling herself over in the process.

Hawke stayed calm. He knew a few old tricks to extricate himself from quicksand and panicking was the worst thing he could do. The extra agitation only served to force you deeper into the trap. He quickly prodded the sand with the butt of the rifle until he found a solid area and leaned into it as he pulled his boot out of the quicksand.

    "Yeah...' he said calmly. "Best not stand on that bit."

CHAPTER THIRTY-FIVE

A few minutes later and Hawke was leading the other members of the team away from the trial by earth and into the third chamber. Han had described how according to ancient Chinese philosophy this would be the trial by water, and being a former SBS man he liked his chances, even in this madhouse, but that didn't stop him worrying about the others.

The reason he had been so sympathetic when Lea told him about her mistake in Syria was because of his own officer past. There was nothing he liked to talk about down that particular memory lane, but right now it rose to the forefront of his mind – now he was leading his team into danger. As a former Major in the SBS he knew what it meant to be in command of others and the grave responsibility that came with it. When they had busted him down to NCO it had come almost as a relief.

But his confidence was whittled away when he turned a bend in the tunnel and saw the size of the third chamber.

It was barely bigger than an elevator in terms of floor space, but the floor was nothing but black water.

"I have a really bad feeling about this," Lexi said.

"Woah!" said Lea. "Flashbacks of our little holiday in Greece, or what!"

Hawke nodded grimly. When he first saw it, he had also thought of the cave system on Kefalonia where they almost drowned thanks to Zaugg and Baumann exploding a hole in the bottom of the bay, but this was different – this was altogether more claustrophobic.

"We have to be careful here," Han said.

"This from the man who should be in hospital," Lea said, shaking her head.

"The wound was cauterized," Han said without emotion.

"You don't need to remind me," Lea said, shuddering. "I was there and I saw it..."

"Then let's get on," Han said. "There are some people inside the cave system with whom I wish to have a short conversation."

"Everyone stay here," Hawke said. "I need to check this out."

He jumped in the water. It was freezing cold and with no light there was zero visibility. He had trained in these exact conditions more times than he could remember, and not only that he had swum in them for real on a top secret mission along the Russian coast, although he was a much younger man back then.

But today there was more at stake than simply fixing a seabed listening device so the Royal Navy could track Russian submarines going in and out of Northern Fleet headquarters in Kola Bay. Today he was trying to stop an insane human-trafficking megalomaniac from getting his hands on what he was reliably informed would be the greatest power ever wielded by man. There's your incentive, Joe, he thought.

Inside the submerged tunnel, memories of Kefalonia came flooding back to him again, almost literally. As he felt his way along the tunnel, pushing deeper into the filthy, near-freezing water, all he could think about was how close he had come to getting all those people killed back in Greece, and now the same had happened to Olivia Hart. For that, someone would pay a heavy price, but he realized the number of people lining up to get their revenge on Sheng was getting longer by the second.

After a while, he saw a grubby, orange light slowly begin to emerge ahead of him. He was nearly out of breath, and he knew he could hold his breath for a full five minutes. Back in the height of his SBS days he could do nearly ten, but that took a hell of a lot of training. How the others were going to hold theirs for so long he had no idea.

Now, he followed the light and swam smoothly upwards until his knees were banging against something – steps. He climbed up them and a moment later his head emerged into a dank little chamber lit orange by the fading, flickering light of one of Sheng's glow-sticks.

So that was the trial by water – he made it look easy, but he knew ninety-nine percent of people would be dead if they didn't have the sense to turn around before they got halfway, and he hadn't even known how long it was when he started out. Normally he would never consider such a suicidal thing to do, but desperate times called for desperate measures, as his Dad used to say.

He took a second to get his breathing back under control and then went back into the water to tell the others the good news. He knew what he had to do, but whether or not he could do it was another thing altogether.

*

The chopper circled the Tokyo Bay Aqua Line main service area as they scouted for the enemy, and then began to descend. Scarlet and the others jumped out into the Tokyo drizzle, rifles slung over shoulders and pistols in their hands. Some members of the public looked startled but were moved quickly away by uniformed police officers. As they marched to the entrance they noticed another chopper with a rope ladder hovering a few hundred yards away.

"The gyrodyne!" Ryan said.

Scarlet nodded. "Ready to kick some arse?"

"Always," Bradley Karlsson said, a wide grin on his face. "It's what I live for."

"Me too, so let's go," Sophie said, pausing for a second to make sure Ryan was ready. "Are you okay?"

"Of course he's okay," Scarlet boomed. "We need you more than ever now, Ryan, remember that. When we've blasted these tossbags into the next life it's going to be down to you to disable that Tesla thing."

Ryan swallowed hard but tried to look cool.

"No problemo," he said, and rubbed a trembling hand over his face.

*

"You're not breathing air into my lungs," Reaper said. "I'd rather die."

Hawke had expected that reaction from the former French Foreign Legion man, now unreformed Merc and all-round nutcase.

"You'd rather die?"

"Of course! I'm a Frenchman. It's not necessary. I doubt it even works."

"Of course it works," Hawke said. "Regular inhaled air is around twenty-one percent oxygen, but exhaled air is seventeen percent oxygen. It works, believe me. I've been there before, and on both ends of it."

Reaper was horrified. "You let another man kiss you?"

"It's not a kiss, Vincent, it's passing oxygen from one person to another."

"You tell yourself that... and don't call me Vincent. The answer is still no. Maybe if you were a beautiful woman like Lea here, but otherwise, no."

"In that case I hope you can hold your breath for a full five minutes or you're going to be dead."

"Of course I can," he boomed. "I think."

Lea blushed slightly. "You think I'm beautiful, Reap?"

"Of course he thinks you're beautiful," Hawke said, annoyed. "He's French. He'd hump a bicycle if you put a skirt on it."

Lea was offended. "Well, thanks a lot!"

Hawke ignored her. "What about you, Han? How long can you hold your breath for?"

"Perhaps five minutes during meditation, but swimming under water... I don't know, Joe."

"Lea?"

"I have no problem *at all* with it, Joe," she said, and winked at him. "In fact I might just pass out on purpose so you can rescue me all over again."

"So now you *want* me to rescue you? I thought your ego couldn't handle that?"

She shrugged and kissed him on the cheek. "What can I say? I blow hot and cold."

CHAPTER THIRTY-SIX

Hawke took Han through first, and had to resupply him with oxygen from his lungs only once. Five minutes doesn't sound like a long time until you're underwater, as his old CO used to say, and Han found that out three-quarters of the way through the pitch-black tunnel.

Next was Lea, who needed two top-ups and seemed to enjoy them rather more than the Shaolin monk had. Finally it was Reaper's turn, and to his eternal disgust he was forced to give Hawke the pre-arranged signal for more air with the end of the tunnel only a few dozen feet away.

"I nearly made it without any help," he said, breathing hard as he clambered up into the tiny chamber. "I can't believe it... I could even see the light!"

"Sounds to me like you wanted a little kiss from Hawke, Reap."

Reaper glared at her, still breathing hard. "I did *not.*"

"Are you sure about that, boyo? You sound pretty excited by it all, what with that heavy breathing and all..." She looked up at Hawke and winked. "And what's this I hear about you being so close to the end and seeing the light and *still* asking for some air. I know if I saw the light I'd probably be able to make it on my own."

"Leave it," Reaper said.

"You love Hawke!"

"Then you better watch out, yeah?" he said, and clambered to his feet. He turned to Hawke. "Seriously though, thank you my friend. You saved my life. One day, perhaps, in the far distant future..."

"You'll repay the favor?" Hawke asked.

"I was going to say maybe I will let you call me Vincent."

Hawke laughed as they moved on deeper into the cave system.

The next bend in the tunnel revealed an enormous cavernous space bigger than any of the previous ones with a single footbridge carved out of the cave's stone stretching across to the other side. Hawke flicked a small stone over the ledge and counted as it fell into the darkness. At least two or three hundred feet, he thought.

Lea joined him and held his arm as she peered over the edge. "How long till you'd hit the bottom, do you reckon?"

Hawke shrugged. "If Ryan were here I'm sure he'd tell us."

"If Ryan were here," she said, "we'd be getting a full-on lecture about the terminal velocity of a human being."

Han leaned over and peered into the darkness. "The question is," he said, "if you fell over that ledge would your fall be too short or too long?"

Reaper coughed and spat over the ledge. "If I fell over there, I would shoot myself before I hit the bottom, no?"

Hawke nodded in agreement. "So let's make sure no one is stupid enough to fall over then. I don't want any of my guys turning themselves into pancakes on my watch."

"Oh, it wouldn't be like pancakes," Reaper said. "I saw a man leap from the top of the Eiffel Tower once."

"Yes, thanks, *Vincent*," Hawke said,

"It looked like someone had dropped a bag of oatmeal and strawberry jam over the side."

"But wait a minute," Lea said, turning to Han, "and by the way thanks very much for *that* little image, Reaps... I thought you said this was the trial by fire?"

Han nodded grimly as his eyes crawled over the cavern. A cold, damp wind blew up from behind them on its way deeper into the cave system.

"Exactly what I was thinking," Hawke said.

Han looked concerned.

They made their way across the footbridge and reached the other side without any problems.

"I don't like it," Hawke said. "That was too easy."

"And where was the fire?" said Lea as they pushed on.

Then everything changed.

They turned the final bend in the tunnel and saw Sheng and his men standing and facing them, all armed with submachine guns.

"How fortuitous that you should stumble upon us here, Mr Hawke," Sheng said coldly. "And how polite of you to volunteer to put yourself first for the next trial."

"Always a pleasure to help the criminally insane, Sheng," Hawke said.

His comment was met with a sharp smack in his stomach by the butt of Luk's rifle. Hawke fell to the floor in agony while Sheng laughed in the deep silence of the cave.

"Through that hole in the rock is the final trial – the Test of Metal."

Lea turned to Han. "What's that?"

"I do not know," Han said. "But he will have to use all his skills now. The final trial must surely be the greatest of all."

Sheng smirked as Luk dragged Hawke to his feet. "After you, please, Mr Hawke."

*

Scarlet and Sergeant Yakamoto led the way as the team jogged into the Tokyo Bay Aqua-Line. The bridge-

247

tunnel combo that stretched across the bay in the heart of the city had taken nearly a decade to build and formed a link between the two prefectures of Kawasaki and Kisarazu.

Slowly they gained ground and found themselves approaching the central point of the construction, an artificial island the Japanese named *umihotaru*, or the firefly. They were now entering a section full of shops and restaurants. Scarlet followed Yakamoto down a glittering escalator and into a lower level which opened out into a broad plaza lined with more stores selling books and snack foods.

People milled around browsing through magazines while others sipped tea or ordered fast food from the many restaurants. Scarlet looked at them and thought only that if they failed in their bid to stop the Lotus, these people would be the first victims of the genocide Sheng had planned for their city.

And it wouldn't stop there. Relations between Japan and China had been worsening for decades, and she doubted Japanese public opinion would tolerate such an attack made by one of China's most visible billionaires.

Yakamoto spoke into his headset in rapid Japanese and then led them down a narrow corridor behind a salad bar. Moments later they were facing a fire escape which the hefty sergeant opened by unceremoniously kicking the panic bar with his Army issue steel toecap boot.

They were now in a staff-only zone, and walking along another narrow corridor toward a series of stainless steel steps which led down to a longer service corridor.

Without any warning, they heard a tremendous roar of gunfire and looked ahead to see the tell-tale muzzle flash of automatic weapons emanating from a door on the side of the service tunnel.

"Looks like our welcoming committee," Scarlet said. "Everybody down!"

They took cover and gradually moved forward using the giant concrete support pillars as protection against the bullets tracing along the tunnel. They reached the service door and Karlsson kicked it down with a savage, no-nonsense blow and before the door had even smacked against the inside wall he unleashed an unambiguously ferocious burst of gunfire, peppering the space with hundreds of bullets in just a few short seconds, screaming the whole time he was firing the weapon.

Scarlet rolled her eyes as the enormous cloud of concrete dust settled around them. "Is that really necessary, Bradley?

Karlsson released the trigger. "Is what really necessary?"

"All that dreadful screaming? It's frightfully bad form, and so very *American* of you."

"In the same way that being such a cold-hearted ice bitch is so very *British* of you, you mean?"

"Ouch," Ryan said, taking his fingers out of his hears. "But she does make a point about the screaming."

"No need to leap to my defense, boy. I think Mr Karlsson and I are going to have a beautiful future together."

"You do?" Karlsson said, beaming.

"Sure, don't you?"

He shrugged his giant bear shoulders and ran a chunky hand over his shaved head. "If you say so, baby. If you say so."

Inside they ran along another corridor and down a series of steps – heading all the time toward the sound of some kind of hammering and then a drilling noise. After another minute they reached a service hatch which they climbed down inside and then found themselves inside the belly of the beast – here, the main support columns for the entire structure were exposed, and at the far end they saw the Lotus and her lackeys fixing what looked like a giant car-jack at the base of one of the columns.

"What the fuck?" Karlsson said.

"They're drilling into the bedrock," said Ryan. "They won't need to go far though if what McShain told us about the device is anything to go by. We need to act fast."

His words were cut off by the sound of hysterical shouting and screaming. The Lotus had seen them and was ordering her men forward to attack. Half a dozen of them took up defensive positions while another three moved forward, firing short bursts from their submachine guns as they crab-walked closer to Scarlet's team.

"Take cover!" Scarlet shouted, and they leaped behind the columns. A savage firefight ensued as both sides fought for supremacy of the tunnel. Scarlet looked down to see the men finish their work on the device as the other goons kept them pinned down. The Lotus strutted forward and pushed some buttons on the top panel, then smiled and ordered her men to kill everyone in sight.

"Why are they fighting so hard?" Ryan asked. "I've never seen anything like it."

"Because we're blocking the only way out," Karlsson said. "Those assholes can't get out of here until we're all dead, and now the timer's running on their personal little Domesday machine down there the pressure's really on. I'm guessing that chopper up there with the cute little rope ladder is waiting for them, but we're not going to let that happen, right?"

The battle raged for another five minutes until Scarlet's team finally overcame them and broke through their defenses. They advanced on the Lotus and her inner guard who were now retreating to a recess at the back of the complex.

"Ryan!" screamed Scarlet. "Get that fucking thing switched off or your balls are mine, and not in a good way."

Ryan scuttled forward, Sophie covering him with her pistol. Ahead of them, Scarlet and Bradley Karlsson raged forwards toward the Lotus and her surviving minions.

Ryan hunched over the device, struggling to take in all the information in such a short time. He looked at the countdown panel.

Ninety seconds.

"Umm..."

Eighty seconds.

"If I recall correctly, the wiring on this was... no – hang on. I'm remembering something else."

"Bloody hell, stop being Ryan for a second!" Scarlet screamed, and fired off another three rounds of her pistol.

Seventy seconds.

Sixty seconds.

"Oh, *dear*..."

Fifty seconds.

"Ah – I remember... if I take this red wire and disconnect it, according to McShain all I need to do then is take out the green one and splice them together. Or was it the blue one?"

Forty seconds.

Then, in the heat of the battle Sophie looked up to see one of the men aiming his pistol directly at Ryan's head. She screamed, and launched herself forward, flying through the air and firing retaliatory shots at the man at the same time.

The man fired.

She fired back – muzzle flash, smoke, bullet released. She passed in between Ryan and the man and took the bullet through her throat.

She collapsed in a heap beside Ryan, hanging over a low concrete barricade like a rag doll.

Her bullet then struck the man in the forehead and killed him instantly.

Ryan was totally shell-shocked. He looked at Sophie, saw the blood pouring from her neck down the cold concrete.

"Is she all right?" he screamed.

"The device, Ryan!" Scarlet screamed, her SAS training kicking in hard now, ruthless, mercenary. "Turn the fucking device off. We'll check Soph in a minute."

Thirty seconds.

Ryan's world seemed to slow down. He looked at Sophie and knew in his heart she was gone. He turned to Scarlet. She was now fighting the Lotus in hand to hand combat. Kung Fu versus Krav Maga. The Lotus planted a solid kick in Scarlet's sternum and sent her flying back, breathless.

Scarlet regained her balance and spun around to land a perfectly timed and devastating spinning heel kick in the Lotus's face, smashing her nose and cutting a deep scar into her cheek with the heel of her boot. The Lotus staggered backwards but kept her balance. Scarlet saw she was searching for her knife but gave no quarter.

Scarlet snatched up a pistol and fired four shots at the Lotus's head. She was so pumped she carried on squeezing the trigger long after the bullets had run out and the sound of the dry-firing filled the cavernous space for several seconds afterwards as the hammer struck down on the empty chamber, *click, click, click, click.* They were all dead now, and she, Bradley and Ryan would be joining them along with the entire population of Tokyo if Ryan Bale didn't work fast.

Twenty seconds.

"As soon as you can, Ryan," Karlsson said, a heavy hand on his shoulder. Ryan's eyes crawled all over the place, from the whirring numbers on the Tesla device, counting down to the destruction of the city above, to the terrible sight of Sophie's body, flopped lifeless over the concrete retaining wall where she had fallen moments earlier, killed trying to save his life.

"I can't do it!" he mumbled. "I just can't do it any more... not now – not with Sophie gone like this." His lower lip began to tremble and Scarlet was concerned he was about to fall apart.

"Listen, Ryan. The lives of twenty million people, and more importantly *my life*, are all in your hands right now, you got that?"

Ten seconds.

Ryan stripped the green wire...

Five seconds.

...and spliced it into the red wire he had previously disconnected...

Two seconds.

And silence.

Scarlet looked at the counter. Two seconds remaining.

"Pussy," Karlsson said, wiping sweat from his forehead with the back of his hairy hand. "James Bond always waited until one second."

But Ryan didn't hear any words. He was staring at the lifeless body of Sophie Durand, and choking back the tears.

CHAPTER THIRTY-SEVEN

Hawke was now face to face with Sheng Fang for the second time since all this began, and as far as he was concerned that was two times too many.

Before anyone had a chance to think, Sheng told Luk to order the men forward, and they proceeded toward the next chamber. Ahead of them lay the final of Qin's lethal challenges – the trial of metal.

Amid a serene sense of triumph, Sheng turned the final bend in the tunnel and saw with horror an enormous shining lake stretching out before him. The glare of the glow-sticks reflected brightly in the surface of the water as he ordered two men to move forward to the lake's shore and report their findings.

The men nervously descended toward the water and Sheng watched with interest as they stooped to investigate. Moments later both men collapsed into the lake, dead. Luk glanced anxiously at Sheng and mumbled something about the curse of the tomb and a burning sky, but Sheng was undeterred.

He called two more men forward and ordered them down to the water to investigate further and collect the bodies. They looked at the corpses on the shore in the cavern below and objected, so Sheng had Luk shoot one of them. Their lives meant nothing to him, so long as they were able to help him achieve his destiny and fulfill the prophecy. Any man who refused to obey his orders was of no use.

The second man looked at the body of his dead colleague and swallowed hard. He was left with no choice but to make his way down to the shore and report back to his leader.

At the shore, he too began to swoon, and then he fell with a syrupy splash into the water. Luk turned to Sheng and spoke next: "It's not water. It's mercury. This is the test of metal."

Sheng's mind began to whir. Mercury was lethal, both to touch or to breathe, and the evidence of that was the three corpses on the shore a few hundred yards below him. He smiled in appreciation of Qin and his sadistic ingenuity when constructing the defenses of the tomb. He ordered Luk to confirm it was mercury and watched him make his way down to the lake.

All of this only strengthened his belief that the map must be hidden in the tomb – why else would the emperor go to such extraordinary and lethal lengths to protect the place? Now, he watched Luk trudge back up the path, holding a black cloth up to his mouth and nose.

"And?"

Luk removed the cloth. "Definitely mercury, and the men are terrified of going any further. They don't want to end up like those three." He flicked his hand behind himself for a moment in a dismissive and casual gesture to indicate the three dead men. "And to be honest, I can't blame them. I've looked around and I can see no way across the lake at all."

"Wrong – there is a way, look." Sheng pointed at the far end of the cavern where a ledge of natural rock stuck out over the lake of shimmering mercury. On the far side of the cavern opposite it was another rock ledge, but much smaller. Once, a long time ago, a natural rock bridge must have connected the two sides.

"No man can jump that," Luk said. "It must be twenty-five feet."

Sheng nodded appreciatively at the distance and

snapped his fingers. Two goons dragged Hawke over to him.

"What do you think, Mr Hawke? Twenty-five feet like my man here says, or perhaps even wider?"

"No," Hawke said firmly. "I'd say your pet monkey has a good eye for distances."

Luk moved forward aggressively, but Sheng stopped him with a raised hand and a few short words barked in Cantonese. Luk obeyed immediately and returned to his place behind Sheng.

"Always with the jokes. Perhaps a little mercury vapor will make you more serious. You will jump that gap and take with you a length of rope in order that we may all cross. If you miss and fall in the mercury, I will kill your three friends here by making them go for a swim in this delightful little lake, understand?"

Hawke nodded grimly and approached the ledge. Thanks to his parkour he knew Luk had been right in his estimation of twenty-five feet, the only problem was that his personal record at a running jump in parkour was twenty-three feet. He knew that two feet didn't sound like much, but he also knew from his parkour how long two feet was if it was two feet further than you could jump.

Sheng pushed the gun into Lea's neck. "Now, Mr Hawke."

Hawke took a deep breath and then a long running jump, and leaped into the air using everything his parkour training could give. For a few seconds, he was mid-air, sailing above the terrifying mercury lake like a wingless bird. Now was too late to reconsider his actions – if he had misjudged the width of the gap he faced a desperate and toxic death.

He landed with a savage crunch in the loose gravel that was strewn over the far ledge. With no small measure of relief, he dusted himself down and returned his gaze to the others standing on the other side. Lea looked so small, standing in between Sheng's goons.

"And now the rope, Mr Hawke," Sheng said "Throw it back, if you please." He raised his gun to Lea's temple. She closed her eyes and muttered something under her breath.

He knew had no choice but to follow Sheng's instructions. He secured the rope around one of the boulders on his side of the cave and tossed the other end back to Luk, who caught it in one hand and then lashed it around a boulder on their side. Moments later, Luk led the way by traversing the taut rope with what Hawke silently acknowledged was a pretty impressive commando rope crawl. Han, and Reaper followed, and then Lea. Hawke watched anxiously as she crawled along the rope, slipping only once, but it was a heart-stopping moment for the Englishman.

Sheng and the last of his goons followed up the rear, and then they were on their way again. Hawke and the others were forced to go in front of Sheng at gunpoint in case there were any other nasty little surprises in the emperor's tomb.

They walked for several minutes until they finally reached an impressive arch carved out of the stone with Chinese dragons carved into each supporting column either side of it.

Sheng gasped when he saw them. "We are here! Behold the dragon – the symbol of the Thunder God. We have finally reached the real tomb, the sacred inner sanctum of the great Emperor Qin himself, and final resting place of the Map of Immortality, kept hidden from mankind until now and it's all *mine!*"

"So, do we get the runner-up prize or what" Hawke said.

"Silence!" screamed Sheng, and Luk punched him to the ground. Reaper darted forward in his defense but he too was struck down by two of the men who had been holding him. "Any more heroics and Luk will start shooting people, understand?"

Hawke clambered to his feet, followed a second later by Reaper.

"It was only a question, Sheng..." Hawke mumbled.

"Wrong. It was an impertinent question, asked by a mortal man to a God."

CHAPTER THIRTY-EIGHT

Through the small arch was their final destination – a tomb of exquisite beauty carved out of the bedrock. All around them, more terracotta statues watched them in perfect silence, their faces dusty from thousands of years of relentless duty to their emperor, and in the center was the man himself – an enormous, intricate tomb of carved stone jutting out of the stone floor.

It loomed fifty feet high, and at its apex was a bridge that connected it to a ledge running high around the top of the cavern. Around its four sides was a series of stone steps carved into the edge of the tomb. At the base was a deep pit, its bottom lurking somewhere below in the darkness, and all around the outside of the tomb hundreds of tiny holes were drilled into the cave walls.

Sheng gasped. High on the upper ledge was the real sarcophagus of the Emperor Qin. They had come face to face with the real man after all this time. The stone face on the sarcophagus was silent, passive, imperious. Mocking.

Sheng pushed the others aside and raced up the steps toward the sarcophagus.

"I am the Thunder God!" Sheng screamed insanely. "This power is my destiny!"

Sheng would soon hold the map in his hands, the first mortal man to do so for thousands of years. Where Hugo Zaugg had failed, Sheng Fang had succeeded and in the most stark of ways. "This is my divine fate! It is my divine destiny to live forever and now I have the map that will lead me to the destiny of the gods."

The Englishman called up to Sheng. "I think you need a cup of tea and a nice sit down, mate."

"Silence, you fool!"

The self-styled Thunder God now reached the apex of the tomb, a full fifty feet above the main floor where the others stood. There, he was finally face to face with the great emperor himself as he stared into the stone statue of Qin's upright sarcophagus.

Lea watched in disgust as he blew the dust from Qin's carved face to reveal a small handle. "Just as the legend says!" He turned the handle on the front of the enormous structure and slowly pulled at the front of it.

At that moment Sheng screamed a raft of orders at Luk, who had been watching his dear leader with increasing suspicion over the last few moments. As Sheng disappeared inside the sarcophagus to claim his prize, Luk moved forward to follow his instructions, which although delivered in hysterical Cantonese were obvious to everyone: kill Hawke and the rest of his team.

Above them, Sheng emerged from the sarcophagus with a small roll of parchment held together with a tiny red ribbon. He held it aloft and laughed madly. As he did so, they heard a rumbling sound and then a dark liquid began pouring from the holes built into the walls of the inner tomb.

"What the hell is that stuff?" Lea said.

"A kind of pitch," Reaper said.

"What?"

Hawke coughed. "It was used as an early kind of thermal weapon. I don't know how old Qin managed it, but any minute now I'd be very surprised if it didn't..."

"Catch on fire?" Lea said.

Hawke nodded. "How did you know?"

"Look over there." She pointed to a platform behind

the sarcophagus and they all saw the tell-tale sight of flames, small, but lots of them and rapidly growing in number.

"Some kind of ancient mechanism's ignited the oil," Hawke said.

Reaper sighed. "Which is not the best news I've had this week – and look." He gestured to the base of the sarcophagus where the oil was collecting in a pool. Slowly the flames from the top level were travelling down the rivers of oil all over the tomb.

With the exception of Luk, Sheng's goons looked at the fire and then ran from the chamber. Luk was panicked, but a few more screams from his boss and he sprinted forward and lunged at Lea with his knife. She took a step back and his momentum carried him forward into the loving arms of Vincent Reno. Reaper tiger-punched him in the throat and he collapsed in a wheezing heap at his boots.

Lea wasted no time in lashing out and struck Luk with an eye-watering roundhouse kick to the back of the head which sent him flying over in an arc and crashing down into the dirt on his back.

He scrambled to his feet and stared wide-eyed at the fire. His eyes darted over to Sheng who was now giving him more orders.

"Kill them! Kill them now, Luk! That is an order from your god!"

Luk looked at the fire and then back at Sheng, and then finally to Hawke and the others, perilously close to the lethal flames which grew larger with every second. The heat was rising, and the sweat poured down from his forehead and trickled into his panicked eyes, which now flicked over to the tunnel that led back to the five trials and ultimately to safety. Without saying another word, he dropped the knife and turned on his heel. A moment later he was in the tunnel and out of sight.

Sheng stared with obvious shock and horror at the desertion.

"Looks like your Luk's run out, Sheng!"

Lea rolled her eyes and moaned. "Oh, for the love of *God*, Joe."

"What? I literally just cannot help it."

"I worked that out the first day I met you, you fool."

"You forget that I have this!" Sheng screamed, waving the map in his hand. "And this means unrivalled power. Luk will certainly rue the day he deserted me, but I have greater things to consider, such as how to dispatch you annoying and pathetic mortals."

Sheng pulled his gun, held it level and prepared to fire it, but as he did so the flames licking at the rope holding one of the beams aloft above his head finally finished their work, and the rope snapped.

Hawke winced, Lea averted her eyes.

Sheng heard it and flicked his head up to see the cause of the noise, but all he saw was the sight of a heavy wooden beam falling toward his face. Half a second later it smacked him hard in the head and knocked him from the ledge. He tumbled off the top of it and crashed into the base of the tomb with a sickening crunch, his neck broken and bent round at a terrible angle.

"That's for Hart," Hawke whispered to himself.

Now, the fire was all consuming, its white and orange flames licking the sides of the support beams holding the temple in place around them. The highly flammable tar mixture continued to pour from the hundreds of holes all around them, and the flames leaped from one stream to the next until the entire chamber was ablaze.

Hawke tried to shield his face from the tremendous heat but it was too much. He could feel himself burning and took a step backwards. Through the shimmering inferno he saw the unmistakable figure of Lexi Zhang as she lunged forward and grabbed the map from Sheng's dead fingers. Her figure rippled mirage-like in the heat as she struggled to cover her mouth with her hand.

"Lexi, I'm coming!" Hawke shouted, taking a step toward her, but the blaze was too much even for him and no matter how hard he pushed himself to go forward his basic survival instinct stopped his feet from going another step.

Lexi waved the map at him and tried to get across the burning river of tar, but then something terrible happened. He watched in horror as she took a misstep and began to windmill backwards over to the ledge. Hawke watched in terrible slow-motion as she slipped over the edge, her arms flailing to try and stop herself going back. In her hand was the cursed map of immortality, flashing in the firelight, and then...

Then she was gone, over the edge, her screams receding into the black pit as she slipped away from them, from life. Hawke stood motionless for a few seconds, taking in what he had just seen. This terrible place and that damned map had taken Sheng and rightly so in his view, but now it had taken not only Olivia Hart but also Lexi Zhang – the Agent Dragonfly he had met in Zambia all those years ago – and now she was dead too, another life claimed by the madness of greed and the lust for power.

"Joe!"

He turned to see Lea holding her hand to him. She was shielding her face from the heat with her other hand and coughing violently in the smoke. "Joe, it's time to go! We have to go now before we all die in here!"

"She's right, Hawke," shouted Reaper. "This is one fire not even we can put out."

"We must leave!" Han shouted.

All around them the fire grew stronger and closer.

Lea beckoned Hawke over with her hand "She's gone, Joe! She's dead, and so is Sheng. We have to get out of here now!"

Hawke snapped back into the moment. Lea and the others were right. All the others were dead, and they would be too if they didn't get out of the tomb in double-quick time. He holstered his gun and jogged over to Lea without looking back for Lexi once. He knew she was gone, and more than that, she had died trying to retrieve the map for him and that was something he was going to have to live with, but now was not the time to think about it.

CHAPTER THIRTY-NINE

Hawke was watching the sun set over Kowloon Bay when Lea stepped out onto the balcony with two glasses of chilled vodka. Tonight should have been about celebrating but instead he felt like a total failure. He had led a mission where Olivia Hart, Sophie Durand and Lexi Zhang were killed.

"How's Ryan?" Hawke asked.

Lea handed him a vodka and turned to look over her shoulder. She was looking back into the room where various people were mingling and fighting for conversation time with Jason Lao, Sir Richard Eden or Frank McShain, who seemed especially pleased with himself thanks to the retrieval of the Tesla device and its delivery back into the safe hands of the US military. But as she looked, she did it as if she were looking for Ryan, but it was a token gesture. They both knew Ryan wasn't at the party. He hadn't come out of his hotel room since their return to Hong Kong.

"I don't know... This has hit him pretty hard, Joe."

Hawke bit his lip. "I know. Who can blame him? He isn't used to losing people around him – not in this way, at least. And it's my fault."

"Joe... you can't blame yourself for Sophie's death."

Hawke downed his vodka and stared at her. "Why not? Maybe as far as Lexi is concerned, but not the others. I was their commander. I was leading the mission. It was my choice to send Sophie out into the field, and it was my choice to bring Olivia into this nightmare."

"Sure, I know, but you didn't pull the trigger, Joe.

Sheng's goons killed Olivia, and the damned Lotus Girl killed Sophie."

Hawke was silent for a long time. Below, the streets of Hong Kong buzzed and rattled their way into another neon night. Above, the first new stars of the evening were appearing in the darkening city sky. Even to Joe Hawke the romance of the moment was obvious – if it weren't for the loss and anger he felt over the deaths of his friends.

"I shouldn't be here," he said quietly.

"What are you talking about?"

"I'm just not up to it anymore. I'm making too many mistakes."

"Now you're just being an eejit."

Hawke shook his head and raised the glass to his lips before remembering it was empty all over again. "I don't think so. Too many details are getting past me, Lea. I lost three good people in the last few hours..."

Sir Richard Eden broke off his conversation with Jason Lao and joined them on the balcony.

"It's bad news, I'm afraid."

Hawke sighed. "The vodka's run out?"

Eden made no reply to the half-joke, but continued. "I don't know how to tell you this, but it's about Lexi Zhang."

Hawke lifted his head and stared at Eden. "What is it?"

"She's not dead."

Hawke was incredulous. "She survived?"

Eden nodded.

"But how? I saw her die just a couple of days ago – consumed by fire and then she fell into the pit with the map."

"We don't know, but it doesn't matter. What does matter is that a woman strongly matching her appearance boarded a private jet in Xian. She was identified by one of my contacts a few hours ago. The plane she boarded was a private charter going to Berlin."

Hawke and Lea shared a glance. Hawke had a very bad feeling about what was coming next. "And?"

"And she wasn't alone. She was with the same Russian who delivered the Tesla device into Tokyo Bay. It's pretty clear she's done some kind of deal and sold him the map."

Hawke's mind spun with the mixture of the bad news and the vodka. Not only had he led good friends to their deaths, but now he'd let himself get betrayed by Lexi Zhang in the process. She had humiliated him, and if that were not bad enough, she had handed the most precious power in the world to an unknown Russian who was happy to drown everyone in Tokyo for a few million dollars.

Eden returned inside where Hawke watched him explaining the news to members of the various concerned governments.

"She betrayed me!" he said, still not really believing what he had heard.

Lea scowled at the thought. "Don't you worry about Lexi Arsing Dragonfly – her arse is mine. Believe me."

"But... *how?*"

"We'll track her down and ask her!" Lea said, her voice suddenly full of optimism. "What a great excuse to tramp all over the world shooting at things, and then we get to have our revenge on the Dung Beetle or whatever she calls herself."

"It's not as simple as that, Lea. Everything's spinning out of control."

"What are you talking about? What do you always say about not losing your spirit of adventure – so where's yours, ya loser?"

Hawke poured more vodka and sank another shot. "Before she died, Hart told me that my wife was the target of the shooting in Hanoi, and not me. It's blown my world apart, Lea."

Lea was silent for a moment. "I don't know what to say... I'm so sorry, Joe."

"And I know you and bloody Cairo are keeping something from me as well – no – don't interrupt or bother to deny it. I don't think I can find it in me to go forward with any of this." He glanced inside where Scarlet Sloane was umpiring an arm-wrestling contest between Reaper and Karlsson.

"Listen, Joe. Keep it together, all right? We can find Lexi Zhang and recover the map – you know we can! As for what the Commodore told you – I'll help you in any way I can to find out who's behind your wife's murder, you know I will."

Hawke started to reply when his phone buzzed. He looked down at the words on the screen and could hardly believe he was reading them.

"What is it?" Lea asked.

"It's Nightingale..." Hawke's face went pale.

"What's the matter, Joe?"

"She says she's being kidnapped. They've got her."

"Oh my God! Who's got her, Joe?"

"I don't know."

"Maybe it's just a joke?"

"Never. Not Nightingale..." His words trailed away and he handed her the phone. On the screen was a blurred picture of a man approaching Nightingale. He was holding a knife. "She says she was hiding in her wardrobe and writing to me from there. She must have had just enough time to send this text and picture before they took her."

Lea handed him back the phone. "I'll do whatever

you want me to, Joe. You know that."

"I don't know what to do... I'm losing it." He stared at the tiny screen with uncomprehending eyes. First Dragonfly, now this blurred figure, the knife... it made no sense.

"You have to go to her."

"I don't even know her name, Lea! I don't know where she lives! If I wanted to track someone like her down I'd ask... well, *her*."

"We can do this, Joe. I'll talk to Richard. You helped him, so he'll help you, and believe me, that really means something. He has serious contacts all over the world."

Hawke looked out over the bay, but his focus was somewhere in the middle distance, in that place he stared at with sad eyes when his thoughts were far away. Any hopes of glory he had arrogantly harbored at the start of all of this were smashed to pieces now.

Yes, he had killed Sheng and ended the threat he was posing to the world, and Scarlet had taken out the Lotus as well, but Olivia Hart and Sophie Durand were both dead – killed on his watch, and Lexi Zhang, the Dragonfly from his deep past had just betrayed him in royal fashion and totally humiliated him in front of Lea and Sir Richard Eden. Now, one of his oldest friends was in real trouble and he didn't have any idea how to help her. All he had to go on was a few lines of text and a blurred picture of a madman with a knife, sent to him from the other side of the planet.

Out there, across the bay, the Hong Kong night drew in around Joe Hawke. It matched the darkness now drawing across his mind as so many thoughts and emotions struggled for supremacy of his soul. He didn't know what to do next, but whatever it was, he knew he had to do it now.

THE END.

AUTHOR'S NOTE

Here is the best place for me to thank everyone who bought and enjoyed the first two Joe Hawke novels. The Hawke series is a lot of fun to write because of the pure escapism in this type of story and like other series of its kind it shouldn't be taken too seriously. I guess if you've come this far, you already know that... It's great to know you enjoy reading about Hawke's adventures as much as I enjoy writing them, and I'm scheduling the final part of this three-story "immortality arc" to be released at the end of 2015 or very early 2016. After that who knows what Joe Hawke will face?

In the meantime, please visit my website at www.robjonesnovels.com for the latest news and updates, and don't forget my Twitter and Facebook pages. Also, I'm happy to reply to emails at robjonesnovels@gmail.com even if it takes me a few days to do so!

And so once again, Mystery Reader – my thanks to *you*, who bought and read this story. It's appreciated, and I hope we can carry on with this journey together. Someone's got to keep Hawke out of trouble, after all...

Signing off,

Rob

The Joe Hawke Series

The Vault of Poseidon (Joe Hawke #1)
Thunder God (Joe Hawke #2)
The Tomb of Eternity (Joe Hawke #3)
The Curse of Medusa (Joe Hawke #4)
Valhalla Gold (Joe Hawke #5)
The Aztec Prophecy (Joe Hawke #6)
The Secret of Atlantis (Joe Hawke #7)
The Lost City (Joe Hawke #8)

The Sword of Fire (Joe Hawke #9) is scheduled
for release in the spring of 2017

**For free stories, regular news and updates,
please join my Facebook page**

https://www.facebook.com/RobJonesNovels/

Or Twitter

@AuthorRobJones

13120615R00171